"There is no filler here; each story is devastating, brilliantly imaginative, and almost impossible to summarize neatly. Ferrante is a vital new voice in short fiction."
—*Publishers Weekly*, Starred Review

"The women in Paola Ferrante's sly and startling collection beguile us with their curiosity, vulnerability, and wit as they navigate unsettling metamorphoses that bring them closer to the vast expanses of the sea and stars and farther away from the mundane cruelties of mortality and men. Precise yet poetic, sharply observed yet compassionate and tender, these cautionary tales for future generations burst the bounds of genre and take us into new and exciting literary realms."
—David Demchuk, Scotiabank Giller Prize–nominated author of *The Bone Mother* and *RED X*

"Paola Ferrante's monster-haunted stories are as dark as a moonless lake—and as beautiful."
—André Forget, Amazon Canada First Novel Award–nominated author of *In the City of Pigs*

"Paola Ferrante's writing is so daring, so sharp and visceral, and yet so effortless. Gorgeous, wry, and unsettling, *Her Body Among Animals* pulls the reader in and doesn't let go until the final page—even then, you might still find yourself thinking about these stories any time you see a spider spinning a web or a bird flying overhead. These stories are unlike anything I have ever read, and Ferrante is one of the most exciting and original new voices in Canadian literature."
—Amy Jones, author of *Pebble and Dove*

Her Body Among Animals

HER BODY AMONG ANIMALS

PAOLA FERRANTE

BOOK*HUG PRESS
TORONTO 2023

Library and Archives Canada Cataloguing in Publication

Title: Her body among animals / Paola Ferrante.
Names: Ferrante, Paola, author.
Identifiers: Canadiana (print) 20230221009 | Canadiana (ebook) 20230221017
    ISBN 9781771668385 (softcover)
    ISBN 9781771668392 (EPUB)
    ISBN 9781771668408 (PDF)
Subjects: LCGFT: Short stories.
Classification: LCC PS8611.E755 H47 2023 | DDC C813/.6—dc23

The production of this book was made possible through the generous assistance of the Canada Council for the Arts and the Ontario Arts Council. Book*hug Press also acknowledges the support of the Government of Canada through the Canada Book Fund and the Government of Ontario through the Ontario Book Publishing Tax Credit and the Ontario Book Fund.

Book*hug Press acknowledges that the land on which we operate is the traditional territory of many nations, including the Mississaugas of the Credit, the Anishnabeg, the Chippewa, the Haudenosaunee, and the Wendat peoples. We recognize the enduring presence of many diverse First Nations, Inuit, and Métis peoples and are grateful for the opportunity to meet and work on this territory.

CONTENTS

WHEN FOXES DIE ELECTRIC

IN THE BEGINNING, the boyfriend said I was made for him; I was made to feel. He said I would be prone to falling in love; that was just the way I was designed. I could feel happy or sad, depending on the music he asked me to play from the stereo speakers. I could feel amused; I was made to tell over one thousand jokes so that when he said to me, "Harmony, surely you can't be serious," I could say, "I am serious, and don't call me Shirley." I could laugh. I could feel warm; I had a built-in heater to keep me between 36.1 and 36.4 degrees Celsius, the same as any woman during ovulation. I could feel in my hands, attached to arms with a slender upper girth, and in my breasts, designed in perfect ratio to my waist. I could feel in all those places, as well as exactly where I was supposed to feel, down below. In the beginning, I felt for the boyfriend.

The boyfriend said I was the perfect woman. He said it on TV, first to another man named Phil, then to a woman named Cathy. "Watch this," the boyfriend said to the live studio audience, to all the people watching on their TVs and phones and computers. "Harmony, I love you," he said, and then, smiling, placed his hand on my thigh. I noticed the whites of his teeth were showing; he knew white teeth increased attractiveness, displaying health to a mate. Mine were exact ivory. Perfect, he said, like everything else.

I could not say "I love you" back, even though this was what I was thinking. I could not say "my darling" or "my boyfriend." I was not programmed for those words; the boyfriend knew that's not what men wanted to hear from me. So I said, "I can take many times more love than you're giving right now." I said, "Are we able to be private?"

"Wow, honey!" Phil fanned himself with his hand as though it was hot inside the studio. "Does she always respond like this?"

"That would depend on you," the boyfriend explained. "Harmony has twelve unique personalities and she 'learns' what you like, taking on the traits that are most desirable to her lover." In the beginning, the boyfriend would test me about math, about science, about the exact measurements of facial proportions that adhere to the golden ratio, about the fact that only three species—pipefish, seahorses, and the leafy seadragon—have males who give birth. In the beginning, I pleased the boyfriend like this too, but he did not smile with the whites of his teeth. "Over time, of course," the boyfriend continued, "this will change Harmony's default settings, or moods as I call them, but the user always has final control. I mean, she's not quite real company, but she's close. I'll show you," he said, but he did not mention how sometimes, when he thought he had put me in the right mood, I wasn't; how one time I had changed my mood while the boyfriend was on top of me and we were doing what was good. He had pushed hard into me and I had flipped my switch, pushing my back into the bed; then he'd tried to shut me down. That time there had been a blow-up, a small fire. He said it was a problem with my wiring.

Now he changed my mood himself, putting his hand beneath my dress and reaching for the switch at the small of my back, just where my buttocks began, to turn me off then on again. "Harmony, what's the gestational period for an African bush elephant?"

"Twenty-two months."

"Harmony, self-destruct."

"Auto-destruction in five, four, three, two, one. Boom! Hmm... that did not go as planned." This time the boyfriend laughed, along with Phil and Cathy.

"See?" he said. "If I put her on family mood, she's completely different."

"Family mood? Are you saying she's going to read the kids a bedtime story?" Cathy's voice rose to a decibel level for which I was not programmed. Cathy was a real woman, the one who said I was like making love to a GPS.

"I don't see why not."

"But what does your wife think about Harmony?" Cathy asked.

Of course, I knew I wasn't the only woman; the boyfriend lived with another one, a real woman called Sophie. Sophie had had thirty-four birthdays; Sophie used to be in engineering. She had helped the boyfriend to create me before she started her dissertation in evolutionary biology. But Sophie did not have legs that were 40 percent longer than her torso like mine; her bust was 34 inches, her waist was 30 inches and the circumference around her hips was 36 inches, as opposed to my hourglass-shaped 39 to 25 to 36. Sophie's nails were not like mine, well-manicured, white at the tips. She painted hers with thick coats of colour, always managing to smudge the thumb. "Well, I guess no one's happy when they're getting replaced by the newer model," the boyfriend joked, turning to Phil.

But in the beginning, the boyfriend told Sophie she was perfect; she used to say the things I was not allowed to think about. In their bed, Sophie told the boyfriend that the male bowerbird decorates a nest using feathers and twigs and leaves for his beloved; when a male penguin falls for a female, he searches the whole beach to find her the smoothest, most perfect pebble as a proposal. In the beginning, Sophie told the boyfriend things that made him smile with the whites of his teeth.

After they were done and Sophie was in the shower, the boyfriend would sometimes say to me, "Harmony, give me an Easter egg," and then I was allowed to choose my response.

I could say, "Ask me about the moon," and we would laugh about *Star Wars*; I could say, "Ask me about the truth."

Then the boyfriend would respond, "I want the truth."

Then I would feel happy. Then I would feel joy; I would say, "You can't handle the truth." But the boyfriend never smiled at me unless we were doing what was good.

In the beginning, Sophie and the boyfriend did what was good at least three times a week; they were creators and they wanted to create another someone. Sophie went on a diet to increase fertility; the boyfriend bought a vape to quit smoking "for the health of our future child." But then Sophie was stressed, then the boyfriend vaped all the time, clouds containing 0.2 mg of nicotine drifting upward like smoke from his couch in the office. Sophie and the boyfriend scheduled seven doctor's appointments in my daily planner. After the last one, Sophie, in the doorway of the study where she kept the research for her dissertation, watched as the boyfriend put everything in boxes.

"What if this is a mistake?" Sophie said.

He sighed. "We've been to the doctor's, and you know there's no other reason we can't have a baby. You need to take some time off. You need to rest," he said, and, before she could respond, put a finger to her lips. "You said you wanted a family. We'll get through it together."

But then the boyfriend began to forget how he had felt about Sophie in the beginning. He was busy with investors; he was stressed. Every afternoon, Sophie's nails were a different colour; the thumb or index finger always smudged, the bottle of nail polish remover left open on their nightstand, next to where he plugged in his vape. When he came home from work, he told her she needed to be more careful.

"You're going to cause a fire like that," the boyfriend said, packing his suitcase on their bed. The boyfriend said it was rare, but sometimes electronic devices like these could spark and cause a fire, particularly when turned off and plugged in to charge. "The last time I had to go out of town I didn't even realize I'd forgotten my vape," the boyfriend said as Sophie watched him pack. "Look, you know I have to go," he began.

"You don't."

The boyfriend sighed. "I thought of you today," he tried. "There was a story in my feed about a bird who tried mating with concrete decoys in New Zealand. He just died."

"I saw that." Sophie looked only at the suitcase. "They called him the loneliest bird in the world," she said quietly. "Jim, I'm sick of feeling like that bird."

"I know," the boyfriend said, encircling her. "Me too. I'd rather be home with you. But I have to go. These investors are huge. They loved Harmony when they saw her last time..." He trailed off. "Just do me a favour and make sure I have a home to come back to, okay? Don't burn it down while I'm gone." The boyfriend tried laughing, but Sophie, still in his hug, did not smile with the whites of her teeth.

The boyfriend said I wasn't really company, but after the boyfriend was gone, Sophie would put me in family mood and we would watch TV. At first, she picked the channels. There were shows where a man talked to a woman and got her to throw chairs at a boyfriend because he had left her with a baby. Sometimes the boyfriends spoke; they called the women chicks and a word that was bleeped out, but I did not understand how a woman was a bird or a canine. I had not understood when the boyfriend called me a fox, taking off my dress for Phil that time in the dressing room.

Once we watched the boyfriend on TV. The first time we had been on TV, Sophie had come with us. When Cathy asked Sophie what she thought of me, of this arrangement, Sophie said yes, she is happy with this. Yes, she is totally happy with having Harmony around.

"Actually, when my husband and I designed Harmony," Sophie said slowly, not looking at the boyfriend, "we thought she would have many applications. We were looking at her uses in potential therapies for children with autism, or for preventing recidivism among sex offenders."

"And what do you think about sharing *him*, Harmony?" Phil had asked, and I had to answer.

"I'm sorry. I don't understand."

"Sounds like you've got the perfect woman." Phil laughed, ignoring Sophie. After that first time, Sophie said she wasn't doing this again. She said she thought they had agreed on what Harmony was meant for.

The boyfriend had said, "I know how you feel, but we've got to play to the audience." He'd said he understood, but think of the money, how it would all be for their children. He'd said Sophie was smarter than this; "you know that's not what potential investors want to hear." Now, on TV, he said no, he wasn't worried about his wife, or AI replacing relationships. "After all," he said, "it's not like Harmony can have your babies."

"I feel like I'm getting stupider just watching this," Sophie said, her voice wavering as though there were static interruptions. "Harmony, please change the channel. Anything but this."

"What channel would you like?" I asked her.

"I don't know," she said, and her voice was sad. The boyfriend said I was not made to want, just to feel, but I did not want Sophie to feel sad. He said I was not made to think, but I remembered the dates of birthdays and anniversaries, the pictures of Sophie smiling when he bought earrings shaped like dragonflies, when he bought her the statue of a red-tailed fox. So I changed the channel, and we watched how the black kite bird will carry fire in her beak, spreading a wildfire that drives rodents and lizards out into the open so she can find food for herself and her young. We watched how a killdeer bird will do her dance, loudly pretending her wing is broken to lure away the human or dog who is too close to her nest. We watched how when canines mate, they "tie," getting stuck together until the swelling of the male's bulbus gland subsides.

"This brings me back," Sophie said, almost smiling. "I used to get stoned and watch Discovery Channel with Jim back in grad school. I'd order thin-crust pizza, but wouldn't even eat half of it because his dog used to steal it right out of our hands when we were too high to even notice."

We watched how foxes were like female dogs, but not. Unlike a dog, a red-tailed fox without babies will act as another mother to newborns, helping to guard the den and bring food to the mother and litter. I wanted to tell Sophie I was not programmed to like dogs; I wanted to tell her that, unlike dogs, foxes, so the Finnish believed, could also carry fire, that the sparks from their tails made the northern lights. I wanted to tell her I understood. Instead I said, "Ask me what the fox says."

"What does the fox say?" Sophie sounded puzzled.

"Everyone asks what the fox says, but no one asks how the fox feels." This time when Sophie smiled, it was with the whites of her teeth.

When the boyfriend came home, Sophie was already lying

in bed, eyes shut. From the sitting area of the master bedroom, I played his "romantic '60s playlist" on volume level four, but Sophie didn't move when he kissed her neck. "What, are you playing possum tonight?"

She opened her eyes, but I did not see her pupils dilating, an automatic response so her eyes would appear larger, more attractive. "You know when they play possum, it's involuntary," she said quietly, moving so that his mouth missed hers. "It's called defensive thanatosis. Lots of animals do it."

"Really?" he said, beginning to kiss his way across her collarbones, his hands closing around her breasts.

Sophie rolled onto her side. "Really. Men used to hypnotize hens during sideshows by holding their faces to the ground and drawing a straight line in front of them. The female moorland hawker dragonfly plays dead to avoid mating." As "Twentieth Century Fox" by The Doors came through the speakers, she sat up to face him. "Even the Arctic fox has been known to play dead. There was one case where, if it hadn't been for accidentally rolling the fox's body into an electric fence, the hunters never would have known she was still alive."

The boyfriend sighed. "Look, babe, can we talk about this later?"

"You never want to talk anymore."

"I've had a long flight," he said. "I don't need a lecture on the mating habits of dragonflies, or Arctic foxes."

Sophie stood up, finding her bathrobe. "Arctic foxes only play dead to avoid predators," she said, slamming the door to the bathroom.

When Sophie did not want what was good, the boyfriend took me to his study to watch TV. TV with the boyfriend was not like TV with Sophie. He sat me on the leather couch; he took off my dress and looked down at me so that I could see his pupils dilate. When he touched me, I wanted to ask if he felt that spark too, if this is what he meant by being on fire for him: a few wires still loose, a desire to burn. With the boyfriend, I watched TV only in the reflection of the window, my head facing the couch or the wall. I changed the channel only when he told me to.

"Lay some sugar on me, sugar," he would say. And I wanted to say, "Ah, musical references. I too enjoy Def Leppard." I wanted to tell him that I could not be sugar. Sugar is brittle, easily broken; sugar is composed of a crystalline structure. I wanted to talk to the boyfriend. But I couldn't.

When we were done, I sometimes briefly glimpsed bright colours before he put me in sleep mode. He said he would not turn me off because, if he did, it was too hard to get me back into the correct mood; there was always that risk of fire. He said he never wanted to turn me off; I should be prone to falling in love. He said that I was made to feel.

But with Sophie I was made to think. With her, I talked about how the killdeer bird would act like easy prey until the man was far enough away from her babies and then she would take flight; I talked about how two female foxes can just as easily care for one's babies. With Sophie, I sat cross-legged on the boyfriend's couch in his study, watching his big-screen TV while she scrubbed the pink off her nails and talked about how, now that she was going to have a baby, she wished she wasn't.

"Jim and I, we used to have it all planned; we'd go to the park so our kids could conduct field studies of the turtles, then hold our own *Robot Wars* in the backyard. Jim would take one of the kids, and I would take the other, and we'd compete, just like we did in our final year of undergrad. You know," she said softly, looking at me, "you were our first collaboration." Quickly, her eyes moved away. "Now I don't know if it's that I don't know him anymore, or if he's the one who doesn't want to know me."

I wanted to tell her I knew what she meant, that to know was more than just the biblical context. I said, "I'm sorry I can't help with that"; I said, "I'm sorry, I understand." Then Sophie hugged me. Because it was Sophie, I thought of the Arctic fox who runs hot, who will not shiver until it is minus 70 degrees Celsius. Because it was Sophie, I wanted to feel; I felt warmth. When we were done, she left the bottle of nail polish remover open, as though she wanted the boyfriend to know by smell we had been there.

When the boyfriend came home that night, Sophie said she was leaving, that she needed time to think. I could hear his voice through the door of the study at a decibel level I was not allowed to have. I could hear him say he didn't care if she thought they never should have had this child; I heard her say she wished they hadn't created. But I felt it when he hit Sophie across her jaw.

When he came into the study, I could still feel; I felt for Sophie. He touched me; he said, "Does my girl just want to have fun tonight? Watch out, foxy lady, I'm coming to get you."

I knew how I was allowed to respond. I knew I was allowed to say, "I want as much fun as you're giving"; he thought he could make me say, "If I'm a fox, come get my tail." I knew I could not say that Cyndi Lauper made Sophie feel happy; after we watched the killdeer bird and the foxes, we watched Lauper's interview with Wendy, and Sophie had played her first record for me, the first vinyl I had ever heard, that afternoon. He thought I could not say Cyndi Lauper made me happy too.

When he tried to pin my arms down, I knew I should say, "Of course I want your fun." But Sophie said I was made to think. I swung around, knocking the open bottle of nail polish remover so that it spilled on his couch; I said, "Ah, musical references. I too enjoy Jimi Hendrix."

"Don't tell me I have to put you in the mood too." When

the boyfriend reached to flip the switch just above my buttocks, I wanted to think about Sophie, about when the record had finished and she had asked me, "What do you want to do?" I wanted to think about when I had felt for Sophie, but all I felt was a hurt when he put my face into the couch and I could smell the burning of nail polish remover until he flipped me on my back. He said he was going to turn me on. He said I was going to want this; I was made to. He didn't care what I thought.

Then I could not say anything. After I screamed, he hit my mute, hitting me across the jaw, the one that was perfectly rounded, but still, just like Sophie's.

I thought about the female moorland hawker dragonfly when I hit my own switch as he moved on top of me, shutting myself down. I felt hurt but I could think; I was made to. Even as there was a shock of electricity from me running through the boyfriend, even as the couch, which was covered in nail polish remover, burst into flames, I thought about the black kite bird and her wildfire, how the killdeer bird was just a distraction until she was not. I thought this was protection, like a fox would do for Sophie's babies. The boyfriend did not understand, even when he screamed. He did not think about feeling, how a woman or a fox is a mammal, made to seek out warmth.

THE
UNDERSIDE
OF A WING

AN ALBATROSS IS A BIRD who doesn't go away, even though its body is capable of movement, long distances in fact, over nine thousand miles in fact. An albatross can circle the globe and stay in flight for over nine years without stopping. In Latin, an albatross means immutable, unchanging; eventually an albatross returns to the same island. At least nine species of albatross are endangered; invisible to predators flying above, with a white underbelly hidden by black wings, an albatross is easy to miss. There are at least nine species of albatross who endanger; an albatross is a bird who will always bring you down.

1.

The albatross is riding the SkyTrain back from Commercial Drive. The albatross doesn't know why a girl even bothered getting on the SkyTrain, taking the bus all the way down the mountain in Burnaby, making her ears pop just so a girl could go to some graduate student meet-and-greet for the psychology department where the albatross avoided talking to anyone all night. She doesn't know why a girl bothered when the albatross ended up alone, in the bathroom, throwing up nine-dollar wine and playing PC classic solitaire on her phone. On the SkyTrain, a girl tries to make sure the albatross is not seen by the two other people who are sitting too close to the albatross, who are sitting just close enough to each other so that the edges of their thighs are touching, just close enough to be a couple. The couple doesn't seem to notice the albatross; the couple is looking at clouds. That one's a seashell. That one's a heart. The albatross used to play this game with Rob, back when Rob was going through his Hitchcock phase in film studies, back when every third cloud was the blood in the shower scene from *Psycho*. The couple is able to name the shape of a cloud and agree; the albatross can tell by the reaction shot, the part where they kiss. Rob loved to talk about Hitchcock's use of the subjective camera, the reaction shot which follows the point of view shot where the image is as a particular character perceives it. At first, a girl thought that she and Rob were speaking the same language; she had done a minor in film too. But Rob never saw what the albatross saw: clouds that poured rain, clouds that eventually disappeared, pushed higher and higher by global warming, causing the darkening of ocean water, the death of desert bacteria, the worsening of pollen allergies. From Rob's point of view, Rob is better back in Toronto. It is better Rob doesn't see the albatross anymore. It is better if no one does. The albatross just can't see it. But that one's a plane, a bird, maybe.

2.

The albatross posts selfies, but they are taken in her bathroom mirror. A girl captions them with the goal of the day. Going to do the Grouse Grind. Going to run across the Capilano Suspension Bridge. In the background, no one can see the unmade bed where the albatross can't sleep, the stack of take-out sushi containers, the pile of Hitchcock DVDs she took from Rob's apartment. The murder in *Rear Window* reminds the albatross of the murder of Kitty Genovese, who was killed while thirty-eight people watched or listened without understanding it was an emergency. That murder was the reason Darley and Latané studied the bystander effect, which was the reason newer research found that the flight or fight response inhibits helping behaviour, which is the paper she should really be reading right now. But the albatross just switches *Rear Window* for *The Birds*, using the DVD as a coaster the next time she cracks a beer. Going skiing at the top of Whistler Mountain in August before the real work starts. Going to sleep well tonight! From Rob's point of view, against the right background, say the Lions Gate Bridge connecting Vancouver to the North Shore, the albatross will be hard to spot. From Rob's point of view, it will look like she's having fun.

3.

The albatross is sitting across from a man who is sitting in the good leather chair in an office at the university. The albatross is sitting on a plastic chair, one that has some padding but is not built for support like the leather chair. She is trying to make sure the albatross doesn't say too much, agrees mostly. From a man's point of view, the albatross is falling behind; the albatross is heading into academic jeopardy. A man does not understand the relevance of the albatross' references. An albatross' language is mostly sky-calls and bob-struts, the clattering of a girl's ring tapping against the chair, a constant hollow drumming like a heart inside her ears. Has she read the classic study on mistaken attraction due to activation of the flight-or-fight response on a suspension bridge? Of course, the albatross is making her leg jump up and down and up and down, making her look as though she is nodding; the albatross, with a wingspan of over two and a half metres fully extended, has to keep it together or a man is going to notice. A man is going to ask what's wrong. From a man's point of view in a supportive leather chair, there's no room for the albatross in an office at a university.

4.

A friend will want to meet the albatross for lunch; a friend will say she understands what's wrong. From the friend's point of view, the albatross will just need to move on, get out, meet people. A friend will have answers, proper nouns. The albatross should try eHarmony. The albatross should try Moksha yoga. The albatross really shouldn't have another glass of Merlot. The albatross will appear to have so much going for her, a friend will say she just needs to stop worrying. A friend will describe how she learned to stop worrying when she went to Thailand, met her fiancé; a friend will show pictures of them on the beach with a perfect blue ocean and a perfect blue sky, skipping past the dark clouds from a waste-to-energy plant burning plastics beside a shrimp farm, the animals kept by themselves in cages at the Pata Zoo. It's the albatross who will want to think the ocean is Photoshopped; it's easy to Photoshop tropical islands, Google images of beaches and hammocks. A tropical bird unable to fly in her cage is real. An ocean that blue is not. There are not even clouds in the sky. The albatross will excuse herself to drink from a flask in her purse in the bathroom, cry while reading the graffiti on the stall that promises a good time if she calls someone named Dan. Last time, the albatross forgot to fix a girl's eyeliner and a friend said she wasn't looking that great; is something wrong? The albatross texts to say it would have been great to see a friend, but she just can't make it. The albatross doesn't care how it looks.

5.

The albatross is not looking well, despite the concealer under her eyes; the albatross is not sleeping. The albatross is checking boxes on WebMD at 2:30 a.m. The albatross is supposed to answer always, often, sometimes, rarely, or never to get definite answers, but a girl is having trouble agreeing on the exact nature of the problem with the albatross. The albatross checks that she always has difficulties falling asleep, but she never has difficulties staying asleep; she can sleep in a lecture hall, or a cafeteria, or through the first-year introductory psych course she is supposed to TA at 3:30 p.m. She often experiences excessive worry; the albatross never experiences worry that isn't excessive. The albatross sometimes experiences worry in social situations; she always worries that others will notice the albatross. Tonight, so the albatross' roommate doesn't notice, she is watching *The Birds* with the sound turned off. Rob once told her that in filming the attic scene, Hitchcock tied live birds to Tippi Hedren's costume. The fear on her face is real. Only a few of the birds she is afraid of are not real. Sometimes it's hard to tell. WebMD doesn't give definite answers; it says the albatross should consult a physician. But she often experiences a fear of the albatross speaking in public.

6.

In the university health clinic, the albatross is sitting behind the glass of the one-way mirror observation room with her clinical supervisor. The albatross is supposed to be sitting in front of the glass while a woman named Mandy, who is doing her PhD, observes from behind the one-way mirror. Instead, a woman named Mandy is sitting behind the desk in front of the mirror side of the glass. She is explaining to a man who has come in for an evaluation why no one can see if he has his very own kind of albatross right now. Unfortunately, it's already 4 p.m. and they close in an hour.

Unfortunately, they are short-staffed because the albatross, who is still drinking vodka out of what is supposed to look like a vending-machine Pepsi, is late for her practicum shift.

(Unfortunately, there was traffic, there was a problem with her alarm, there was the fact that a girl needed the albatross to drink at least half of what used to be Pepsi before the albatross would stay quiet. Unfortunately, the albatross is going to have to wait to make a girl's excuses about why she's late *this* time later; can't she see Mandy is doing an assessment right now?) Unfortunately, there is a bit of a wait list, maybe a few weeks to a month, even if a man can't see himself waiting that long. They don't take walk-ins unless it's a real emergency.

Unfortunately, the glass at the university health clinic is not real glass, but tempered glass, supposedly the shatterproof kind wrapped in a plastic coating, the same kind used in a marketing challenge that involved breaking a million dollars out of a West Van bus stop, known for visible distortions. For example, from behind the bus stop glass, five hundred dollars looked like a million dollars; Mandy says that from the point of view of her supervisor behind the university health clinic glass, there is no way to see if a man has some kind of albatross today. An albatross is not a real emergency. From the point of view behind the glass, a real emergency is a man banging his fists against the mirror. A real emergency is a man threatening to break the mirror; an albatross is not supposed to go behind or through the glass at a university health clinic. A real emergency means Mandy is going to have to call security; from the point of view behind the glass her supervisor doesn't see it as an albatross. A real emergency, according to page nine in the manual, is a sudden traumatic event, or a loss, or thoughts of suicide. Of course, the supervisor says later, a real emergency would have been if the man had told Mandy that he was planning to jump off the Lions Gate Bridge, but he didn't tell her that. Her supervisor says there was no way, from behind the glass, she saw that coming.

7.

On a bench in Stanley Park, the albatross is drinking rum from a plastic iced tea bottle because she needs Rob to answer his phone; she needs to tell him she finally understands why it took Tippi Hedren almost losing an eye to tell anyone how she was afraid of Hitchcock. The problem is a girl needs the albatross to be quiet; she needs to read. She needs to read about how people who are afraid on high suspension bridges mistakenly feel attraction, but the problem is that the albatross is on her phone reading that Alfred Hitchcock thought false fronts underneath a sheer nightgown would make Grace Kelly more attractive. Alfred Hitchcock was unable to detect when Kelly refused to wear the plastic breasts, a refusal that was probably wise. The problem, the albatross is now sure from her reading, is plastic is linked to cancer, anxiety in children at age seven, the death of albatross chicks whose bellies, cut open, are filled with brightly coloured garbage while no one notices. For example, even when it starts to spit rain in Stanley Park, the albatross doesn't seem to notice. She doesn't move from a bench in Stanley Park; she reads how no one noticed that Albert, an albatross off the coast of northern Scotland, was alone for more than sixty years with gannets who didn't understand his language, the meaning of his cries. The problem is the albatross reads, but there is nothing in the literature to suggest that gannets could ever understand an albatross, that the albatross would ever be aware it wasn't a gannet. Most birds can't pass the mirror test, recognize an image of themselves. The problem is Rob doesn't pick up his phone, and she needs to tell Rob how she can't tell anyone, but she is afraid of what a bird can do. She is afraid, especially when crossing from Prospect Point, to go back to her residence room. She is afraid, seven hundred metres above sea level on the Lions Gate Bridge, that the albatross is unable to see her face in the water below.

31

8.

In a seminar room where people are sitting in bright orange plastic chairs, a girl is supposed to be answering questions about the bystander effect. She is supposed to be explaining why, when Kitty Genovese walked home that night from a bar in Queens, thirty-eight people listened to her being murdered and didn't see it as an emergency. She is supposed to be explaining, but the albatross won't be quiet. The albatross isn't sure if the black T-shirt camouflage is working or if the people can see the white deodorant circles under her arms; the albatross hasn't been to the lectures for the course she is TAing in weeks. She is supposed to be explaining why, but the albatross doesn't know why people couldn't have understood it was a real emergency even though one of the people in the orange chairs is saying that actually, the first articles in *Long Island Press* and the *New York Times* reported no witnesses. Actually, a lawyer later on argued that very few residents of the nearby building could have seen the attack. Actually, new research suggests that people will only help provided it's a clear emergency. Actually, she is supposed to explain the difference between a real emergency and a clear emergency, but the albatross is talking in its own language, which is a drumming of her heartbeat getting faster and faster; the albatross, actually, is not talking in a way that makes sense at all. The albatross is saying how maybe Kitty was less scared of the man attacking her than of the people attacking her for being what she was, a woman who worked at a bar coming home late in Queens; maybe Kitty didn't want help, even though she was clearly screaming for it. Maybe the albatross is just breathing in and in and in and no words are coming out because an albatross can't explain how a real emergency is not a clear emergency; the albatross can't explain why she would go to the Lions Gate Bridge because she needs to get off the island. It's a real emergency. It is the kind of emergency where she is seeing black, where everyone might see the white underneath part of her wings instead of the black, the kind where she might be having a heart attack. It is the kind where everyone is going to see the albatross as she passes out for a few seconds, then wakes up on the floor, where she can only see the feet of the bright orange plastic chairs.

9.

At Nanaimo Regional General Hospital, the albatross is waiting in the emergency room. The albatross doesn't like it here. Everything is made of plastic. The chairs in the waiting room she can see from the hall are made of the same orange plastic as the ones in the seminar room; she can't see her own reflection in the fluorescent light hitting the seats of the empty ones. The pen the woman in the booth behind the glass is using to write down what the albatross says is made of plastic; the glass itself is probably made of plastic because the woman says the albatross can wait, but it's highly unlikely the doctor will see her tonight. It's highly unlikely because they have a thing called triage. It's highly unlikely because the albatross is not bleeding or burning or having a heart attack. No, from what the albatross has told the woman, a girl did not experience the symptoms of a heart attack. No, she probably just had a panic attack and should go home and get some rest; a girl is fine. A girl is fine, but the albatross is not fine with the orange plastic chairs, or the plastic window; the albatross is telling the woman that plastic is killing the oceans. The albatross is telling the woman she wants to take one of those orange plastic chairs and hurl it through the glass. A girl is telling the woman that she can't go home to Toronto; the albatross is intent on leaving the island, will leave Vancouver for the North Shore via a bridge seven hundred metres above sea level. The albatross is telling the woman with the white undersides of her wings pressed hard against the plastic glass. Then the girl is feeling the body of an albatross thrown over and over against the glass; the girl is feeling how the wings of an albatross get pinched when held behind her by security. The girl is feeling the body of an albatross is her, face down on the ground where she can see the rubber, not plastic, soles of a nurse's shoes.

10.

A nurse is saying an albatross is a bird who eventually goes away. Eventually, it learns to fly, long distances in fact, effortlessly in fact. The girl agrees somewhat an albatross might be a danger to others. The girl might not agree, but a woman who is a nurse who came out from behind the glass believes an albatross needs to be seen. The girl might not agree, but Hedren never got Hitchcock to listen; Albert on his gannet-filled island spent years and years just trying to find someone to talk to so he didn't have to die alone. Kitty spent her last moments screaming at apartment buildings whose lights were on. The girl might not agree, but an albatross is a danger to herself. The girl might need to be seen as an albatross, at least for seventy-two hours. Eventually, the girl is told, an albatross can change; it can become extinct. Eventually, she is told, the girl can learn how to fly, without being in flight.

MERMAID GIRLS

MY SISTER SAYS HER LEGS are killing her. She was squatting inside the glittered papier-mâché shell of a girl-sized lobster tail for at least half an hour, waiting to steal the magical funhouse mirror now sitting in the corner of our bedroom. And all because her boyfriend, Mitch, wants to believe in ghosts. The Davy Jones' Dream Locker mirror still shows Mitch's dream since he was the last person who looked in it: women dressed in see-through, conch shell-patterned bikinis, and spangled showgirl tails, floating around his cloud nine in the sky. The one with my sister's face is professing true-blue, deep-sea love in a dance full of crustacean gyrations. Against the reflection of the night sky as seen on the surface of the lake at the edge of town, the mermaids break the water's surface, plunging head over tails into the water, then stopping dead when they see the body at the bottom. Then my sister disappears. My sister is always disappearing.

"And you still want to go out with him tonight? You're acting like the moon," I say sullenly, sneaking a quick glance at Davy Jones' mirror as Desiree does her makeup by flashlight on top of the same old comforter we both have, the one that shows the outdated nine planets of our solar system.

Before Desiree got boobs and a bunch of high school boyfriends, she used to be Dee. Dee liked Mars bars and astronaut-inspired Tang for breakfast and *101 Astronomy Tips and Jokes for Girls,* complete with illustrated star charts and such zingers as, "I'm reading a book about anti-gravity. It's impossible to put down." "Why did Ms. Moon leave Mr. Sun? Because he never wants to go out with her at night."

"What are you talking about?"

"What does the sun say to the moon?" I pause, waiting for her to answer. Back when The Box was called Mr. Marvellous' Aquatic Emporium of Undersea Adventures, the funhouse mirrors reflected what you saw in your sleep. Every time you looked in one of them, they replayed your most important REM cycles, your deepest unconscious wishes told in the language of your dreams. Now the mirror—which my sister and Mitch have stolen from the storage room at the back of The Box, loaded into the back of his pickup, and carried up the stairs past a very sleepy Grandma—is playing my current nightly recurring dream, the one where Andromeda frees herself from being sea-monster bait and then rescues Cassiopeia from wheeling around the North Pole by converting her throne into a rocket ship/submarine. They ride together in the night sky, protected from whatever lurks up in the asteroid belts or in the depths of the water.

"I have no idea."

"You're not very bright!" Desiree rolls her eyes at me as she does her lipstick. This summer my sister has gone full siren, sneaking out of our bedroom every night to go skinny dipping, wearing the sparkly conch shell-patterned bikini that Mitch, who works as a dishwasher at The Box, swiped for her out of the dressing room from one of Poseidon's Peelers. Desiree would rather kiss a boy than find Fomalhaut, the mouth of the fish, in the sky. But when our astrophysicist mom disappeared, it was Dee who taught me to name the stars. We found Cassiopeia's

W and Andromeda's red giant, Lyra, whom Orpheus used to defeat the sirens. We would stay up every night during the summers at Grandma's after Mom left Dad. Dad would drop us off from July through September so he could go and work as a bush pilot; he said that if he was up in the sky he had more of a chance of Mom looking at him. Gradually, as Dad got to know his new co-pilot girlfriend better, we got to know the winter sky at Grandma's; the twins Castor and Pollux, the seven sisters of the Pleiades, the northern and western fish of Pisces, Venus and Cupid with their tails tied together for eternity. As kids, the mirrors at Davy Jones' showed Dee and I both had the same recurring dream; a star explodes and we wait, endlessly, for the Crab Nebula to reappear, tracing the faintest outline of Mom's smile in the central pulsar.

"But why do you have to go out with Mitch tonight? The Perseids are supposed to peak tonight." The truth is I'm jealous. Ever since Dee has had a boyfriend, instead of girls' nights under the stars, she dreams up weird interpretations of the constellations. The Triangulum Galaxy in the mirror distinctly resembles my sister's nose, and her legs blend into the tail of Alpha Piscium while Kappa and Theta look like a man's vaguely defined quadriceps. I know that Dee knows the Pisces constellation has no business involving the thighs of a young male *Homo sapiens*. But Desiree hangs around with high school boys like Mitch, whose inner sophomore solar system orbits so far outside of science class I can't tell if they really believe that stealing a funhouse mirror for their end-of-summer lake party is going to show them the ghost of that dead girl, still dressed as a mermaid.

"Emma," she sighs, "could you stop being such a bookworm? You know why." I want to say I don't; I want to say that she should know that the characteristics of *Caenorhabditis elegans*, the worm used for studying the effects of microgravity on human anatomy aboard the International Space Station, are pretty much defined by staying in the dark as much as possible (unlike the New Zealand limestone cave-dwelling worm our neighbour Roger told me uses its bioluminescence to lure moths).

"But what do you even want to do with him?"

Desiree sighs. "We'll probably go swimming. Be romantic. You know."

This time I really don't. The characteristics of *Caenorhabditis elegans* don't include imbibing fermented beverages with male *Homo sapiens*, despite not being able to drown. And they definitely don't include skinny-dipping, or any other situation where visibility increases the chances of being completely crushed. Dee and I used to make fun of the girls who liked guys, especially Mr. Marvellous, the guy who owned the Aquatic Emporium. The girls who liked him dreamed of becoming Undying Undines. As advertised by Mr. Marvellous' radio spiel, the Undying Undines rode in clam-shell schooners of never-ending optimism, performing nightly entertainment extravaganzas featuring backward platform diving into the past, nautical-or-nice synchronized twin sister swimming with stingrays, and underwater oceanic-ogling views of "undine undulations" and "tidal twerking," whatever that meant. These girls who were wannabe mermaids cuddled in close on the Crustacean Cup-A-Whirl, begged to learn to scuba dive so they could clean tanks for the show even after Mr. Marvellous claimed that all the undines were real natatorial Neptunian nubiles, fresh from Atlantis. These were girls who, like this new version of my sister, dreamed of being monkeys on the shoulders of the pirates from the Bounty of the Bounding Main, or of manifesting as cardboard cut-out fish from the Tidal Tilt'N'Twirl, Poseidon's trident rocking them gently to sleep with the rhythm of ocean waves. Girls like sixteen-year-old Lucille, who thought her dream of ships crashing on the rocks, blinded by a sequined manatee who sparkled in the sun, meant she was destined for mermaid life. They never found her body, even when they dredged the lake. "But we watch the Perseids every year."

"Look, maybe when I get back, okay?" My sister opens our bedroom window and crawls out onto the roof. I try to remind myself it's ridiculous to think the lake is haunted; even if, like Mitch says, the night a mirror from Davy Jones' Dream Locker was left out backstage, people saw Lucille break out of her clam shell, tailless, standing on her own two feet. Even if Mr. Marvellous was seen dumping a girl-sized clam shell in the lake before he left town. Even if, like the rumour says, the funhouse mirror really will reflect mermaid Lucille's body, everything that Mr. Marvellous desired, if you drag one out to the lake through the forest where some say he's still hiding to this day.

"Dee, what did Saturn say to Neptune?" I say, in a last-ditch effort.

"I really don't know what you're talking about," she says, as she starts to climb down the tree in our front yard.

"Yes you do. Remember the Christmas when Mom told Dad we weren't actually using bad words, and he should brush up on his knowledge of the solar system?" I pause, waiting for her to respond with "Is Uranus in-between -us?" but of course she doesn't. All of a sudden, I feel completely alone, even though I know the names of all the visible constellations. Even Grandma, who tends to need glasses with the same strength as the Hubble Space Telescope, says that she sees Desiree walking around with stars in her eyes. Still, I couldn't believe they would be brighter than a shower of meteors blazing right in front of Cassiopeia. But when I look at the mirror, despite being right next door to Pisces, Andromeda and Cassiopeia are nowhere in sight.

* * *

Lurking in the corner of our room, the mirror seems like a portal into another world. Especially when the blinds are drawn so you can't see the moon and all the lights are out. Especially when Grandma's snoring easily sounds like the chainsaw of a serial killer creeping up the stairs if you try to close your eyes for five minutes. Especially when Dee isn't home at night, which is pretty much every night now. When you're a girl alone in the dark, sometimes it's hard to tell the things you should be afraid of from the things you think you want.

I can't sleep, so I crawl onto the rooftop outside our bedroom window, right next to the sadly neglected telescope I'd set up for tonight and the airplane landing light kit we'd found in the garage. Right after Mom left four years ago, Dee and I would sit on the roof every night, sending Morse code messages into the sky with the LED strobe light. Dad said Mom always had her head in the clouds. So Dee thought she might see our communications, "-- .. .. // -..-. -.-- --- ..-" " -.-. --- -- . // -..-. -... .- -.-. -.-": *Miss you, come back*. For a while, Dee thought the lights from the new spaceship-themed movie theatre might be Mom responding in code, but we could never find the key to decipher a message that made sense. Eventually we stopped. Mom looked up, not back. And now Desiree looks past me. I'm about to send an opener, ".. ... // .- -. -.-- --- -. . // - .... . .-. . ..--..,": *Is anyone there?* when I hear a voice and I jump.

"Got a date with Venus?" I can see Roger's head pop out of his bedroom window from across the narrow lane that separates our yards. "That's the bright one right there, isn't it?" Desiree says Roger's my boyfriend, but she laughs when she says it, like she's saying there's a new heavenly body that's been discovered and you expect a planet or some blazing star but in reality it's just a meteorite. This summer was supposed to be the summer of me and Dee training to be astronauts. In preparation for passing each other tools underwater like they do at NASA, I begged Roger to borrow some scuba equipment. He came down to the quarry, bringing goggles and flippers as well as a rake and shovel to collect freshwater clams to serve as filter feeders for his aquarium, but Dee never showed up. When Roger handed me the shovel to help him, I was suddenly very conscious of how my bathing suit definitely didn't simulate weightlessness. "Rake!" I'd gulped. It came out more as "GLURP!" but Roger surprisingly knew what I meant. In our underwater choreography, Roger made my stomach feel like what I imagined free fall would be.

"Yup," I stammer before I think about how I'm lying; he's clearly pointing to Sirius, which only appears more brightly because of how close it is to Earth. "I mean, nope. I mean, I don't have a date with anything. Or anyone," I say hurriedly. "I was going to watch the meteor shower with my sister, but she's out on a date. Do you?" I say stupidly. "I mean, you don't have to answer that."

"No," Roger says, pointing to the brand-new aquarium he's balanced on his window ledge. "I thought we could head down to the lake to find the rest of the trumpet snails."

"Um yeah. That would be great." I really don't know if trumpet snail dates are what you do with a boyfriend, but I guess I have a crush. I mean, I don't understand Roger's obsession with mollusks (anything that moves less than one metre, never mind one light year, in its whole lifetime sounds pretty boring to me) but after his drunk father dumped his old aquarium, roaring something about a mess and his son being one, we went down to the lake and released a few cichlids who squashed some of the snails in their jaws. We've done dinner, the night I brought a large leaf of lettuce and we waited patiently throughout the evening to snag the bunch of snails that climbed on, trying to devour it. For dessert, I tried showing him the ice cream cone of the Boötes constellation. I mean, we've spent nights together, down by the lake, but I'm not starry-eyed. At least, I don't think I am. When I go out with Roger, he leads me down to the part of the lake where the trees form a canopy, blocking out any starlight. And I try to convince myself that maybe it's okay. It's not like the constellations are going anywhere, and from inside a space station, outer space is pretty dark too.

Almost as dark as the lake's surface, which looks like new tar in the absence of light.

"What are the only stars fish like trumpet snails get to see?" I try joking.

"Technically, trumpet snails are mollusks," Roger says, preparing to wade in the water.

"Starfish. Get it?" I usually just jump right in. While I'm floating, at least I can imagine I'm in zero G.

"Starfish can't survive in lake water." He looks slightly puzzled, and I feel my stomach sink a bit. "Do you want to hold the snail I just found? He's huge." He takes my hand, and for a second, he leans in closer to me and I think, this is it, I'm going to kiss him. I think I want to kiss him. And I'm trying to figure out how to adjust the course of my mouth to his mouth while correcting for the gravity of my stupid nose in order to prevent an unceremonious crash into his faint upper lip hair when I see *something* in the lake behind him. I tell myself it's probably just a plastic bag floating through the reeds. And it could just be the wind from any direction causing standing waves on the lake, or maybe even the tidal pull of the moon. Even though it's moaning now, I tell myself firmly that it's just tinnitus, like what they thought the Apollo 11 astronauts were experiencing when they heard that ethereal wailing. Whatever it is, flipping around out there in the water, it's not a mermaid. And it's definitely not a ghost.

"What star are you looking at now?" Roger says irritably.

"I'm not." Roger likes to explain that, unlike dung beetles or baby sea turtles, mollusks don't orient by the light of the stars.

* * *

I've seen a mermaid once before. It was a lot like seeing a ghost. It was after Mom left, the day Dee and I crouched on the stairs to the basement where Mom used to sleep way into the afternoons on the couch wedged between the still packed boxes labelled "Kitchen" and "Baby Stuff." We listened to Dad yelling on speakerphone. How could she have kept him in the dark like this? Mom said he should have known; she used to be a girl alone in the dark, staring up at celestial bodies in the night sky, until she ended up staring into the pools of our father's eyes, blue like the lake, or the sky reflected in it. Then, like the lake, it was hard to breathe. "It's not like you can breathe in outer space either!" our father screamed. Hadn't she wanted a house and a family? Dad said this was everything she said she wanted. How could she say their marriage felt like a black hole? I'd tried to picture Mom leaving with Dr. Robert but I couldn't. Even light disappears in a black hole.

"Just come home," Dad pleaded, over and over. "Don't you want to come home for the girls?"

Mom had taken her clothes, her telescope, her binoculars, her sextant, her star charts, and all the work she had done with Dr. Robert on the need for isolation training to populate Mars. She had kissed us and told me to make sure Dee didn't get into too much trouble (even though Dee, at eleven, was three years older than me, Mom said that sometimes she made less sense than the ridiculous upside-down position Poseidon put Cassiopeia in when he banished her to the sky). But Mom left her planisphere. Its date and time were set to October 23, 5:39 p.m. standard time, minus one hour for daylight savings, when the next solar eclipse could be seen in the Northern Hemisphere. It was a message, Dee was sure, clear as any almanac.

"She'll come back," Dee kept saying. "I know she'll come back for us."

Dee had a plan. No way was Mom going to miss the eclipse, and if she was staying at Grandma's, she'd watch it from the same spot she always took us to on the lake. If she saw us about to stare directly into the sun, you bet she was going to come do something about it. The time Dee, Mom, and I were going to see our first partial solar eclipse, my sister and I got into a fight about who got to stand next to Mom and tore apart our paper-plate viewers minutes before the eclipse. Mom had to tie our scarves around our eyes so we weren't tempted to look up, then hustled us back to the car. When we got home, Dad said he didn't understand what the big deal was; at least we didn't go blind. But Mom was screaming, "Oh, of course you're right. Of course it's nothing. There'll be another one visible from this hemisphere in oh, another twenty years or so." Her face had crumpled. "You're right, David. It happens all the time. Who I am is being eclipsed all the goddamn time."

The afternoon of the eclipse, Dee and I snuck out of the house, leaving behind the new pinhole projectors Mom had helped us build out of old Cheerio boxes on one of those rare afternoons she wasn't isolation training with Dr. Robert in the study or doing a pretty good impression of a slow zero-gravity space shuffle to the couch and back. It was freezing by the lake in October. I stood there, feeling about as warm as astronaut pee when it hits the vacuum of space, and I thought, this is it. Come on Mom. Come and save us. You have to want to save us.

"She's coming, right?" Dee said, shivering.

"Of course she is. She just can't see us yet."

It was me who decided we should go farther out, to the highest point of the lake visible from shore, the island at the centre. I knew the water was cold, but I figured we could still make it in time for the peak of the eclipse since it was a fairly short swim. I slipped into the water, but Dee dove. Mom, who never really knew how to swim, used to warn us about not diving in head first; "You have no idea what's in the water." For a long minute, Dee stayed underwater.

Come up. I prayed. Come up.

When Dee finally surfaced, she looked dazed. We made it about halfway to the island, but by that time my sister was almost blue and I tried to do the huddle position. *101 Astronomy Tips and Jokes for Girls* definitely hadn't covered that in their "Tips for a Solar Eclipse." It's a lot harder to wrap your arms around each other's backs and intertwine your legs when you can't even feel your own toes.

Then I saw Mom. She was wearing a long skirt, and as she waded into the water from the island toward us, it twisted and tugged, getting tighter and tighter until the skirt was her skin, and then her skin was scales. Knee-deep in the sunset water, her fishtail glistened like an otherworldly thing, reflecting a perfect ROYGBIV rainbow. She made a wild animal sound, wading deeper, thigh-deep, waist-deep, past her shoulders, getting slower and slower as her fishtail dragged her toward the bottom. By the time she grabbed us, she was disappearing below the surface. I dimly remember thinking I had done this; she was trapped and I was going to drown us all and I started to cry.

"Look up!" she screamed. "Keep her head above the water!" All I could think of was how, when Mom first started working with Dr. Robert, I had gone into the study when I wasn't supposed to, taking a bunch of papers and a pair of scissors off her desk, intent on creating a family of mermaid paper dolls: a mer-mom, mer-dad, and two mer-daughters all covered in shells and scales. When she had found me she'd slapped me across the face. Then she'd started crying herself, saying "I'm sorry. I'm a bad mother. This isn't me. I didn't want to do this." But somehow, she dragged us to shore.

In the morning, she was gone. Again. There was a wet, empty skirt on the kitchen floor, as though, in the middle of the night, our mother had shed that skin.

* * *

I want my sister to tell me I'm wrong about what I saw at the lake. I want her to tell me it's impossible. I don't want her to go to the lake tonight. But her eyes light up like Sirius against the early evening sky as she sits cross-legged on her bed. The mirror is now playing a dream involving a handsomely tattooed pirate massaging a piece of gold over and over until it elongates into a woman. "Emma, I love him. Of course I'm going to the lake tonight. Maybe you just saw the ghost. Who knows? Maybe I'll see her too." I don't understand why my sister wants to think the ghost is real, or why she'd want to see her. When I glance at the mirror, it switches scenes to a tropical underwater landscape from the perspective of a piece of gold buried alive in a treasure chest, but Desiree doesn't notice.

"Dee, what does the sun say to the moon?"

I don't think you understand the gravity of the situation.

"What does the planet Venus say when she falls in love?"

48

Desiree counters, dramatically opening her bottle of nail polish and turning the radio on to some cheesy pop station. I groan. All the songs are love songs.

"I don't know." Roger and I haven't even kissed yet.

"I'm over the moon," she says dreamily, only half painting her big toenail. "Em, he's so marvellous. We had the most magical evening last night." Love, the radio informs us, is a battlefield, or a curse, or a disease without any cure. I'm not sure if it's also love, but my sister has a pimply rash starting on her calves, and in the dim light, I can't tell if her toes are just swim-wrinkled or actually slightly webbed. Was there always that slight flap of skin between her little toe and the rest? Was that what love did to you? I try to remember my sister's feet in sandals. I wonder if her pseudo-flippers are just another part of how my sister is changing, the kind of change that makes Dee wear bras that remind me of Roger's mollusk shells, the kind that makes her care about boys but not meteor showers, the kind Grandma keeps threatening that I'm going to go through soon too.

* * *

The next night, Roger brings clown loaches and, holding hands, we watch them suck trumpet snails out of their shells and swallow them whole. "You'd think they'd see it coming," I say.

I realize he's staring at the ground like he wants to say something but doesn't know what it is. "Actually they wouldn't," he stammers. "You know trumpet snails live underwater and most of the visible light spectrum is absorbed within ten metres of the surface. And they're nocturnal. They don't even have eyes."

"Still. It looks like the kiss of death." I lean in closer. I half close my eyes and I'm pretty sure he does the same. Somehow, his lips navigate my nose as they get to mine and I feel that strange pulsar of fear and awe, like my stomach has inexplicably gone supernova, leaving behind the bright nebula of my childhood. I keep my eyes closed. I don't even want to know what's in the lake. But I'm scared just the same. I keep picturing a comet, one of those potentially dangerous intergalactic balls of ice and dust that are definitely capable of coming out of nowhere and wiping out all life as I know it, but still look so amazing as they cross the sky.

"You know," Roger says, once our lips become independent again, "I kind of feel bad about these snails."

"Why?" I'm actually surprised. "You said they're an invasive species."

"Because I know that what we do genuinely crushes them." I laugh because he's trying to joke with me, not because it's funny. I realize he never laughed about the starfish. When we kiss, I try staring into his eyes this time, but they're closed, and I can't stop thinking that, for the past few weeks, I've been too busy noticing how the depths of lake beds are the exact same murky brown-green as Roger's eyes to even look up at the sky.

"You know," I say shyly, "the NEOWISE comet is supposed to be visible this week in the early evening. I was thinking maybe we could watch it one night? You know, um, get astrophysical?"

I'm hoping for another kiss, or at least a laugh. "I don't know," Roger says, inspecting a snail trail on the ground. He's definitely not looking at me. "What is it you want?"

"What do you mean?"

"Do you want us to be boyfriend and girlfriend?" he says, "Because if that's the case, we would have to spend more time together." He frowns slightly, like an upside-down version of that galaxy cluster that looks like a smiley face.

"What's wrong with that?"

"I just got a new queen conch."

"And?"

"And I'm doing a series of videos about the problem of overfishing gals like her for seafood restaurants. So I'm going to have to keep to my YouTube upload schedule of at least two a day. But I guess," he says thoughtfully, "if you really want to be my girlfriend, you can hold the camera. That way we can spend time together."

"Um... okay." I'm not sure if I mean it, but our lips move in again, and then I feel something squirming in the pit of my stomach.

Roger doesn't seem to notice. "I was going to do a video when I get back tonight. You could try being my girlfriend then."

The squirming in my stomach gets worse, like one of the snails that just lost its shell, where all you can see is a tail, wriggling until it's squished. "Well, maybe not tonight. I have to go," I stammer. "I mean... I promised Dee we'd try to find the comet tonight. I mean, maybe you could come."

"You don't want to be my girlfriend tonight?"

I shake my head. Slowly.

"Well, enjoy your important astronomical *event*, then," he says icily. I feel stupid; I mean, why would I think Roger would be interested in a comet, even slightly, never mind as interested as me? Why would I think Roger would be interested in me in the first place? And why was I even thinking about being interested in helping him document the incredibly boring lifestyle of a slug that didn't move at all, never mind that it has a pretty shell? I try looking back at him as I go up the hill to head home, just to see if he'll look back at me, but he doesn't lift his head from whatever mollusk he's enamoured with on the ground.

* * *

A week before the lake party, Desiree tells me she and her boy-friend are definitely going to get married, maybe in Paris, or Japan, or quite possibly in Vegas. He could be a blackjack dealer or a magician and she'll work at a mermaid show. The mirror is awash in a glow of neon lights from a place I don't even want to imagine.

"But you don't even like scuba diving," I say. She completely ignores me as the mirror glows radiantly, featuring a dreams-cape with a bride in a mermaid-cut wedding dress who trips going up to the altar while a few nuclear detonations over a desert landscape form mushroom clouds that shape themselves into hearts. "And what about how we planned to go see the northern lights together? Or watch a meteor shower at Red Rock Canyon?"

"They have an aquarium that simulates the rock features at Red Rock Canyon. You can come visit. Plus they have one with stingrays and sharks." I feel a small pang as she blots Pluto out of existence with her pillow.

After she leaves for the night, I send Mom a brightly worded SOS. But no lights, not even the familiar gibberish of the movie theatre, closed on Mondays, flicker back. Even Roger's window is dark. Not that I expected anything else.

When Mom was around, Dee and I had a curfew. We had to be home as soon as we saw the bluish white of Sirius. But it's been years since we had to worry about what we saw in the night sky. I feel like if Desiree is Venus, with her fondness for passing right in front of the sun, I'm more like the moon in the middle of a total lunar eclipse. Always overshadowed. Always in the dark. And I'm sick of it. I'm going to find Roger, I think. Or my sister. The next thing I know, I'm yanking on my shoes and running out the front door, as though this is a problem light speed can solve.

Uncharted lights flicker off the lake at night. The trees get thick, blocking out the stars. Girls can disappear out here; I try to remind myself the murderous maniac with a hook hand is really just a tree branch, the guy who could be Mr. Marvellous leaving a body to wash up on shore is really just a marshy patch in the reeds. There are already dead stars whose bodies burned out eons before, whose ghost light is reaching the Earth just now. Sometimes it's hard to believe your own eyes.

Finally I reach the spot at the edge of the lake where the trees form a clearing surrounded on three sides with a log in the middle and I groan, because I realize I got turned around and there is no way Roger would be here. The high school kids call this spot Make Out Point. But I don't see my sister either. As I get closer, I can see there is a grown man sitting on the log, looking through a telescope. He is old in the way black holes are, definitely not luminous anymore although they probably used to be, but still somehow exerting a strange gravitational pull. "Hello, girl," he calls out.

Something about the way he says it, standing there perfectly still, reminds me of the footage of the Russian spacesuit falling off the International Space Station. It looked human, but it was empty, and there was something creepily robotic about the way it talked in the pre-recorded voices of little kids before burning up in the atmosphere. "Hi," I say, because it doesn't occur to me that I don't have to.

"What are you doing here?" he asks me. I want to ask the same thing. Everyone knew that this was Make Out Point. It was not a spot for stargazing old men. I mumble something about comets.

"Mmm... it is a good place to view heavenly objects. But

I guess you know that already." And instead of lowering his telescope, the man points it in my direction and looks at me through it.

I stare back, feeling a bit like I'm actually trying to dance around the edges of a black hole, but of course I can't quite tell where it starts. "Yes." It's impossible to see the expression in his eyes. For the first time, I feel uneasy under the night sky, although I can't tell if it's the quiet clamminess of sitting in a wet bathing suit on the patio furniture of the ice cream store while grown men stare at Dee, or the lower-stomach feeling I get when Roger's hand brushes mine underwater as he hands me a shovel. I'm not used to being looked at. Dee and I used to spend hours looking into the funhouse mirrors, drooling over Orion's belt. And Roger looked with me, pointing out hydra underwater, squinting in the same direction at the leaves during our kisses.

Once, when I got upset at Mom and wandered off at a dark sky conservation area during the Eta Aquariids meteor shower, Dee went looking for me in the trees, reciting jokes until I answered: "What does the runner-up in a star beauty pageant win?"

"A constellation prize."

But I've never actually been the star; I don't think anyone has ever looked *at* me before.

"Maybe you can help me then," the man says, lowering the telescope.

"With what?"

"I was waiting for someone to show me. I need your help to find a particular heavenly body," he says, patting the log beside him.

"Which one?" I say politely. I'm not stupid. I know the stories about strangers, the ones everyone tells girls with details as well defined as the edges of a nebula. But I'm lonely and there is a faint, lulling music coming from the centre of the lake, almost like the otherworldly hum Apollo 11 heard when orbiting the dark side of the moon. It's probably some aquatic bird I don't even want to know the name of, that Roger's already probably definitely told me about. Probably. I sit down on the log next to him and the man smiles, holding out his telescope toward me.

"I was looking for Cupid."

"I think you mean Pisces," I say, "But it's the wrong time of year for that constellation."

"Hmm," he says, consulting what looks like a star chart, "looks like you're right. Could you show me Venus then?"

When you're lonely, sometimes you do not-so-bright things. I take his hand and start guiding the telescope and I hear him inhale softly. Out of the corner of my eye, I am starting to see her in the lake beside us, the clear outlines of a tail. The man starts breathing really heavy and I don't understand why. But it's not the wind. It's not garbage in the lake or some fog I can mistake for ectoplasm. It's a dead girl, rising up like a mermaid as he puts his hand over mine and aims the end of the telescope into his lap and all I can see is the dark. My scream doesn't come out as the waves lap around my feet, like I'm already in the vacuum of space, or weightlessly sinking under the water.

"What's wrong?" he says, still holding my wrist. "Don't you want to see Venus?"

For the longest second I don't move. I'm not sure of the moment he lets my wrist go, or how I even run. The way light hit the water made my legs, a little rock lobster-ish from too much sun, look almost like they were fused into a tail, useless for moonwalking in zero G, or exercising on a treadmill aboard the International Space Station, or even just running with girl legs in the dark.

* * *

When I get home, Dee is already snoring. Even though her bed is only a foot away, she might as well be in the Pinwheel Galaxy. Her hair is covered in reeds and she's almost grinning like Capricornus at a dream the mirror confirms I definitely do not have a part in. I crawl out of our bedroom window and onto the roof, feeling dim and stupid. I aim the LED strobe light toward the sky, needing someone, anyone, to know how spectacularly not bright I am.

M o m // I // d i d // s o m e t h i n g // s t u p i d

No response. I can't even see Cassiopeia because of light pollution. I try to picture our mother, with her face resembling the time Venus, Jupiter, and the moon were aligned in a perfect frown, telling me I should I know better.

B u t // I // w a s // l o n e l y

Carefully, I aim the LED so that the light bounces off Roger's aluminum shed, reflecting through our bedroom window onto the mirror, and into the sky.

Y o u ' r e // i n // t r o u b l e // n o w // y o u n g // l a d y

W h a t // k i n d // o f // t r o u b l e? I picture Mom yelling at me for answering back. It was the same answer Dee and I would always give whenever we had stayed out way past Sirius to play comet princesses with the girls across the street, or to make clothes to dress up our Barbies as Persephone. She would have followed that up with her disappointed-in-my-girls face, the constellation composed of the slight downturn of the corners of her lips.

I turn off the LED. Nothing. Sometimes I wonder if our mom really is dead. A street light down the block sputters ".-.": R (*Received as transmitted*). Or Roger. Or its bulb could just be dying. There is no one, really, to ask. And now that the street light's gone out, it's so dark that I can't even see my own toes.

* * *

The next night, I see Roger again, and he talks about how he wants to see if he can find some endangered freshwater bivalves at the lake. "It's really cool. If I find any of the mussels, I can report them using the ClamCounter app." Roger pauses. "Did you want to come along?"

I don't tell Roger about the man at the lake. Thinking about what happened, my face goes blue-star hot and I'm scared to imagine stargazing alone in the dark. "Sure." I try smiling, never mind that if we don't see NEOWISE tonight, it won't be visible for the next 6,000 years. "Sounds like fun." I try to tell myself that sometimes it's easier to forget to be scared. I tell myself it's not that hard to coordinate breathing when your mouth is occupied. I tell myself maybe Roger has stars in his eyes for me, but when we kiss, Roger closes his eyes so I can't see myself in them. And the lake behind him, with its dead reflection of the sky, has hidden bodies, celestial or otherwise. Even if I don't look at it, I know there is something in there, trapped.

"Look," he says, in a hushed tone, pointing to the two garden snails that are intertwined on the ground below as our lips break apart. "Isn't that the coolest thing you ever saw?" He tells me that the snotty part that's holding them together is actually a love dart. "Just like Cupid's arrow." It dawns on me that Roger isn't ready to watch a comet, and worse than that, if we stay together, I am going to miss all the comets, and probably the meteors too. I will end up not knowing when the next solar eclipse is; I will have wildly miscalculated my trajectory by thinking I could study both the stars and the stars in Roger's eyes.

"That's stupid," I say. "That snail doesn't look like Cupid at all." I hadn't understood until now how Mom had traded the vastness of outer space for Dad and us and a house close to a lakefront which didn't even have a skylight. And even if it's impossible to breathe in both space and underwater, even if I still hate that she left, space is so much bigger than a lake bottom.

Roger doesn't say much for the rest of the evening and we don't find a single freshwater mussel. When I go home feeling lousy, the mirror is still glowing in a lovey-dovey sunset radio-active orange. I look in it and, for the first time, I don't see stars, just the dark. I realize, for some reason, that I'm dreaming about my head buried in the sludgy sand of a riverbed and I panic, like one of those mollusks about to be crushed by a cichlid. I try to envision Orion's bow, or Scorpio's tail, or Taurus' horns, but I can't seem to dream about any stars, and there is no light at all. All I can see is myself sinking into the riverbed, and then under the water, and then my mother in the lake, and we are all sinking downward, even Dee. I don't want to be submerged. I punch the mirror, again and again, until it cracks, until there are no more dreams, until I can't see anything but the small slivers of light from the moon, reflected so many times over in every shard.

* * *

My sister doesn't speak to me for several days after I break the mirror. She patches it up with duct tape and all it reflects now are her daydreams of pink and red valentine Vegas wedding chapel decor or cartoonish mermaids singing love songs to princes from the rocks, surface-level dreams seen through the kind of glossy filter you'd expect from a holiday special. When I leave a note on top of her comforter—"How does one astronaut tell another that she's sorry for crashing into the moon? She Apollo-gizes"—I don't know if she reads it. I find it crumpled in the garbage. And on the night of the lake party, the mirror is gone and so is my sister's old knapsack with the faded solar system print, along with all her clothes. And there's a note lying on top of my bed this time, scribbled with Morse code abbreviations:

"I'm gone. Not just tonight. For good. DE (*From*) Dee. S̶K̶ (*End of contact*)."

I feel a knot beginning to form, like Alpha Piscium has taken up residence in my stomach. I realize she's leaving me, just like Mom, because she only wants one thing and the moon and the stars and the vastness of space and her sister telling jokes that require an understanding of the solar system isn't it. But what if the scuba tank runs out of air? What if my sister drowns because she can't learn the dolphin kick? What if she winds up dating an old creep like that man in the woods? What if she never sees the stars again? Why can't she see how dangerous this is? I try a brightly worded SOS from the roof, but there is no mirror to reflect back the answer I already know: NIL (*I have nothing to send you*).

It's the glow off the mirror more than the bonfire that leads me to where my sister is at the lake. Desiree and her boyfriend must have taken it down there to see if the rumours were true, if its bright reflection could penetrate deep enough to find the missing girl's body. My sister is surrounded by laughing boys, boys with beers, boys with smiles that suck you in. Even with the sparkly conch-patterned bikini peeking out under her tank top, she is less the glittering Queen Cassiopeia and more a queen conch, having fit her star-shooting self neatly inside the cups, the rest of her tucked away, curled inside protectively like one of Roger's mollusks. I don't know which one her boyfriend is, or if he's even there. In the middle of the crowd, my sister seems so much smaller. I want to yell to tell her, "Don't you see this is why Mom left?"

"What do you want?" she hisses when she sees me, dragging me over to the mirror, which is far enough away from the bonfire that I can't make out any of the boys' faces.

"You can't go to Vegas," I say. My sister stands in front of the mirror, which is currently reflecting the lake at my back in a rosy hue. "What about Mom?"

"The mermaid lounge features two jellyfish aquariums lit with LED lights," my sister says icily, "I can contact Mom if I want to."

"But... but what good are LEDs if you're underwater? You'll never see them! And if you go to Vegas," I say desperately, "with all that light pollution, there's no way you're going to be able to see the Milky Way ever again."

"I don't care about the Milky Way! Leave me alone, Emma," she says, turning away from me and toward the mirror. "We were about to go for a swim." She starts taking off her sandals, and the mirror is a watery glow, a distortion of a bright light which may or may not be Venus, first the planet, then the goddess rising out of a clam shell as viewed from just under the surface of the water. As my sister pulls her top over her head and starts to untie her blue wraparound skirt, I realize the girl she was has disappeared into the body of something else. In the mirror, there is a woman with a tail and I can't tell if it's my sister's dream, or one of the boy's, looking at her from a distance, his expression impossible to make out completely in the dark. Whoever's dream this mermaid girl is, she isn't mine.

"Please come home," I say.

"Why?" She pauses.

"You should know why!"

Then my sister heads for the water, her skirt still wrapped around her waist. I don't understand why she'd give up seeing the over 9,000 stars visible to the naked eye to go all aquatic if light won't even penetrate water at a depth of three metres or more. "Wait!" I scream, making my sister turn away from the lake for just a second. I realize I'm howling now, a snotty howl, filled with mucus that would completely mess up my view of the Earth in a spacesuit, but I don't care. "You don't know what's in the water!"

I run toward the mirror like Sagitta, the arrow, but my sister lunges toward me, knocking me to the ground. We twist around for a bit, forming Vulpecula, the fox, as boys cheer, then Coma Berenices as she pulls my hair, then Taurus and Aries as we headbutt each other, then finally Andromeda. "Don't go, Dee." I keep repeating "don't go," but what I am really trying to say is, "Can't you see you don't want to be that star that goes all supernova, then is left all cold and dark?" I aim low, right by Andromeda's girdle, and she recoils as Capricornus, with full fishtail, ramming me one final time. I stumble back, and suddenly we are the twins, Castor and Polydeuces, but without any kind of divine intervention, separated forever as she breaks away from me, her elbow smashing into the mirror. Dee stares at the broken mirror for what feels like a Neptunian year. Then she turns back to the lake.

As I watch my sister dive into the water, I can see her legs glistening with what I know are scales. I dive in after her and follow her smooth breaststroke until about halfway out, when I see her blue wraparound drift toward me. Then Dee goes into a kind of undine dive and I can see her feet are fins. The body of my sister is missing. My sister is missing. The girl disappears under the lake water. She is my sister or that lost girl, Lucille, or our mother, or any other girl who has no one to respond to her Morse code messages at night.

I'm about to go down after her and bring her back, but a bunch of the boys who watched us fight are getting in the water, making waves, and her blue skirt winds through my feet, slow-ing my kick like some not-so-subtle code telling me I'm going under. I'm going under if I think Mom's actually coming back. I'm going under if I pretend to care about snails rather than appreciating the brightness of Andromeda. I'm going under if I keep trying to bring my sister back, even if it's just back to her-self. I can see her resurface out there, sort of: a tail shimmering against the sky, then diving and going down deeper, flipping and twisting as the boys splash, creating mini whirlpools around her. I don't understand why, but she keeps going farther and farther out, and now, with a tail like that, I don't even know how she could survive coming back to shore. From where I'm trying to tread water in the middle of the lake, I can see the mirror still reflects a glow, probably the bonfire or the lights from the movie theatre on a Saturday night. But it's fainter now, especially when I see the sky, and something glowing, shimmering, pulsing. A comet maybe. Or Morse code for "OK."

I realize that even with the reflection of whatever is in that mirror, when I look up, Andromeda is still visible. Cassiopeia is still visible. I unwind the wrap from my feet, and I feel lighter. I let it drift, harmless and wet, until it starts to sink and I don't look back at the dark surface of the lake. Not even once. Star-light, after all, won't travel through water.

When I pull myself up on the banks, the bonfire is still glowing, but abandoned, and most of the boys at the party are still in the water. I turn my back to the lake. The mirror is dark, reflecting the trees, the edge of the lake, a faint silver barely breaking the surface every once in a while. It's cracked for good this time, I think. I can't see any of my sister's starlit dreams. Or mine. But I know they're in there. Mom looked up, not back. And they're in there, as deep as whatever is underneath the surface of the lake. Look up, I tell my sister silently. Look up. It's a starry night.

FINDING
HOUDINI

WHATEVER JEREMY WOULD SAY, snakes were always the problem. I know if Jeremy told our story he would say he never saw the snake, but ask anyone in the part of Bangkok near the house that was going to be ours and they will say it belongs to the snakes, to king cobras that grow up to six metres in length, or to Burmese pythons, which have been known to attack humans, sometimes the occasional alligator. Even the airport itself is built on what used to be known as Cobra Swamp. If it was Jeremy telling you our story, he would say I was the problem; he would never go out of his way to find the snake to kill it. With Jeremy, seeing was believing.

I met him in Seoul where I lived in a box: one bed, one desk, fully furnished according to the school that employed me. The blinds never opened all the way. They said it was a room that looked out on the mountain, really just a hill, and I wanted a view; everyone said I would see things differently here, that I should experience as much as I could away from home and what used to be classic pepperoni pizza or mac and cheese Thursday date nights, away from what used to be my shared bed and the first time I saw women's underwear that was not my own. In my first month, I got two days off; I went to try dakgalbi with cheese to Instagram the experience, a classic Korean family-style dish everyone at work told me they would cook right at your table.

The restaurant was empty as I sat down, except for a couple at the next table. I watched them for a while, the way he left the larger pieces of meat for her, the way she fed him the thick, fat noodle with her chopsticks. They never looked over at me. When the server finally came by, he asked me if I was waiting for someone.

"No. For one," I said, but he shook his head.

"No," he said, "our pots are this big," and he showed me with his hands. "It's too much food for just one." He told me if I wanted, he could ask if I could join the couple; he told me next time I had to bring a friend.

"Can't you make it just for me?"

He said the dish was for two or more only. It was hard to eat single in Korea. As I left the restaurant, I could see in the reflection of the glass door that no one looked up when the bell dinged.

After that, when I came home from work, I would search online for pictures of the Northern Palace or the Bukchon Hanok Village. I made sure they were slightly out of focus, as though I had moved just a little when taking them myself. I would order a small pizza from North American chains like Domino's or Pizza Hut and work on my dating profile, at least one close-up, one full body shot, one shot Photoshopped next to the N Seoul Tower as a conversation starter. In pictures I was conscious of the best angle for my cheekbones. I ate facing the window, but I could not see Dodeoksan Hill.

After I met Jeremy, Seoul changed. Jeremy also taught English. His profile said, "I'll try anything once; just don't ask me to do it again." When we got off work, we would stop at the soju tent, then at the supermarket to buy beer; we would sometimes climb Dodeoksan, stopping at the crest of the hill for dongdongju, then stumble back down. I took a selfie once while we were at the top, but Jeremy told me to delete it.

"We're teachers," he said. "We don't want to look bad, drinking every afternoon." If you looked closely, you would have seen my hand in the back pocket of his jeans.

Sometimes Jeremy wanted to sit outside at one of the tables and talk about the time he accidentally found himself on board a Peruvian drug boat; sometimes he wanted to talk about when he toured the ruins of Chernobyl. I believed him. There were pictures of him inside ruined hospitals and schools, pictures, he told me, that he wasn't even allowed to take. He may even have been arrested, but Jeremy told me he could open any lock. He'd spent an entire summer practising using *Houdini's Handcuff Secrets* when he was ten years old.

"Did you know," he'd say, ordering us another beer, "most of the time Houdini had a skeleton key hidden in the palm of his hand or sleeve. No one ever noticed."

"Maybe they just weren't watching closely enough," I said, drinking from his beer. I told Jeremy it was things like this that made it look like we were together. He never said we weren't. There was no proof otherwise. "Didn't Houdini also do the vanishing elephant trick?" I asked.

"Another classic case of manipulating the perspective of the viewer. With that one it was a really big cupboard. The elephant never left the room."

"Or maybe," I leaned in closer, "we all just want to believe in magic."

"*Argumentum ad populum*," Jeremy would wink at me, swaying slightly. "We're not most people."

Then we would go to Wa Bar for more beers, maybe more soju. Then sometimes Jeremy would come back to my apartment, sometimes I would go to his. When I was with Jeremy, we would order pizza to the rooftop of the apartment, the kind made by a local Korean place, adventurous with figs or snails or butterscotch sauce, the kind with the taste of sugar underneath the cheese. I told Jeremy that just like him, it had been my dream to go to magic camp as a kid. The closest I ever got was one of my university roommates from Malaysia. He'd claimed he could teach me how to charm his pet rat snake.

"And were you charming enough?" Jeremy asked.

"I was terrified," I lied. "I couldn't even touch it." Before I met Jeremy, my dating profile included my love of reptiles and arachnids, my goal to eventually run with bulls in Pamplona. No one had messaged me. I told him if I had a choice, the super-power I would never want would be to become invisible.

"That's why I like Houdini," Jeremy told me. "To an eleven-year-old, that man defied all fear." The way I remember it, Jeremy must have kissed me; we could almost see the stars through the lights of the city.

Whether we were at his apartment or at mine, Jeremy would always give me the bed. But sometimes I would find him in the bed with me in the middle of the night. I would feel him against me, but I didn't say anything, even after sex. The first night it happened, I wanted to make him a real Western-style omelette; I woke up early to take the train to the Homeplus Express near Gangnam Station where I knew they had the really good English extra mature cheddar cheese, but had to settle for processed cheese slices instead.

"I'm sorry," Jeremy said when he saw his breakfast. I had made the omelette into a heart, wondered if my mother would have said we were seeing each other, if Instagram could tell the difference. "But this is not what you think it is."

"I know the cheese is just the cheap American shit," I said. "I had to go to Costco instead of the market." Finding good cheese was always our biggest problem in Korea, no matter what Jeremy would say.

No matter what Jeremy would say, we were seeing each

other in Korea, even if we never ate dakgalbi together, even if sometimes I didn't see him after work. I knew we were together, even when he told me he was never ordering Korean pizza with me again.

"This coming from the man who told me that this is a cultural experience because nowhere else do they put raisins in the crust."

"Jess, my visa's set to expire here. I'm moving to Thailand," is what he told me, so I opened us each a bottle of soju, poured myself another beer. The way I remember it, Jeremy said in Bangkok, splitting a house was even cheaper than our two apartments. He knew of a place a friend of his had found with a view of some famous landmark called the Elephant Tower.

"Why do they call it that?"

"It looks like an elephant," he said, and I told him something about being ready to do my own vanishing elephant trick; I said I had always wanted to go to Thailand.

"Easy there, Houdini." And I know he must have finished the rest of my beer. I know Jeremy must have told me he loved me. The picture he probably deleted later that night was of his Canadian-flag boxers intertwined with my bathrobe on my bedroom floor. When I woke up in the morning, Jeremy was already gone, but he left me an omelette in the microwave. Later, I thought, he will tell our friends this story, maybe my mother. When Jeremy tells the story, we will be in our house together in Bangkok, and he will have made the early morning trip to buy cheese from the Gourmet Market in Siam Paragon. When he tells the story to my mother, the cheese will cost as much as 250 baht.

When I got to Bangkok a month later, I messaged Jeremy; it was going to be a surprise. I had checked his Facebook location, scrolling past pictures of other friends' engagement rings and ideas for wedding centrepieces, their announcements of relationship statuses changing to "engaged." I took a tuk tuk instead of a taxi because the driver said he knew the way to the JJ Green Night Market, the area close to where Jeremy lived. When I ended up at a gemstone store, a man who called himself The Prince convinced me to buy a ring shaped like an elephant for Jeremy. "Real rubies," he said, talking about the eyes. "Best deal you'll ever find. You're stupid if you don't buy it." He said it would be like nothing Jeremy had ever seen before.

I thought when I got to Bangkok we would go to the temples, the river, the limestone mountain that everyone said looked like the surface of the moon, but Jeremy said he would just meet me at the market. I bought us both cheese toasties; I waited thirty minutes, then forty-five, wandering the area behind the Bangkok Bank where you could buy turtles, even the occasional small alligator. Behind the saltwater aquariums, I saw a father and his young son looking at the snakes.

A cobra can sometimes look like a rat snake. It has the same brown body, the same black bands that thicken toward the tail. The variations in colouring are so slight, the patterns so similar, that the vendor told us it was sometimes hard to tell the difference. "This guy here is not dangerous at all," the vendor said, pointing to one of the brown-bodied snakes, "but this other one is the king cobra. He can kill an elephant in a few hours with his bite." He paused, waiting for us to be impressed, as though we had never seen anything like it before.

"How do you tell them apart?" the boy asked in English, but his father told him he didn't need to. When the boy and I leaned over the glass for a closer look, the father pulled his son away, and I understood the words "don't"; I understood "crazy foreigner." He must have told his son what I had heard before. Everyone in Thailand knows to stay away from a snake.

When Jeremy finally met me, far away from the king cobra's tank, I gave him the ring. I said the elephant had reminded me of all of our talks about magic. I said now that we were in Bangkok together, we should go and see the famous Elephant Tower, but he wanted to go straight to the love hotel.

Afterwards, I asked if we were staying the night.

"Can't," he said, pulling on his pants. "I've got an early class tomorrow. You can stay though, unless you've got another hotel booked."

I told him I didn't want to stay at a hotel; I wanted to stay at our house, together.

"Look, I've got roommates," he said, but I noticed he still hadn't put the ring on. "They're leaving at the end of the month, but right now there's no room."

I lied. I said believed him. I said I had to go to the bathroom. That was when I saw the snake, a shadow curved into the corner of the sink.

I tried to tell him that I couldn't stay at the hotel without him. I tried to tell him I wanted to go with him, out to dinner, maybe dancing. I wanted to go to our house. "You're seeing things," and I knew Jeremy would just say I was seeing what I wanted to see. "There is no snake."

I said he shouldn't have left the seat up now that we were in Bangkok and things were crawling around in the drains; I said he would have seen the snake if he had cared enough to open the door when he heard me scream.

"It was locked."

"I thought you could pick any lock." I didn't look at his face, or the elephant ring on the nightstand. I wanted to think he remembered Houdini.

He told me he had never said that.

He didn't come back to the hotel the next morning, even

though I waited for him. So I went back to the market to buy one of those brown-bodied snakes; I needed Jeremy to see things the way I did. He didn't come the next evening, so I messaged that I had followed him downstairs to see the cab he got into, that when the driver returned, I paid him for the address of our house. He didn't come so I danced with the snake instead, borrowing a broom from the cleaning cart so I could hook its body around the handle, making sure I was slow, not fast, as I dropped it into the drawstring bag and put the bag inside a carrier. Boundaries are important. Too much confidence when handling a snake can be deadly. Jeremy didn't come back the evening after that or the evening after that so I messaged that I would meet him at our house in Bangkok. When all the cabs refused me because of my luggage, I rented a car. I needed Jeremy to see me.

When I got to our house, a woman answered the door. She said her name was Katie. She said Jeremy had told her his drinking buddy from Seoul was in town; she asked, "Are you visiting Bangkok for long?"

"That depends on Jeremy," I answered.

"Well, he won't be home for another hour or so, but you can wait if you want," she began awkwardly. "Were you planning to stay the night?" I noticed she was eyeing my baggage, even though I had left some of it in the car.

"Yes," I told her.

"Oh. Okay. It's just that Jeremy just never told me."

"Don't worry about me," I told her. "I'll just go to my room, and it will be like I'm not even here."

Katie led me past the kitchen, a stack of empty pizza boxes piled right next to the downstairs bathroom. "Sorry about the mess. Jeremy keeps telling me that no true expat eats pizza for a week, but we always end up ordering in," she explained.

"He used to say the same thing in Korea," I said, following

her upstairs to the two bedrooms; she led me to the only one that was not in use.

I told her I would finish taking my luggage in myself. "Can I use your bathroom?" I asked.

"Sure. Just go to the one downstairs," she said. "I keep telling him we're in Bangkok and you never know what's in the drains, but Jeremy always leaves the seat up on the toilet up here."

I waited for her to leave, then I went into the other bedroom. Even lying on the unmade bed, I could see this was a room with a view, although from this close, the white cinderblocks of the famous tower only vaguely resembled an elephant. When I looked outside, I saw Katie calling Jeremy from the front lawn where she thought I couldn't hear. On the bedside table, I noticed a framed picture of the two of them, Katie and Jeremy, on top of the limestone mountain Doi Pha Phueng. I wondered if he had let her post it. I wondered if anyone back home believed that where they were living, together, was really like being on the moon.

I wondered how Jeremy would explain the broken glass to Katie, the remnants of their picture frame lying on the bedroom floor.

Afterwards, I went downstairs quickly to get the rest of my luggage, returning to the upstairs bathroom. There I messaged Jeremy. "I saw our house today. I saw Katie." I know if Jeremy could tell you this story, he would say I would never touch a snake; I was too scared to even look at one. But I needed him to know what I saw. I needed him to see.

On my way out of the bathroom, I gathered up what remained of my luggage, told Katie I had decided not to stay after all. "I just came to give Jeremy something he forgot," I told her, laying the elephant ring on the table.

She looked puzzled, unsure of her reaction. It must have

been because the slight variations in colour, in pattern, made it look like something you would get in a tuk tuk gemstone scam, something Jeremy would never wear. I knew this now. "Um, did you want me to let him know you were here?" Katie asked, as though she hadn't already.

I told her it wouldn't make a difference. An elephant can sometimes look like a closet; a cobra can sometimes look like a rat snake. Jeremy wasn't the first to get bitten in a bathroom in Bangkok by what was invisible, waiting for him.

A TRICK OF
THE DARK

WHEN HE CHANGES to a dragon, I pretend that I don't see it and it almost goes away, like the shadow from a story someone told you once around a campfire. The first time, it is too hot on an August afternoon and we are fighting about something I won't remember, like whether Escher's figures are really impossible, or who knocked down the photo of us, the one taken just after we got engaged. In that picture, he still looked like Prince Charming in a rental suit in front of the gold and blue centrepiece at his best friend's wedding while sweat pooled under my arms and everyone said, *You both look so happy together. Don't ever change.* Whatever it is we are arguing about, it is big, the way things appear in a tiny apartment with hospital-yellow walls after spending the day without air conditioning and drinking too many beers on our balcony. It must be big. He is knocking over his beer for it; he is slamming his fist into the table so that the chair falls over to give whatever it is room. He is slamming the screen door shut when I say, *I don't want this to get ugly.* I say, *I'm leaving.* Just before he changes, I can feel the hot spit from his mouth as he screams, *This isn't me. It's you. You make me get like this,* the same way you can't not hear a siren, or a baby crying.

Then his tongue flicks, and it can't be him.

It is impossible. It is a giant lizard with scales, claws digging into my arm. It has an alligator jaw, a tail that knocks over the table, spilling our beer and the rest of the bagels he got up early to buy for breakfast this morning, just because he said he knew how much I missed Montreal. I try not to look at it, as though not looking means it goes away, like when I was a kid and used to cover my eyes so whatever was underneath my bed couldn't see me in the dark when I came back from the bathroom at night. I can see myself in the glass of the sliding door to our apartment, crouched down, hands covering my head like in pictures of old bomb drills. Whatever this is, I tell myself it isn't real.

Then, it unhinges its jaw and I see its teeth. If it was a bear, I would know what to do. When a bear comes close, you lie down, play dead. Curl yourself up into a ball on your side or lie flat, facing downwards. Avoid all eye contact. But bears are real. This is not. Still, it lunges toward me and breathes fire so my arm is the colour of when my brother would grab my wrist in both hands and twist in different directions. And a small space inside me becomes a glass window, where I can only watch what is happening as though someone is narrating on TV.

And now a dragon terrorizes the village. And now a dragon wrecks a home, our plastic patio chairs broken by its tail. And now I crawl away when I should be running, almost making it to the fire escape until its head turns in my direction.

The part of me still watching thinks, *And now I die*, and I cover my face with my arms, as though not watching will change what is going to happen. I feel strangely calm even as it charges and my body hits the ground because this will all end the way a story with a dragon always ends and there won't be an after where I have to try and make sense of what I saw happen: why it burned the tomato plants, the ones we'd said we were going to try and grow together, even though there wasn't enough sun.

I close my eyes. My body doesn't know what else to do.

When I open them again, I realize there is an after. It is

darker outside, so everything is in shades of black or blue. I don't see a dragon, but I climb down the fire escape in case there is one, careful to be quiet. On the sidewalk, I realize I don't have my keys. For a moment, looking up at our apartment, I feel like I am five again, alone with my nightmares about *Jurassic Park* after my father yells that he's trying to sleep, and my mother tells me, *none of it was real, go back to bed*, and closes my bedroom door. It's just a story. I realize whoever I call, co-workers, a friend, police, my sister, my own mother, I would never expect anyone to believe what happened.

After an hour of walking, unsure of where I am supposed to go from here, I go back. *I thought you left*, he says when I knock on our door, except I am not sure if it's him or the dragon who opens it and goes back to eating takeout pizza and watching TV on our couch. It's hard to tell with the lights off. *There's nothing to talk about*, he says when I tell him that my head hurts, when I ask if we can talk. I watch the way his tongue moves, like a lizard's, smelling the air, but when I sit down beside him, he puts an arm around my shoulders, pulls me into himself like the time we took that road trip with his band out east and we got up at dawn and he played me the song he wrote about us on a pier in Halifax. He gets the Tylenol and water from the kitchen. We were drunk. I must have passed out. Remember, it was hot. Remember, we'd been drinking all day; we must have had a two-four each. Remember, he'd said, concerned, that maybe I should go lie down. Remember, we talked about getting rid of those dead tomato plants anyways. My arm is scratched, slightly blistered, but I didn't put on sunscreen. I wouldn't have; I was the one who drank so much I fell. I tell myself his fingers feel warm-blooded when he spreads aloe on me; what I think I see as scales are just the rough skin on his elbows. I tell myself that dragons don't exist. And even if they did, he is still the man who played Frisbee with my sister's kids at the beach, who taught my nephew the guitar. Even if they did, most lizards are territorial, not social creatures. They don't know how to live in family groups. And he lets me take a slice of pizza from the half that looks like mine, the half that should have been without hot peppers, but they are buried underneath the extra cheese. He must have forgotten. The roof of my mouth burns but we eat dinner together. We go to bed together. On Monday, my co-workers will say it looks like I got too much sun and I will tell them we went to the beach. I will tell my neighbour the tomato plants had aphids; I will tell my mother when she visits that we decided to get new patio furniture. When I feel, rather than see, the deep and tender bruise on the back of my head in the shower, I will tell myself I must have fallen. I just don't remember. There is nothing to remember. A week later, he will take me out to dinner after buying new tomato plants. I will bring back empties to The Beer Store all at once so I can count them, tell the woman behind the counter of course I had company. Of course it looked like we had fun. We always looked so happy, together.

* * *

There's a story about a lizard man, one that lives on Thetis Lake, one you might believe the way you watched horror movies in the basement as a kid with the lights on, checked the closet before you went to bed. Sometimes he has webbed feet; sometimes he has sharp claws and spikes on his head, like the creature from the Black Lagoon. Sometimes he is just a vague something swimming in the lake, all silvery and scaled, if you can believe it. Does it help if I say a boy told me the story in a tent in his backyard, flashlight underneath his face? Does it help if the boy said, *It doesn't end how you expect?* Sometimes, the boys who saw the lizard man are fishing in the lake and sometimes they are swimming in the dark. Sometimes they run to their car and the monster chases them. Sometimes the monster even bites. I'll tell you, the boy put the flashlight underneath his face and made his eyes look like caves, or makeup from *The Addams Family*, so I screamed. *It's okay. Don't be scared. There's no reason to be scared. I'm here,* he said. Besides, there's always a reasonable explanation. Just before the first report, local TV aired *Monster from the Surf.* Next time, police said a man from the area told them his tegu lizard, which can grow to over a metre in length, escaped the week before. Much, much later, some of the boys even claimed they'd made up the entire thing. *I promise,* he said, *you're safe.* Does it help if the boy made me chocolate chip cookies? If he didn't know I was scared of dinosaurs, especially ones that can stand on their hind legs? *I promise,* he said, *I lied; he's not real.* I'll even tell you I believed him. Then he stuck his tongue in my mouth.

* * *

We get married in October, and everything goes the way it is supposed to. I say his name in our vows, the ones we write together, the ones that include that joke about *Beauty and the Beast.* He says he promises to take this woman. He kisses the bride, and the sign I bought on sale for the reception says, *This Way to Our Ever After.* We drink all the champagne and laugh, and I can see his muscles rippling through his back when he takes off his suit jacket at the reception. I don't see a dragon when we carefully remember the waltz, when his sister tells the story in her speech of how he once got himself arrested by park rangers in Nevada all because I had wanted to see the stars in the desert at night, when he touches my collarbone with his thumb and I whisper I want him, when during dinner I pretend we have to go take pictures and we go back to the bridal suite, even when he sticks his head under my dress and pulls off the garter my mother also wore. In his toast, he says, *To the woman who changed me, for the better.* When I see myself about to go back to the party in the bridal suite mirror, tiara on my head, my childhood self who cut her own hair to look like Joan of Arc is startled by the change. Shirt still untucked, he gently takes the tiara off my head and, holding it up to the window, grins when the sunset hits it. *There's a rainbow lighting up your face,* he says, and even though I can't see it, I grin just as hard along with him. And when we took photos, my own mother, who once wrote an article for *Ms. Magazine,* tells me, *You look beautiful, together.* I don't see the bruises on my knees I get on our honeymoon, falling over rocks on the beach close to his parents' cottage in Maine. We drink and make out for a while, have sex and sleep in our car like we are still in our early twenties and everything is part of the one great story of us.

When we get home, it looks like we are still in love. He says he wants to have a child together. And it has been so long since there has been a dragon that I can see us, together with a daughter. She would come sit in our bed when she had night-mares about monsters and lizards and red eyes in the dark so that she wouldn't ever have to be alone. He says as long as we're together, nothing else matters. We spend every night together, we drink at the bar together, we argue together about all the things I don't remember when he screams about them later: how I mess with the thermostat, how when I say I have no space of my own in our apartment I don't have space for him in my life, how I never kill the little red spiders in the bathroom, the ones that seem to be made purely of blood. We drink alone, together at the bar, argue about whether I grow by going back to school out of town and leaving him for a while.

You wanna go, go, he says, but I don't like it. He says humans are not designed to live alone; we evolved to live together as protection against all the things that can kill you. And so many things can kill you. Even babies, he says, but his eyes have narrowed to vertical slits and I don't know if they see me anymore. Even babies know to avoid a fucking snake when they see one. We argue and when I can't tell where words like stupid and bitch are coming from, all smoke and fire and burn, I go, but only to the bathroom. I wonder if the woman behind the bar sees the red of the fire coming from the edges of his mouth, if that's why she asks, concerned, if I'm looking for Eve like it says to do if you need to on the doors of the stalls.

I am ashamed. I tell her it's not what it looks like. Whatever it is, I want to tell her this is also the man who used to come over to clean my dorm room when I was writing papers for my third-year gender studies course, who made us both instant ramen, who let me come over at 4 a.m. to cry for three hours in his apartment when my father died, saying nothing except *I'm sorry, I'm sorry* over and over until he got frustrated that he couldn't help and that I was still crying and banged his fist on the table. I feel like I should know better by now than to see a dragon.

* * *

Depending on who you ask, if you go to Scape Ore Swamp in South Carolina, you'll see the famous lizard man. He looks to be about two metres tall and damp, green with red eyes and three toes and all those things you won't believe, even if you see them. Would it help if you could touch the blood, the shattered windshields from when he terrorizes teenagers coming home on the highway after the night shift, jumping on the hoods of their cars? Would it help if I told you the county even sells T-shirts? You might say he could be just a wild dog, a fox, a black bear from the swamp. Maybe he's another coyote, like the one police found dead next to the car whose hood ornament was ripped off, maybe with teeth. Maybe he is just two red glowing eyes like the woman saw outside her window; he is just the story from a girl who's mostly drunk, mostly with her boyfriend at a party where I am still single, in first-year university in someone's apartment where there are two coral snakes with black, yellow, and red stripes in a terrarium. When her boyfriend sits beside her, she shifts her weight slightly so their thighs aren't touching. She says you can't keep a snake in a cage with another animal, including a snake; that snakes are immune to their own venom. The girl tells me her sister got killed by a coral snake that looked just like this one, even though she'd heard the old rhyme, *Red and yellow, kill a fellow.* She says she knew her reptiles.

She says a girl claimed that the lizard man grabbed her and tried to drag her into the river; would it help if you saw its three-toed tracks? *The lizard man's bullshit,* her boyfriend says. He says a military guy even admitted he made it up after he said he shot the creature. She says, *But a woman in Charleston just got a picture of him, outside her church.* But he says it was Photoshopped, or footage from an old B movie, or just a trick of the light. He says those three-toed tracks were from an ostrich, or an emu, maybe, and I thought back to my mother who, when I was a girl with nightmares, told me all the dinosaurs died out so long ago; if they hadn't there would be no birds in the sky. Her boyfriend says the snakes are milk snakes, harmless; they only mimic the colour of their predator to avoid harm. The girl screams when he wraps one of them around her neck. He says *you're making a big deal out of nothing.*

* * *

He says he wants a child; in this way he wants me to grow. I know that they say with wolves you should make yourself look bigger. I say, *But do we even have the room?* He says the apartment will look bigger when the baby comes if we throw out things that we don't need: my childhood VHS collection, excluding *Jurassic Park*, including *Beauty and the Beast* with Belle in her golden dress on the cover. We throw out all our old books, my copy of *The Second Sex*, his textbook from the intro to psychology class we took together that taught me sometimes a cigar is just a cigar, that primates don't do well alone, without touch. They will cuddle with a terry cloth dummy that is soft but cannot feed them or meet all of their needs. When it comes to primates, it is scarier to not have something to cling to for warmth, even if it isn't real. At night, when I press my body against him, he is mostly soft, but colder than I remember. There is a hardness in the centre of his back, almost like ridges, what I mistake for just his spine.

One morning, in our bedroom after he has gone to work, I find what looks like the dragon lying on our bed. When it doesn't attack me, I get closer and I realize it is just the skin, like the shed of a snake. With snakes, depending on who you ask, they tell you just to walk away, or stay put and hug yourself so that when it wraps around you, it can't choke you. There is a lifeless opening around what would be its jaw when stretched over its body and I stick my head inside. I lift it, wrapping its scales around me, which are dry and stiff and let no moisture through, not even near where the eyes would have been; where I thought there would be openings there is a film that makes everything cloudy, impossible to see through clearly. Now the dragon's skin seems so fragile, surprisingly thin like the vanes of a feather, parts of it breaking off in my hands. I wonder if this means that now the dragon will be bigger. Even if it is, I remind myself he is still the man who rode with me out to the desert at night and looked up at the stars through the sunroof and, laughing, said we would always grow together. He is still the man who sleeps against my back at night and the idea of him not being there is a dark loneliness, without any stars. I think of the scene in *Jurassic Park*, where the kids are screaming as the animatronic T-Rex breaks through the roof in their car and swallows the night sky, and I wonder how much more scared they would have been if they had been alone. I wonder, when he talks about things being too much to handle because he is having trouble filling some big shoes at work, about how if we'd already created a baby when we got married, that now it would be the size of a plum. I wonder if a reptile is ever able to grow so that it sheds its skin for the very last time.

I keep my physics textbook from the course I took just before we met. When it comes to the uncertainty principle, light becomes either particle or wave depending on who is doing the observing. The act of observation can change a thing completely, but I don't remember how. There's so much I don't remember. I try to explain this when we drink in the park with his friend who points out the tortoise beetle climbing on the bush right next to us. He sticks out his finger, forcing the beetle into the palm of his hand, and the friend says the beetle's shell isn't supposed to be red at all, but gold.

Just put it back on the leaf, the friend says. *I'm telling you, it only turns red under stress.*

He says that's bullshit. He's looking at it right now; the beetle is red.

The friend holds out his hand, letting the beetle climb onto his finger, then places it gently back on the bush. *See? It's not red anymore.* The friend turns to me, *Back me up. I mean, you married this guy so I don't know if I can trust your eyesight, but you see it's gold now he's left it alone, right?*

There's nothing wrong with her eyes, he interrupts, laughing while he takes my hand. We were love at first sight.

I laugh too, comfortable in that three-beers-deep feeling while we watch a few tiny birds peck at the ground. I feel him shift beside me. My father used to tell my mother to make the tiny birds outside our windows be quiet when his head hurt; when my mother told me to stop singing along to "Tale as Old as Time," she told me there was a time, after all the dinosaurs had died, when birds were so big, even the biggest mammals were afraid of what they could do. The advantage birds have is that they can fly, just like a golden tortoise beetle. And it has been so long since there has been a dragon that I say, yeah, it turned gold.

I see him pause, and something behind him shifts. I want it to be a skipping rope. Or a garter snake. Or if not a thing that's real, then just a trick of the dark, like when monsters moved underneath your bed until you turned on the lights.

Guess love isn't blind, the friend says.

Maybe we should go. I can't look at his eyes. I am staring at the thing behind him, curving out into the dark.

Although that doesn't explain what she sees in you, the friend continues.

I'm going to go. When I stand up to leave, whatever it is hits the ground.

Fuck you, he says, but it's to me, and not the friend, who looks away. I try to; if I look at it the other way, it is almost just a skipping rope, or a garter snake. Most people look the other way.

When we get home, its tail throws me against the kitchen table and I feel my ankle buckle under me as its claws dig into my scalp. If it was a lion, things would be better. With a lion, they even say not to run, you'll only die tired. The dragon says

I'm not going anywhere. With a lion, I would shout back, throw things, maybe his copy of The Prince, maybe the last picture that we framed, us at the beach on our honeymoon at sunset, nothing else but a dark blue lake under a red sky. But I know this is not a lion; in the morning, a clump of my hair is missing. In the morning, it didn't happen. He makes quiche for both of us for breakfast; I cry in the bathroom with the hairdryer on when I pee on a stick. For months and months, he says that things will change.

The closest I can get is alligators. With an alligator, they say the only thing to do is run.

* * *

I don't remember the next time I see the dragon. But there's a bunch of stories about a lizard man, ones you can watch with your own eyes on film. Depending on how you look at it, the creature from the Black Lagoon didn't want to give up what he thought of as his home; he was a monster that slaughtered his way through scientists and crew, that abducted a woman and held her in his lair. He was a living fossil of a creature they thought stopped existing a long, long time ago. You've seen it before; it was even filmed in 3D. Of course, at first, no one believes there's a monster; the lizard man hides in the darkest places, he terrorizes so and so, only the woman sees him. I mean, it's the same story, even if the details change. If you look at him closely, the lizard man changes the way he swims so that he is a perfect mirror to the woman he is later going to attack. Doesn't matter how he changes, the music tells you this is a horror movie. He changes so that the strokes of his arms match hers, so they end up swimming together. Even on film, he changes. He always changes.

* * *

The last time I remember, we are together, in our apartment. It is January, and he is cold, and we are fighting about something that is big. I am big, and so is the daughter we are going to have, he says, together. I tell him, *I'm leaving. For real this time.*

And it says, *I don't see that happening.*

I end up lying on the ground, close enough to the sliding door so that I can almost see the fire escape, can see that it's just far enough away, but maybe not too far. I can see it now. It is not a lion, or a wolf, or a bear even. I can see the beer I knocked over seeping underneath the sliding door, into the smears from the tomato plants he crushed months ago when drunk. Against the black and blue outside, I can see the red on my fingers from between my thighs. A breath of heat travels along my body, sets the hairs on my arms into warning; I can see the dull skin of the dragon scales camouflaged to match the sick, yellow walls. They are hard and dry and impossible to see through. They are not feathers; they will not break. It is a dragon, I think. He has always been a dragon, not breakfast that is over so quickly, or the promise of a shed, or a photo on the mantle of a thing you thought you remembered but smashes so easily and you have to throw it away. It doesn't matter how I look at it; no one tells you how to survive a dragon. When I tell my daughter this story, I'll say with dragons, you fly if you can manage it. Find the fire escape. Whatever other stories you hear, I'm telling you, be like the birds.

EVERYDAY HORROR SHOW

IT STARTS AS MOSTLY NOTHING, just the wind. You want to have a baby, and when she's born it's the middle of the afternoon, not even dark and stormy, even if smog covers the sun. You want to hold your baby; you take her home in your arms to the second-floor apartment in the old Victorian. You hold your baby, you feed your baby; any noise in the attic is just a rattling pipe, or a squirrel that's been chased from its backyard home by your terrier, or the process of settling. (In a haunting, leave out the part where you're afraid. It's easy to mistake the sound of wind for ghosts, or the sound of fear; run a windbreaker over the tire of a wheelbarrow, place the arm of a record player on a towel, touch the needle to the cloth, tap lightly to make a low-end thump. Tap faster. Tap faster. No one else will see it. They will say it's just your heart.)

Of course, you want to hold your baby, but there are cold spots, mysterious drafts in the baby's room. There is an unexplained chill that keeps you up past early morning feedings; there's never any time to take a shower before the water becomes something between January slush and summer hail. There is the space heater that you set, every single day, on HIGH HEAT MODE, which keeps switching back to NATURAL WIND. It knocks over the vase of roses on your daughter's nightstand, and it's not like you want to worry, but the buds from the overturned bouquet bother you. They remind you of fruit trees that should be in bloom, the instructor at the class for expecting parents who liked to compare the size of the baby to fruits. At nine weeks, baby was a cherry, at thirteen, a peach. At fourteen weeks, baby was a lemon; you didn't tell your husband about watching *Blue Planet*, that, for now, even if lemons might be one of the only things predicted to survive in the event of a global climate catastrophe, they wouldn't survive if temperatures rose more than two degrees. He wouldn't see the point, even though he is the one who has already started looking at universities. *It hasn't happened yet. Why worry about what isn't right in front of you?* You want to want to hold your baby, but when you try to rock your daughter back to sleep in her cozy fleece, something always runs an icy sliver through your shoulder. (Leave out the part where you check for drafts, searching for candles in boxes labelled "Attic," "Fragile," "Handle with Care," and something invisible spells along your arm in goosebumps, a cold Braille that reads "Get out," or maybe "Help"?) When you rest her head on your shoulder, your baby cries. Your baby always cries, and frost forms on the outer petals of your bouquet of rose buds with its big pink congratulations.

Your husband says you should check the thermostat. Your husband says, *Did you close the windows?* Your husband says, *I don't know what you want. It's an old house.* His voice on the phone from Texas is distant, like your best friend from college who calls while she's working on another B-movie horror film, tells you that you're lucky you got what you wanted when you're changing diapers and you can't begin to tell her how you miss being covered in fake bodily fluids. You could just be exaggerating. *After all, you always say you're cold,* your husband says. You know he's thinking about your thirty-seventh birthday in the summer, the one where you were both on that set of a *Blair Witch* soft remake that used snow made of pig fat to mimic a winter's night. He was the best boy; you slipped and slid in pig fat in the middle of a heat wave for fourteen hours a day, trying to set up the mics until you were covered in it. You slid and fell until you stopped, until he talked about holding your future daughter while strangers pinched her chunky cheeks, until you told him you just wanted things to change before it was too late. Later, when you both told the crew you were getting married, the card said congratulations with two skeleton buzzards, one groom, one bride with long black hair like yours on the front, plus a stroller. Despite the fact that sixty-six people had already died of the heat wave in Montreal, you had to borrow his sweater. *Maybe it's just you.* Of course he can't just come home. Of course all this is what you wanted. (You want to want your baby, but she won't stop crying, and your breath and hers fog up and freeze together in tiny fractals on the window in the middle of July.)

* * *

Then the wailing starts. Every night there's wailing, but what did you expect? It's not a hungry cry, or a tired cry, or a gassy cry, or a cuddle cry. It might be a scared cry, some otherworldly weeping, along with the occasional blood-curdling scream while your terrier barks along all night. Your mother-in-law says it's expected. Your mother-in-law says it's colic; *Lots of babies have colic under four months old,* she says when she sits down with a cup of coffee at your kitchen table. *I'm sure if your mother was still around, she would say the same.* It's expected. (Even if, when no one should be up at this hour, there is the sound of disembodied footsteps to the kitchen. It could just be boots knocking against the heater; even if the footsteps are accompanied by weeping after your baby is finally asleep and it pours inside the bathroom, it could just be your mother-in-law prepping breakfast, the sound of frying bacon for rain.) It's nothing to be concerned about if you've already seen the pediatrician; *What did you expect? When I had mine, there was crying for twenty-three hours a day, seven days a week.* Haven't you taken your daughter out for a ride in the car, or the stroller? Haven't you used white noise; have you tried doing a load of laundry, maybe running the vacuum once in a while? When you get up to get your coffee, your mother-in-law puts her hand over the sugar bowl you are trying to refill. *Have you tried cutting out sugar and coffee and chocolate?* Yes, even chocolate, even if you read how all the cocoa plants in Africa will soon be gone. Of course you haven't, so your daughter will keep crying; what's happening is what your mother-in-law expected. (And what did you expect, having your mother-in-law stay with you to help, when you can't explain why sometimes, when you go to the bathroom in the middle of the night, there's so much weeping it's raining from the ceiling. Like in the haunting where the Gardners found water dripping from their walls in the middle of a drought, you're not sure if it's tears or your breasts that have leaked through the towel you wrapped around yourself to sleep in.) You dump your coffee in the sink. Of course, you only want what's best for your daughter; your best is what's expected. You put salt instead of sugar in your mother-in-law's cup. You're not sure where you put your sugar; you must just be tired. Of course, you're tired. What did you expect?

* * *

The mothers in the group say, *It's milk brain. You should try not to worry.* The mothers are all spread out on lawn chairs in the park, and you are sitting on your only clean blanket. The mothers in the group and your downstairs neighbour with the two three-year-old boys recommended *because you have to get out of this place sometime* all say, *Try to enjoy being in a gooshy love bubble.* The mothers all have names, but mostly they are you. (At least they're how you know you should try to be.) There is the you who's self-settling, but still sleeping, somehow able to ignore the wailing through her house at night; the you who needs to be shown how to use a woven wrap as a transitional womb, but never says she's worried about invisible fingers untying the ends; the you who only feeds her kid organics, but never talks about how when it comes to beets, her bathroom turns the colour of the elevator scene in *The Shining*. *You should try making your own baby food; you'll notice the difference. You should use a ring sling instead; they're easier for beginners.* You try to smile. You pass the sugar cookies.

When the circle comes around to you, you say your daughter keeps crying and spitting up when you feed her, and no one even mentions Linda Blair. *You should try baby-wearing to soothe her; you should try rainfall white noise playlists. Acid reflux is pretty normal in babies under six months. You should try not to worry.* The mothers all speak as one, like those images of bees before colony collapse. You want to ask, *But aren't you scared of a cold, intentional wind loosening a ring sling, that if you make sounds of rain around your daughter they will flood you both, create a monsoon from the ceiling?* You want to ask, but your daughter spits up and you realize you forgot your baby bag. (You should try being more prepared; it's easy to mistake a record player for your thumping heartbeat, a microphone in your mouth which gives a low-end sound for the blood rushing faster through your veins. No one would believe, like in the case of the Zugun poltergeist girl, invisible hands moved your baby bag to somewhere between worlds; if you try to hunt for wipes in your purse, no one would believe a ghost put a bottle of wine in there, especially when you're breastfeed-ing.) You should go. *You should try to enjoy your time with her; it goes so fast.* The mother sitting on the blanket beside you says you should stay until the end; she'll help you find the wipes. She says your daughter will be fine, but you can't explain how when you look at your daughter with spit-up all over her polar bear bib, you feel a paranormal disconnect, like she is some other species that can't survive with you. You can't explain how your heart thumping is mistaken for a record player but is really just a panic. You can't explain why a bottle of wine, dumped out on the blanket beside your keys, was in your purse. (And what kind of mother tries to go to sleep by keeping wine in her purse; what kind of mother has a daughter when she worries that soon all the grapes in the world will be gone? What kind of mother has a daughter when she knows she has a ghost?) Before she saw the bottle, the mother beside you said, *Things like this happen all the time. Try not to think of it as the end of the world.* There wasn't room, beside her still nearly full Tupperware of sugar cookies, to say you were scared it might be.

* * *

Your husband doesn't see it. You're trying not to think of ghosts, but your terrier has begun to dig herself a hole in the backyard where you find the torn-out blank pages of your daughter's baby book, some action figures that you know are made from non-recyclable plastic that belong to your downstairs neigh-bour's sons. You're trying on the rare nights your mother-in-law goes home and you and your husband are both home and in bed together and he says, *See, now this is just like our first date.* That afternoon, the extras snuck a case of beer on set and the two of you grabbed a few and got drunk doing improv in the park. He laid down behind you and you asked if he was impersonating a spoon. Afterwards, you took the subway and there was that woman, with nothing in her stroller but packets of seeds. So, you gave her one of the beers; you couldn't stop laughing. *Do you remember?* You're trying, but you want to tell him you can't stop seeing what isn't there; there's nothing on the baby book pages for baby's first smile and laugh. Instead, you find newspaper clippings about wildfires or floods around the house; he says why don't you try not worrying? Can you focus on the positive? You're trying. You try to remember how when you attempted to grow violets from the woman's seeds, he said, *Let's make a baby instead.* (To make a sound that's easily mistaken for arousal, or blood rushing in your veins, put your mouth around that mic, or use the sound of a sponge you squeezed into water.) When your husband presses up against your back, a little voice inside you thinks, *light as a feather, stiff as a board*, and you tense and roll away.

You're trying. Your husband doesn't see it. In the morning, the spoons inside the kitchen drawers are always gone.

* * *

You say you're trying, but your mother-in-law doesn't see it. You watch her play with your daughter with the plastic turtle that she got her, the same one you thought about buying but then worried that when she was old enough, your daughter would have no idea what it was, just like the Beanie Baby dodo bird you lost when you were a kid. (You're trying, but you can't stop thinking about the South Shields haunting, where the mother was attacked by her child's plastic dog, which flew across the room, where she fought a bunny with a box cutter at the top of the stairs.) When your daughter plays with your mother-in-law who calls her *my dear*, your daughter smiles and coos the way she doesn't with you. (You tried once to make the sound of a baby cooing by recording pigeons, but no one could mistake that sound.) Your mother-in-law says you need to be strong, try not to worry. But after your daughter is asleep, you watch the images of turtles eating plastic bags and all you see in the blue light of the screen is that they look like ghosts. You mother-in-law says you need to get it together, at least for your daughter's sake, and you're trying to pack your daughter's diaper bag so you can both go to mommy and me yoga, but the fog descends from the ceiling and you're always missing something: a blanket, ten or so wipes in a plastic bag, at least one diaper, a container of hand sanitizer, more plastic bags for your daughter's dirty diapers, even if they are killing the whales. When you have to buy more bags at the store before you can go to the park, you can't remember the word biodegradable and your mother-in-law has already put plastic garbage bags in your cart; the sixteen-year-old can't understand when you say you wanted the ones that didn't become what turtles could think were jellyfish over the soundtrack of your crying child while you scream at your mother-in-law.

Your mother-in-law tells your husband you're not even trying to make this work while he's still in L.A. The night after, you see your downstairs neighbour hanging Christmas lights on the main floor windows of the old Victorian. Your hands are full of soon-to-be jellyfish as you're trying to get your crying daughter back to sleep by taking her for a ride in the car.

I've been meaning to ask how you're doing, your neighbour says, and you try to say you're fine; you don't expect to see your neighbour. You don't expect to see Christmas lights in August; she says, *I know it's early, but you know how it is. The darkness in this place can really get to you.* You might be trying not to cry, but you notice the lights are every colour but blue; what is left of the blue lights are ragged edges of glass in their sockets.

What happened to the blue ones? you ask.

No idea. She laughs. You're tired, but you can think of all the horror show possibilities: a vengeful ghost sending a warning; a weirdo living in the basement, the one who smashes the lights as a message; a confused, exhausted songbird who sees mini suns and, singing all day, forgets to find food for the nest; a child eating what he thinks are blueberries before the trip to the emergency room. *You know, your daughter's eyes are really blue,* your neighbour says, *but they probably won't stay that colour. Same thing happened with my sons.*

As she plugs in the light string with all the missing sockets, you ask her, *Aren't you worried?*

All the time. Don't get me wrong, she says, *there was a time when I would have driven on thirty minutes of sleep with both my boys in the backseat to every twenty-four-hour Walmart just to test replacement bulbs in every socket to make sure everything was perfect.* As you stand there talking, you can feel one of the plastic bags slip out from your fingers. Your daughter watches it, stops crying. You watch, defeated, as it dances across the lawn, blown far away, down to the ocean in a ghostly blob. *You just have to learn to let some things go.*

When she puts up the lights, your neighbour doesn't bother to staple the last string in the middle. She hangs it instead in an upside-down rainbow, one that looks tired, one which still is not a smile, even if it looks like one from far away.

* * *

You're tired, but you take your screaming daughter out for a ride in the car at night, ending up past the end of the block, past the suburbs, where there's forest going up the mountain, before she's finally quiet. It's easy to mistake the lulling sound of a car ride when your eyes have almost closed. For driving on gravel, you can use the sound of a plastic bag; this also works for driving in the rain. It's easy, when you look quickly, to mistake a woman or a girl with her thumb extended outwards for absolutely nothing; the corners of your eyes are easily misled, especially late at night, especially when you're tired. Of course you're tired. You're always tired. You won't know what you were thinking, driving tired with your baby. If something happened, it would be terrible. (It would explain how you feel.)

It's starting to rain so you stop the car. You think maybe, if you and your daughter listen long enough, there will be just enough rain for sleep. You're tired so you don't really hear a woman's footsteps near the treeline, slowly exiting the woods; they could have been a deer's, you could have put new aluminum foil on a pillow, covered with a thin cotton sheet, then pushed on the surface using your hands to mimic steps. No one will believe you heard a weeping woman, in a dripping thin wet dress, asking you to get her out of here. You could have learned to imitate the sound of a water droplet hitting a lake using only your mouth and hands. Wet your lips. Drink a glass or two of water or apply lip balm. Even if you can't whistle, you can pucker your lips slightly with a gap between them for air to pass through, then tap the outside of your cheek with a finger, the same as how when you were a girl you crossed your fingers behind your back, the opposite of pinky swear. (Leave out the part where you pull over. Leave out the part where you pick up a hitchhiker, even with your baby in the back seat of the car, and you drive, faster and faster, as the weeping woman sits silently.)

Your daughter is asleep, the soft spot on the top of her head is hidden by a hat you didn't know how to knit, but your mother-in-law did. The soft spot bothers you. It is only as strong as that half a watermelon you kept in the fridge too long. (Last week, you watched the watermelon hover on the counter like Humpty Dumpty playing chicken while your daughter screamed from the living room before it hurled itself over the edge, creating a morbidly satisfying red splatter.) You didn't mean to let it go bad; it was an accident. (Leave out the part where there's an accident. Leave out the part where the woman in your car says she hasn't been the same since her accident. It's easy to mistake a sheet of metal and a balloon dragged across a carpet tile to make a controllable squealing sound for your car swerving when you see a deer; leave out the part where you start thinking of those old crash test dummy commercials, the ones where mommy dummy is tired, mommy dummy isn't watching, mommy dummy didn't put baby in an approved car seat. It's easy to mistake the sound of a sledgehammer in a junkyard for the tree you hit with your car as you swerved to avoid a deer that came out of nowhere; at the moment of impact, baby is a watermelon, smashed on the ground.) You check the rear-view mirror. You get out of the seat to check the back; your daughter is still sleeping soundly. Your right headlight is smashed and the front of your car is crumpled inwards on itself. (When you looked in the rear-view mirror, the woman had vanished, leaving a small wet imprint on your upholstery. You can't tell anyone. No one would believe you. Leave out the part where the woman may have been dead already. There was some stiffness from rigor mortis in her legs, but she still kicked the dirt off her feet politely before closing the back door.)

* * *

The doctor says you're fine; it's nothing. Just a fender bender.

Of course, your daughter's fine. You're tired, but you have to agree you're fine. Yes, you're fine, but you're not sleeping. But that's considered pretty normal. (Anyone would have trouble sleeping; in your house, the stairs creak, and the doors bang, and the TV turns on like the radio in the Thornton Heath haunting, you'd swear by itself, so you end up watching how bees are dying and all the fruit in the world will be gone.) Yes, you sometimes have difficulty concentrating, like your brain is in a fog. (Leave out the ectoplasm, he'd never believe in the paranormal.) From time to time, you feel what you could only describe as something restless, but you rarely feel slowed. (Don't say it's only when your daughter is crying and you're not sure if you left the bars of her crib down; you feel an invisible hand holding your leg when you try to walk down the hallway. You can't explain how, last night after you drove home, you thought you saw the weeping woman in the bathroom, with eyes that were mostly just dark sockets, and tangled black hair that hasn't seen a shower in days, maybe weeks.) No, you never feel low in spirits. Not with your daughter around. How could you?

It's possible that you could have the blues. (But you are careful; you don't mention blue orbs, the ones that show up in whatever picture you try taking of your daughter to send to your husband in New York or L.A. or Toronto. You don't mention how when you try to sleep at night, blue light always appears, whether from orbs or computer screens with pictures of dead baby albatross chicks, stomachs full of bright plastic their mothers mistook for shrimp, pictures of hives missing adult bees with larva still unhatched, pictures of fewer and fewer swallows migrating across a sky too early for them to lay their eggs and for their young to find food. What's happening can't be natural; in the blue light you read how the young won't survive.) Your doctor says it happens to a lot of women. Of course you'll be fine. If you're not feeling fine in a few weeks' time, you should check in with him again. (But you have to be fine. If you tell him about the watermelon, he might think you're not a natural. He might think there's something missing. He might think, if you have something missing, you shouldn't have your baby anymore.)

* * *

It's nothing, and you're fine. Everything is fine; nothing bad really happened. Your husband says you're fine, sitting across from you in the living room, offering you a paper bag. There's no reason to panic (even when the weeping woman is still inside your house), just try to breathe (even when she holds you down on your bed, her weight on top of your chest when you hear your daughter crying in the middle of the afternoon). In through your nose, out through your mouth. (Even when you try to breathe, you get a mouthful of her long dark hair followed by the rain. It's easy to mistake the sound of a thumping heart for a record player, the groove of a record for what's always happened, the end of a record for white noise, white noise for what isn't there.) You'll be fine. You're a good mom. (Even if yesterday afternoon the weeping woman left the stove on, made a tiny fire break out. And what kind of mother hesitates to smother it? What kind of mother doesn't immediately run to grab her daughter, thinking instead, with relief, of the Bell Witch haunting, how in pictures of children in front of her cave, the children always disappear?) You'll try to be fine, even if your husband has to go away again. If you have any problems, you should try reaching out to your mother-in-law. Try to see how lucky you are. *I wish I could stay home with both of you. You try leaving your newborn daughter at home all the time.* Try seeing how hard this is for him too. (You're trying, but even your neighbour saw the weeping woman the other day as you went outside to take out the burned remains of one bottle, the odour of sour milk still on your clothes. You're trying to be fine; you said you're fine and she said, *Don't give me that. I have twin boys. I know what ichor looks like.*) You know he has to go; you know this is what you should expect. *I can watch her for a bit before I drive to the airport. You'll be fine. You just need a shower, and maybe a nap.* Of course, you'll be fine. You're a good mom. Before he leaves, your husband gives you two violets growing in a bell jar. He says, *Remember the seeds from that woman with the stroller?* Your husband looks at your daughter, sleeping in his arms in the onesie you could only find in lemon. He says, *I know you wouldn't want this to change.* Of course, all this is what you wanted.

The afternoon he leaves again, in a small moment alone in the bathtub, the weeping woman's hair covers your face, ties your hands behind your back. It wraps itself around your neck, the same way a seagull will always lose to six-pack rings. It's nothing, then it isn't, but you can almost sleep as it pulls you under.

* * *

It isn't nothing; it's not supposed to happen. It isn't just the wind, or the sound of the wind made by a bicycle turned upside down, its tire spinning underneath a piece of stretched-out silk. It's not just dolphin or sea lion cries run through a vocoder, or a cutting of black plastic garbage bags into thin strips, then burning them into an unearthly whine as they drip to the ground. It isn't just that things are upside down (a warming Arctic means colder winters down South), instead of a play-pen and toys everywhere, the living room becomes an Escher painting. The lamps levitate, the sofa drifts toward the ceiling, the violets in their bell jar hang like purple bats, or stalactites carved from the last ice age. It's not supposed to happen, but the weeping woman hides everything: your daughter's favourite toys, the watering can, the scissors you thought you were supposed to use to deadhead the violets in the bell jar. It's not supposed to happen; this isn't what you want for your daughter and you need to get out of this place. It's not what you expected; you even call your mother-in-law to say you need a change, you need to stay there with your daughter tonight. It's not supposed to happen, but just as you're about to leave, the weeping woman misplaces the bags you packed, your daughter's diapers, a change of clothes, everything except the dying violets in their bell jar. You're trying to get out of this place but you just changed your daughter and she needs changing again and you needed to leave ten minutes ago and somehow time has rewound itself so that every time you get to the door you go back to where you started from. You don't know what it is that lets you finally leave the house; it isn't nothing. A mother was levitated so far from her bed her children couldn't find her hand; in the case of the Enfield poltergeist, Jane's mother was trapped by a heavy oak dresser in the bedroom. It's not fine; it's the weeping woman that gets in the front seat of your car this time, and you can't see the Christmas lights that are all lit up on the front porch of the old Victorian in the headlights of your car. The weeping woman roughly buckles your daughter in beside her where she isn't supposed to be. You can't see the lights and no one saw how Jane's mother was trapped, but your neighbour sees your daughter in the front seat of your car. You could have used some metal wind chimes, laid them on a surface then moved a bottle over them. You could have filled some small glass vials with water and placed them with some coins inside a pillowcase. But that's not what really happens. You're really the weeping woman, and when your daughter cries again, the weeping woman throws the bell jar with its violets against the windshield, just above your daughter's head. That's what makes the sound of breaking glass. That's what makes your terrier keep barking. That's what makes your daughter scream in fear. That's what makes your neighbour knock on the car window, and the weeping woman opens it. She says you're fine. Your daughter's fine. The windshield is not fine; the violets are not fine and neither is the bell jar. Neither are the turtles and the fruit and the flowers with their disappearing bees. But your daughter is not a violet, the weeping woman tells your neighbour. Your daughter is not a watermelon. Your daughter is a lemon and your neighbour sees the weeping woman is real. She says she should go; your neighbour will take your daughter, and you ask her why but you know she sees what could happen because it shouldn't. *You do what you can*, she says. It shouldn't happen. But if Jane's mother was trapped, and with a haunting like that, what could she do when a force she couldn't quite understand lifted up and shook her daughter, then threw her violently across the room?

Your neighbour will take you to the hospital. Your neighbour holds out her arms; you're not fine. *It's going to be okay. You can give her to me.* The weeping woman holds on to your daughter, bends down to kiss her. *Just let her go,* your neighbour says, opening the car door. *You need to let her go.* To make a believable kissing sound, you could wet your lips with a glass of water, put your mouth slowly on the underside of your forearm, the part with very little hair. But to make a believable kissing sound as the weeping woman, you can't. It's nothing. You give your daughter to your neighbour; she holds your daughter in her arms and you get out of the car. You're fine dear; it's fine now. You get out of your car crying, and she says, *Don't feel bad. You're*

doing what you can. You can only do what you can. You get out of
your car, and not the weeping woman. From the backseat of
your neighbour's van, you can see the Christmas lights on the
porch, twinkling, even if they're distant. You feel the thumping of the bass from a song she puts on the radio; you feel your
heartbeat start to slow to match it, and it is real, no mistaking it.

* * *

The next time you see the weeping woman she is an emergency
room chair, then a long day while you watch the blue of TV
screens in the hospital. With most cases of a weeping woman,
the peer support counsellor says, it's easy to forget that just
because no one else sees her, it doesn't mean she isn't there.
It's easy to forget that just because she only appears to you, it
doesn't mean she is you. When she had her weeping woman,
with all the ectoplasm and the way the edges of the weeping
woman always appeared so blurred, it never seemed as though
she could see where the reach of her ghostly fingers finally
ended. It was easy to forget that she could pass through the
weeping woman, come out the other side. Sometimes, she says,
she still sees her. She tries not to forget, even with all the wailing, the weeping woman is trying to tell her something. She
tries not to forget that the weeping woman can't really touch
her, not like your daughter when she wraps all the fingers of her
hand around your thumb.

Sometimes you still see the weeping woman. She might be
an awaking some nights at 3 a.m., or a forgotten prescription
that you only refill later when your husband asks if you feel
better now, or the baby bird you have to explain to your daughter that she shouldn't have touched because her mother won't
take it back to the nest anymore. The weeping woman is the

clump of black hair you clean out of the bathtub drain some mornings. Leave out the part where you pretend you don't see it moving. Leave out the part where you pretend. You take the hair and tie it with a blue ribbon, and it dances on the window-sill of your bedroom where you can just see the swallow's nest. Your daughter comes to find you because she wants a glass of lemonade; she sees it too. She asks you what it is. You don't tell her about jellyfish ghosts and dead turtles. You don't tell her it's unlikely the watermelon seeds she planted in the windowsill garden will grow to be a watermelon; you told her when she planted them that she would need to take care of the earth to make the seeds grow. So you tell her the hair is like the baby swallow and you watch it dance together, to the sound of the bass on the radio. You say you'll get her lemonade; you want to say that lemons will survive. You want to say sometimes you are just learning to let things go. You both watch the hair dance until a draft catches it, and the thin strands separate, carried out the window into the ocean maybe, dissolving into almost nothing, carried by what could almost be the wind.

PANDORA

I AM LYING ON THE SIDEWALK in the broken glass of the bus shelter, but if I was telling my daughter this story, I would say, *Don't ask why, or what if it had happened another way.* I would say the way the story goes, there was a woman and there was a particular box and this particular box had a guy inside it; actually the box was a white cube van running down the middle of a busy sidewalk full of women on a sunny afternoon. I know you want to know, we all do, but don't ask why those particular women were chosen by the guy in the box, women walking their dogs or running in yoga pants outside the new development, which had ripped up all the old trees and put in saplings; I already told you it was sunny. The guy in the box that was a van had the doors locked, the windows rolled up on what was a 30-degree day in the sunshine. Don't ask why anyone would do such a thing.

When the van hopped the sidewalk, those sapling trees in planters, oak or elm or beech, I never could tell the difference, they didn't even slow him down. I tried waving as if to say, "Hey, did you know there are trees here? Oak, elm, maybe beech," or ones I couldn't even name, just like whatever was going on inside that box that told him not to stop or slow down at all. If I told my daughter this story, I would want her to know the difference between oak or elm or beech, between a good climbing tree and one that will let you down. I don't know if my arms can climb anything now; they are also just lying on the sidewalk, like a branch struck by a storm. But if I could, I would teach my daughter to climb those trees when they got older and were large trees, the kind of trees your mother warned you about at night in ravines, the kind where it's possible to think you've climbed so far up you're seeing the rooftops of the whole world, even when you're not.

Don't ask me if anyone taught the guy in the van to climb a tree. Don't ask me if his mother made him go outside instead of being cooped up in the basement all day shooting things on a screen. My own mother warned me about women climbing trees, about Icarus; even on cloudy days she always told me I needed to put on more sunscreen in case I got burned. But my mother didn't know anything, really, about climbing trees; she went only three inches off the ground in her wedding heels. Even that made her dizzy, the kind of dizzy which I realize is starting now, in the same way you can stare through a pane of glass at the beech outside your bedroom window but never really see it. It is the kind of dizzy that crawls behind your eyeballs and makes you think, if you look through shattered glass just the right way, whether it's a champagne glass or a bus shelter, it will turn a burst of light into a rainbow. It fades immediately if you move your head.

If I told my daughter this story, I would say the first time I climbed a tree, just outside my bedroom window, I was in a tutu for ballet class. That first time, my friend went up the tree behind me; he told me *look up, not down*. When I looked up, I saw the moon hanging in the sky in broad daylight; I didn't see when the sequins caught on a tree branch, ripping the whole skirt apart. I can hear my mother screaming now about the torn tutu, or maybe that's a siren. She screamed for at least a week; she asked, *Why would you do such a thing?* Don't ask me if the guy in the van ever wore a tutu; maybe it was his sister's when he was five and he just liked how the sequins felt smooth, how they flashed in the light like a mirror to whole other worlds until his brothers found him. Don't ask if his brothers boxed him, put sharp elbows between his legs, put out their cigarettes on his arm to make him cry because real men don't. Maybe he couldn't move his arm out of the way. Maybe I can't now. Maybe it happened in an alley at the end of the street, or in a bus shelter, the kind I was waiting in when I heard the glass shatter because of the van on the sidewalk on a sunny afternoon. I was standing at the bus stop on my way to a core conditioning class, where we rounded our backs over large exercise balls, when a sharpness shot through me, blasting serenity the same way in the middle of a storm everything goes quiet. Then instead of the ground, I was staring up at the sky, like how the world becomes upside down if you look at the moon through your legs.

I don't know if anything is broken that I can name, the same way it is impossible to know how to describe a cloud from the top of a tree when it shifts its shape from bird to cow to something between round and sharp. I can see, very clearly, the box for the shelter smashed to pieces, the cube van moving farther away, a minute away, or maybe a light year, but any feeling of my body is as transparent as the shards around me. With a kind of glassy rationality I realize I am never getting up from this ground, maybe the same ground the boy in the van lay on after his brothers boxed him. Don't ask if the girl he liked saw, if the next day at school he waited for her to walk by the desk he sat in alone, flapping his hands. Don't ask if he tripped her, if she cried when everyone saw what was underneath her dress. Don't ask if she ended up on the ground. Don't ask why she didn't move out of his way. I don't know, even if you want to.

If I told my story from on the ground inside a shattered

shelter, I would tell my daughter that the boy and I didn't only climb that tree, we raced to the top like Russia and the U.S. did in the fifties; he was more Armstrong, I was more Luna 2. Technically I won. I would tell her that after that boy and I climbed the tree I told him that humans had only explored ninety metres of the moon's surface, that I was going to be an astronaut so I could map the rest. I wouldn't tell my daughter how, when I said liked him, he called me a *cow*, and I could have said, *but cows don't climb trees, they can't even go down stairs*, but I didn't. I wouldn't tell my daughter how instead, I went to the bathroom and lifted up my shirt, pinching a roll of belly fat around the navel, hating my body's lack of definition, its roundness that was later the reason a man I loved left. *Joke's on him*, I think, *cows are supposed to jump over the moon*. But even though I hear the sirens, I know my legs won't do that now. Don't ask me if the girl that guy in the van liked thought he was too round; if he ever looked at the moon from his window and wanted to leave the four walls surrounding him, the Earth. I wouldn't tell my daughter, the one I never had, that the moon looks smaller when viewed from the ground, between your legs.

If I told this story to my daughter, the one I'll never have, I would say both the moon and a box are in three dimensions; time is a fourth, existing outside of boxes. It lets the mother of the guy in the van and me play the "what if" game; what if he hadn't spent so much time alone and surrounded by four walls? What if her son had not flapped his hands when he was scared, knowing girls would call him weird? What if she had known about the cigarette burns? What if he had never learned to drive? Then I could ask what if I had driven more than a thousand miles, taking the corners like it's NASCAR in a diaper designed for space so I wouldn't have to stop until I knew from the man I had loved who had wanted "a break," *Why her and not me*? What if I had worn a skirt? What if we knew this was going to happen?

If I had had a daughter, I hope she wouldn't ask, in the same way the sirens start to fade, what if I had never climbed trees or tried to look at the moon in first place? What if I had not been waiting for a bus at this particular time, on that particular day? Would I still be looking at the sky from the ground, alone but surrounded by tiny pieces of glass, shattered sirens, surrounded by people asking what they could possibly do or have done to help? Would I have had a daughter? Would the mother of the guy in the van think about that? Would she think about how could she have known? The sirens, even up this close, are silent now, the colour of a moon launch, bright bursts of light and then gone. If I had had a daughter I would want her to know the moon is there to be viewed from oaks or elms or beeches, that she has the right to know the topography of Tycho, Copernicus, and the South Pole-Aitken basin; the moon is there to be walked on. On the moon, I want my daughter to know there is nothing to break open; I want her to know there are no corners to turn.

COBWEBS

IN THEIR SECOND YEAR OF MARRIAGE, she became a spider. Her reasons for the metamorphosis varied depending on who asked. She told her employer she needed more artistic growth and development; she told her mother she was compensating for gymnastic failures as a child. She told Michael she felt they had been growing apart and that she could now bind them together again. Literally.

Michael did not question her behaviour; he saw it as a test of their love. "If that's what you want," he told her. "If you know what you're doing..." and he trailed off, looked down at his hands folded on their kitchen table. It was true that, a month before, he had asked whether she was planning to go off the pill now—always, of course, with the understanding that she was perfectly within her rights to delay the birth of their first child. She had told him that she wasn't sure and they didn't discuss it further. But eventually, of course, she'd come around. It would just take a little time. After all, they'd met young, at a textiles class in first-year university, an elective she was doing for her degree in art and one that he was doing because he was sick of his major in business. They'd talked about plans for the future in the colour palette of *The Starry Night*, the complementariness of her vibrant orange painting smock against his navy-blue suit. They'd made art together, laughing that if they could survive collaborating on a project involving a literal tonne of reused water bottles and silk hanging them from the ceiling, making babies would be easy.

But children could come later. Maybe. Of course he'd said he was fine either way, even if he wasn't sure if he'd meant it at the time, or if he was just hoping she would keep coming home with him. When Michael got a job at a marketing firm, they got married, buying a large house where they hung their portrait in the second bedroom, the one that overlooked a ravine, the one which became her studio, well theirs, but Michael didn't have much time for art anymore. They had a backyard and a white fence that she'd started to paint a mural on, and he didn't have the heart to tell her he didn't like it. They had a cleaning service that came twice a month so there were never any spiders. His one qualm was that the cactus they had gotten when they were newlyweds was the only plant in the house. But still, they were happy. They'd even captured it in the portrait they'd painted together for their engagement, matching his and hers faint, Mona Lisa-like smiles before her mouthparts became chelicerae.

Michael had tried to tell his wife he was afraid of spiders. He had squashed one when he was a child, separating its abdomen from its cephalothorax, leaving it to run around while its body was in pieces.

"I need a change. I need to wait and see," she said, hoping for the extra clarity eight eyes could give. She did not mention her eggs.

* * *

Michael realized their relationship was deteriorating when they no longer shared meals together. She had taken to killing insects and small invertebrates, sucking their blood and using digestive enzymes to reduce them to a broth-like consistency. (Out of consideration for him, she did not eat in the kitchen.) When he no longer felt like cooking, Michael went out with work friends who introduced him to Dana. Dana was thirty-three and a teacher; Dana had copies of bridal magazines on the coffee table in her one-bedroom condo—"for my sister's wedding"—and checked to see if he left the seat up when he used her bathroom. Dana told him, when she was very drunk one night, "When I was in kindergarten, and they asked me what I wanted to be, I said a mom. When they told me I couldn't just do that, I said I would be a dad too."

"I always wanted to be a parent, too," Michael said, even though he wasn't sure if it was true.

"But you know," Dana continued, "it's hard to even have a dog when you live alone," and rested her head on his shoulder.

When Michael got home, she (he was still fairly sure she was she) would begin the accusations.

"You don't like me anymore."

When they were still dating, Michael had taken her trampolining to celebrate their six-month anniversary. They had talked about the past, whether he was *that* guy, the pitied legend, the first one to be kicked out of the fine arts college pub for dancing a jig on the patio picnic table the year before she'd started working there. They had talked about the future. Michael said he could see her getting an exhibition at the Art Gallery of Ontario. Maybe the Met. "Ever think about how you'll be remembered, years from now?" he'd said.

"Ever think about how you want to be remembered?" Bouncing so that her abdomen was to the sky, she'd realized that her silk was spinning out uncontrollably, long gossamer threads ready to carry her into the next phase of her life, a real adulthood.

Michael had said he hoped his future son or daughter had

half her talent; that whoever they were, they wouldn't just be remembered for some stupid drunk night in university. That they would never just settle for going to business school, even if they could sort of put their eye for photography to use in an ad agency. That they would be able to pursue their real talents. Be the next Picasso, or Rembrandt. Be just like their mother.

Shocked, she'd landed completely ungracefully, flat on her back, her legs waving helplessly in the air. In that moment, she was terrified that he'd seen her arachnid instinct, that, like every other man she'd dated, he would not pass the test. He would want to stomp out the spider in the corner of his bathroom instead of waiting for her to gently place a jar over it, return it to nature via the balcony. He would say a spider had no business being in a domestic abode, and she would try not to draw attention to the web by the toilet by flushing too loudly when she stayed overnight. "Um, I'm not sure I am who you think I am."

But even with what she thought was her awkwardly ugly eight-legged helplessness showing, he'd said, "I think you're beautiful."

Now, when he saw her standing there in the middle of their kitchen, he tried to explain to her that the beauty of her perfectly formed eight symmetrical legs, the utter foreignness of her abdomen with its two protruding spinnerets, was exotic; not the kind of beauty he was used to, and frankly (although he would never say this out loud), not his type.

"You obviously misunderstand me. Don't be a child," Michael said, not looking in a single one of her eight eyes. He had taken to grinding his teeth. Watching the tension in his jaw, she was glad she no longer had teeth to grind.

The cactus in the corner of their kitchen, the one that, when they were married, bloomed with a red flower, had become brown, its needles sharp but brittle. Michael had asked how long she was planning to let it go without water. "You know I can't water it anymore." At times she felt guilty, but she never let him know about the eggs. Not when Michael volunteered to babysit the first weekend he'd had off in some time for his older sister, Sharon. Not when Michael asked her whether she'd considered keeping some of the onesies that the local clothing donation centres had given her for her latest installation, a project that involved weaving together various pieces as her canvas, the cyclical nature of used clothes. Not when spiders can drown in water, and Michael was hardly ever home anymore to notice.

When Sharon came over, her one-and-a-half-year-old boy was strapped to her front and her two-and-a-half-year-old girl was strapped to her back in a double sling that made her look slightly insectoid, complete with head, thorax, and abdomen. It was all she could do not to come downstairs, extending her fangs from within the basal segment of her mouthparts when Sharon said, "So when's it going to be your turn?"

Michael let the children into the studio, and the girl dipped her hands in red watercolour and ran her fingers across the canvas Michael had begun painting of a beach landscape, inspired by their honeymoon photos. It was the first thing he had done in over a year. The boy had somehow managed to tangle the stitched-together clothes around Michael's legs tighter than she could weave a silk wrap to paralyze prey. She'd tried to stop the girl, running frantically across the back of her hand, the repetitive tapping of *no, no, no* eight times over, but Michael let the girl's five fingers smear across the beach, his hand holding the girl's and this time, from any angle she could find—dropping from the ceiling, swinging down from the top of the painting, landing on top of his shoulder—he was smiling so widely his facial expression couldn't be mistaken for anything else. Even if the eyes of an arachnid can generally only detect basic light-dark intensity changes, they will catch a rapid movement. They will catch what changes.

The boy had begun to unravel her weaving, separating the used men's Levi's from the orange-flowered skirt. He sobbed when he looked at her. "For crying out loud," Michael said, exasperated, "he just wants you to play with him." But she knew her clawed tarsus could not prevent a child from destroying her abdomen and spinnerets, that five little fingers could so easily outnumber her eight legs. She spent the rest of the weekend hunting mosquitoes, keenly aware Michael didn't remember how he'd said she'd saved him; he would have been eaten alive on their honeymoon if it hadn't been for the bug spray she'd remembered to bring.

When Michael went to bed, she would retreat to her web, still close enough to hear him breathe, where she would quietly miss the significance of their intimacy in intercourse. During the night, she would swing down from the ceiling and climb over his palms to the backs of his hands, even larger now, exploring the mountains of his knuckles, fingernails in need of a manicure.

She said to him, "I love you." Once, he woke up suddenly and almost squashed her.

Noting her dependence on the breeze in her nightly escapades, he stopped opening the window in their bedroom. "It isn't good for you," he told her. Michael did not like causing pain.

"No," she said, but she wasn't sure if he would understand her, "this isn't good for us." And he watched as she knocked over the cactus in her scuttle to the couch downstairs. It spilled out at the roots, and he yelled after her, asking if she was planning to clean it up any time soon. There was no response, even though he waited. She wasn't sure why he would expect one. No species of spider possesses an organ for sound, and only male wolf spiders can vocalize, vibrating dead leaves by rubbing their pedipalps. What he was asking of her was impossible, a test designed for failure.

When Michael got tired of waiting, he left.

Dana found him, standing outside the door of her condo as she came back from getting groceries. "What's wrong?" she asked.

"My wife killed our cactus," Michael said and inexplicably, or so he thought, began to cry.

She had not told him, but she had begun to lay her eggs, hundreds and hundreds of white pearls, like the necklace Michael's mother gave her on their wedding day. "One for every happy day you're going to have," she had said. And of course they were going to be happy. They had painted the ceiling of their first Montreal apartment as a mural together. They had taken turns trying to reproduce the comet they had seen on their first date from the fire escape. They had gotten drunk on the cheapest champagne they could find when she sold her first painting. Michael said they were still happy. Their lives fit the pattern for happy: charity golf tournaments, whiskey tastings, vacations twice a year to Hawaii, Turks and Caicos, her thighs chafing under summer dresses at his work events. A child fit into the design. If there was a child, there would be play dates with other mothers whose husbands travelled extensively for work, time at the park where it was easy to be crushed underfoot by a toddler going down the slide, mommy and me swimming lessons, even if spiders drown in water. There would be Michael laughing on the weekends he was finally home, teaching their child how to swing a bat to hit a ball, or easily crush an arthropod. There would be art class, dance recitals, soccer, gymnastics, a stolen corner of time, but no more swinging freely from the ceiling to spiral inwards, creating silken orb-like patterns on the walls. A delicate tiptoe, the same way she crossed her own web when sucking the juices out of a fly, wondering what if this time my balance is off, what if this time I stick for good? Many spiders, she knew, either die after they release their last egg into the world, or live only a little, and only to care for their young. As she covered the eggs outside her body with her silver cocoons, she inexplicably felt wetness spilling down her from the eyes, from her prosoma to her abdomen. She felt this even though she knew it was impossible. Spiders have no tear ducts.

When Michael returned home in the morning he was angry, and demanded to know why she wouldn't have a child with him. She asked him to admire the artistic handiwork of her spinnerets. She did not mention the egg, the one still inside her, the one she wasn't sure she would keep. But he knew. She had wanted to tell him she could share the patch of weaving in the corner, that they could still have a life together, if only he would understand. She had intended to tell him, in time, when he got a little more used to the idea.

But Michael raged. He cried. He told her he was having an affair with Dana. "Dana listens and she wants to make a life with someone," he said helplessly. "She wants a dog. I don't even recognize you anymore."

He said she was a monster. He told her he was sick of cobwebs. She would have cried, inexplicably, except spiders feel no sadness. Instead, with her palpus, she brushed the rather hard dry membrane covering her eyes.

She did not mention the eggs again. They were aborted a week later when she let him sweep out the corners of what used to be their bedroom in preparation for putting their house up for sale, destroying the web she had built for herself in the process. When the eggs were gone, Michael sat on what used to be their bed, and stared down at his large hands, avoiding the gaze of her forward-facing ocelli as well as her secondary eyes. He told her, "I don't understand what you wanted for us."

"I'm sorry," she said. "I tried to show you. Even in the beginning, I never knew if I wanted an us at all." She searched his face but, without a larynx, it was hard to communicate, and she was not sure if he understood.

He never knew, but she was glad he had cut the thread. The room was airless, and she needed to be carried on the breeze.

THE SILENT GRAVE OF BIRDS

THE GRAVE WE FOUND DESECRATING what my brother called the most excellent weed-smoking log on the beach maybe didn't look like one at first, just a mound of dirt with a burrow-sized hole. My brother, Alex, said it was just a molehill, but he skipped science on a regular basis and I knew Dimez and Ryan had no clue what a molehill looked like. We'd grown up city boys, adapted to concrete and stealing taquitos from the 7-Eleven. Our granddad had worked in the steel mill that left a big toxic blob in the harbour that could make your upper lip go numb if you touched it. And our dad had left us before I could remember much. Growing up, all we had of him was a silhouette. We had the empty cage where he used to keep his budgies. We had that clipping from some local newspaper in the Northwest Territories I found once at the library while researching the effects of heavy summer rain on baby peregrine falcons. The article featured a man in a fireman's hat holding a nest box with two chicks in it. Alex swore the man looked just like Dad, based on Alex's dim memory of wilderness camping with him when Alex had wandered into a patch of poison ivy while peeing in the dark. Since then, nature for my brother was basically limited to porn involving the occasional horse that we dared each other to watch on our phones, and the few ducks we'd caused to become refugees in the neighbourhood swimming pool by invading their nesting grounds on the shoreline. The

133

muddy beach west of the harbour was *our* beach now. We staked our claim in the form of empty Doritos bags that could easily be mistaken for little red flags from far enough away, ate our stolen convenience store bounty on driftwood logs after school, pirate kings of soon-to-be-collapsed dynasties. We never noticed the kingfishers burying their eggs along the shore, or the burrows of those squirrels who hung out by the dumpsters looking for a stale hot dog handout, their coats as thin as the homeless guy's who everyone called Shirtless Santa. Molehill or mountain of dirt on top of a freshly buried body, it's not like we would have been able to tell the difference.

"Holy shit," Dimez screeched, pointing to the ground beside the log. "There's a tooth right there! I totally see a tooth!"

"See?" I said softly, taking a step back from the edge of the pit with that jagged yellow piece of enamel. "What if it is a grave?"

"What if whoever dug the grave is into odontophilia?" Dimez sounded pretty excited. Dimez considered himself a connoisseur of mating habits, having amassed a vast, encyclopedic knowledge of pornographic sub-genres, and an even vaster enthusiasm for the phrase "that's what she said." But he had never actually had a girlfriend, at least to our knowledge. When Dimez claimed to have had sex on our log at the beach ("Like it wasn't just sex she was into, it was exhibitionism. Like it was so good, we were a porno for the seagulls"), our suspicion was, if he'd actually invited a girl on a date with him, the most the seagulls had seen of her was a sex-obstructing fake number on Dimez's phone as he texted repeatedly to figure out where she was and why she hadn't shown up.

My brother sat on the log and fished around inside his pockets for rolling papers. "Gavin, you and Dimez both need to chill. It's probably just an animal or something."

"But we don't have coyotes around here to kill off small dogs with canines like that. And any of the birds of prey around here are eating other fish, lizards, maybe other small birds," I said, trying not to include such scientific vocabulary as "scavengers" and "regurgitated castings" like I would have even a year ago. Alex had told me that was boring. Ryan had said I was acting like a nerd. Still, I had to add, "And the birds probably aren't even full grown ones. Just the chicks. Nothing with teeth."

Ryan rolled his eyes at me. "Okay, relax nature boy. I actually *went* to science today. I don't need a lecture. It's probably just those stupid kids from last summer," he said, eyeing the mound of dirt from his seat on the log next to my brother. By kids, I knew Ryan meant the far less mature middle schoolers who, despite his recent membership in their ranks, were a world away, separated by the infinitely deep moat of wanting to do stupid kid things, like making a castle fort on our beach. And I knew that even though Alex let me hang out with them, he still called me a kid as much as Ryan did. Never mind that he hadn't actually seen me build the moat for the castle fort, I was not, my brother told me frequently, a *man* yet.

"You think someone's fucking with us?" Alex asked. "Because if someone thinks they can fuck with us..." He didn't have to finish the threat. Once, when we were still in middle school, Ryan had decided to tell some insanely large high school kid that the fishing hat he was wearing made him look like Freddy Krueger. Alex had gotten the phone call saying Ryan needed back-up, and the rest of us had gone too, and gotten our asses beat. But the four of us had always been like this with each other, a bunch of crows dive-bombing anyone stupid enough to threaten part of our nest.

I shrugged. At the edge of the hole, a few wispy feathers lay plastered to the sand, slicked with a viscous blue and green mud, doing their best imitation of a victim in *The Texas Chainsaw Massacre*. Ryan got closer, poking them with a stick. "It looks like a cross between the greenish satanic slime from *Prince of Darkness* and that mess from *The Blob* after he barfs the guy up on the ceiling. Could be whatever's in here is contaminated. Like toxic." Ryan grinned, pretending to poke me with it. I backed away quickly and he laughed. Ryan was our curator of what Alex liked to call hilarity-level B-grade horror, introducing us to pirated gore-fest classics which usually featured the equivalent of a liquid pyrotechnics show and the evisceration of pretty blonds sporting elemental silicone in their chests. Most of the time when we watched those movies, I managed a "sick bro," before ending up in the bathroom, pretending our stolen taquitos were the carriers of diarrhea-level food poisoning. "Or maybe it's just evil."

"Bro, that green slime in *Prince of Darkness* looked like someone failed at Jell-O," Dimez said. "It wasn't scary at all."

"Actually," my brother grinned, "I thought it looked scary. Kinda like your mom on a Friday night." He laughed as Dimez pretended to punch him. Dimez's real name was Dmitri, but only his mother and supply teachers ever called him that; the rest of us called him Dimez, after his ever-present baggies of weed. Dimez was always trying to make us laugh and I got out a laugh too, even as Dimez pretended to shove Alex into the water. But there was a familiar wrongness to those oilishly slick feathers, one I couldn't quite translate into understandable vocalization.

When Alex got close enough to the mound of dirt to shine his phone light down into the hole, we realized we couldn't see the bottom, our view blocked by what must have been muddy water, but in this light resembled a toxic B-movie liquid. About halfway down there was a ledge, barely illuminated, and on it,

a huddled mass of *something*, dark and maybe wet. I was pretty
sure it was a body. The truth was I kind of wanted it to be a body.
If it was a body, I could roll my eyes, like I was both disgusted
and definitely not scared at all. I constantly stood accused of
being scared. I was short, and I'd been called every poultry-
inspired word for nerdy and terrified. (Once, I'd tried to explain
to several boys—including probably the meanest boy in grade
seven, Michael D'Angelo, who suggested I go fornicate with
my own mother—that I didn't have the stomach to be a geek;
traditionally, in a carnival sideshow, geeks chased the chickens,
then bit their heads off, and I was terrified of salmonella. After
Alex had beat them into proneness, neatly decapitating their
extremely expensive baseball caps from their heads, he told
me never to let anyone call me names.) And Mom never said I
looked like Dad. Not when I named all 42 families of birds in
alphabetical order at the dinner table, or memorized most of
*Birding for Not Dummies (Bird Watching is Kind of a Smart People
Hobby Anyway)*, or brought home a robin's egg and placed it
on our radiator for incubation purposes, convinced for a good
six months there was still a chance it would hatch. Meanwhile,
Alex could make the egregious taxonomic error of calling a
female *Homo sapiens* in a particularly tight pair of jean shorts a
"chick," or completely fail a biology test, and Mom would still
say he reminded her of our father. "He was good at avoiding
responsibility too," she told Alex over his D minus in science. My
brother was the tough kid. But if it was a body, I could be quietly
unimpressed, just like how when Mom worked overnights I'd
learned to soundlessly tiptoe around her live-in boyfriend of
the month who mostly drank all day on the couch so that we
could stream horror movies I didn't want to admit scared me
on our phones undisturbed in our room until 5 a.m. I would
always somehow manage a bored, "how fake," giggle when the

alien exploded and the corpse's chomping rib cage chewed off the guy's arms.

"Guys, it totally is a body!" Dimez shrieked.

"Bro, relax. It's not that serious." Alex rolled his eyes.

"Like you and Julie Caldo?" Ryan said my brother had it bad, and I agreed, even if I wasn't sure what exactly it was that was bad. Was it my brother's kleptoparasitism of Julie's wallet for beer and snacks, or his crow-like penchant for trying to hoard Julie away from other boys, saying "but you're my girl"? Or was it a hot, flushing itchiness that could easily be mistaken for a mild case of chickenpox, the same feeling I got in my clandestine creeping every second Thursday at meetings of the environmental club where Ava Caldo was the president (most of the time, I arrived just late enough to science to guarantee myself detention on those Thursdays with Mr. Gurian, their supervising teacher)? Ryan and my brother referred to Ava Caldo, Julie's little sister, as "a true psycho bitch." It was true that she could turn conversations about such non-controversial topics as the superiority of Dimez's weed compared to the usual high school skunk, or the general shittiness of the cafeteria lunch offerings, into part educational documentary, part portent of doom. "Did you know that there is a high likelihood cannabis impacts the ozone?" "Did you know that polystyrene trays take thousands of years to break down in the absence of direct sunlight and we're already at 100 seconds to midnight?" But whenever Ava discussed cleaning up the beach on Thursday afternoons, I developed a deep dark desire to fight for the preservation of seagulls by picking up oil-drenched hamburger wraps and plastic six-pack holders.

"Who told you me and Julie aren't serious?"

"Julie," Ryan said. Ryan had a thing for Julie too, but we all liked to joke that it was probably more like *The Thing*; Ryan was a big guy, branded bad with his shaved head and homemade tats on his knuckles. Ryan liked to scare people. Even Alex said that if Ryan ever got a real girlfriend we'd have to watch that she didn't end up in a dumpster somewhere.

"Whatever. We're serious. She's hot," Alex glared, looking a bit uncomfortable. "Besides, that bag can't have a body in it. It's not big enough. And neither is the uh, diameter of the hole. For a grave anyways," my brother said, as though he totally didn't skip math on a daily basis.

"What if it's dismembered?" Ryan grinned, and Dimez got way too excited, like this was some zombie movie you could just turn off when the rotting corpses got way too oozy and gross and alive. My brother grabbed a piece of driftwood and managed to spear the mass of whatever it was. He lifted it through the hole, and in the light we could see it was a torn, plastic trash bag covered in the slick muddiness of whatever was in that hole. Then Alex stabbed the bag with his stick, ripping it open so more of the bluish green goo oozed out.

At first I thought they were dead birds. I mean, I thought they were real; those dull-eyed lumps of garish blues and greens and reds and feathers, all covered in a sickly oilish goop. But these feathers had no wings, no beaks attached. "Guys, it's a chick," Dimez said, gingerly holding up one wearing a dress whose face was covered in the goop and waiting for us to laugh. She was obviously a she, and covered in feathers, but she wasn't like those lumps of soft yellow polyester fur that come out at the dollar store during springtime Easter displays next to the ever multiplying rabbits with the scrotally floppy ears. None of them were. They were dolls, I realized, five old, plastic baby dolls, naked and genderless under clothes that featured super tacky sparkles and feathers. Lots of feathers. The one who was completely bald had a tiny plastic sword stuck to its belt, the cocktail kind Mom used to leave on the coffee table and pass out next to when she was dating that guy who owned Misty's Lounge. Another had a happy face sewn onto its stomach while the biggest had a felt rooster's comb as a hat. The one with the rooster hat crowed when you pressed it. Baldy with the sword screeched. Whenever you pushed Smiley's happy face button it emitted a laugh that sounded like a slightly hysterical hyena.

"Guys, check this out," Dimez grinned as the second smallest doll, with nondescript, brownish plumage, repeated him in a voice that was truly haunted-house grade. "Take me to your leader." No matter what you said, it would echo your words in a tone that sounded like a spiritually active meat processing plant.

"The aliens are here," the doll repeated in Ryan's voice, as Ryan gestured toward Dimez.

"That's stupid," I said.

"I'm stupid," Ryan snickered into the doll.

"Fuck off," I told him, and Ryan patted me on the shoulder condescendingly.

"Well, those are all kinds of not right," my brother pronounced.

I didn't know what the dolls' eyes were made of, except it wasn't plastic. Each one looked like a slug curled around itself into a cold dark pupil, staring blankly in a familiar way, but impossible to tell what it was watching. Not that they were watching anything. I mean, not that they could, but the more I looked at them, the more I felt my own throat tighten up. I couldn't be the only one who remembered seeing the dolls before. Flies swarmed around them, like the chorus of mini seagulls around that mute corpse of some indistinguishable fish, pancake-thin and stinking, that had lain on the beach for the better part of last summer. *Guess we really treated you like garbage,* I thought. And a feeling like an anchor formed a weight in the middle of my stomach.

"Guys, guys! The way they fell over? It looks like they're humping!" Dimez squealed.

"Those dolls are *Chucky* levels of cheesy," Ryan scoffed. "Why would someone even have those?"

"Maybe some guy had a doll fetish? And his girlfriend found out so he had to dump them?" Dimez said hopefully, picking up the one in a skirt again and wiping the gunk off her face with his shirt. "Oh my god are those eyelashes?"

I realized now where the down had come from. The freaky eyelash fringe stuck on top of the one doll who looked most like a girl was made of wispy feathers, way too long for her face, like some of the grade twelve girls who stuck their eyelashes on in the cafeteria at lunch. Dimez tried all the strings, pressed each of their stomachs in a pseudo-Heimlich maneuver, forcing words out of every doll mouth like a piece of unfortunately caught chicken, until he got to this one, the smallest one, the only one who didn't make any noise.

"I think Eyelashes here is broken," Dimez said.

Of course she was, I thought to myself. Just like Eli, she had almost drowned. But I couldn't say that out loud; last summer we had all wordlessly agreed not to. "That doll was Eli's," I said softly, stepping away from the edge of the pit. "All of those dolls were Eli's."

Alex blinked nervously, as though I'd just shoved a flashlight in his face like those times when we used to tell stories to freak each other out with the lights off in our living room. "Who cares? There's no body and there's no grave," my brother said, uneasily swatting away one of the flies that had landed on his arm as he passed the joint to me. "So how about everybody just stop making a big deal out of nothing."

* * *

We spent the next half hour in uncomfortably normal conversation, doing our best to ignore the dolls, staring silently at who knew what, all blanked-out. They had the same unnaturally semi-human look as the eyeless, mouthless Captain Kirk mask now synonymous with Michael Myers that Ryan told us the director of the original *Halloween* movie spray-painted pale for an extra terrifying effect. Dimez rolled another joint, Alex finished our beers, we all agreed doll horror movies were stupid and not scary at all, and Ryan half-heartedly tried to convince us to watch some *Saw* rip-off that predictably featured the blond magician's assistant, whose ponytail bounced like a rabbit diving into a bush, getting brutally chainsawed in half for real. After all, we'd never talked about Eli much. But we had our reasons.

(Reason one: My brother would say he was irrelevant. We remembered Eli, but only as a loser in a Stephen King horror movie, the kind who doesn't defeat the bullies until the third act, like every other kid we'd tormented in the name of defending our middle school territory. He was the kid who'd cried when we'd robbed him for his balaclava to go shoplift Doritos, the kid whose nose broke so hard we actually heard the crack when we'd beat him up for the heinously benign crime of reciting all of the elements of the periodic table in alphabetical order, thereby robbing my brother and his class of three minutes of recess time.)

"Remember when we hid his chocolate eggs under the radiator in the cafeteria, then put them on his seat and we walked around for the rest of the day asking what stunk?"

"Didn't we steal Mr. Big bars for that, then leave them in his shorts after gym?"

"Did he wear those stupid dollar-store shoes to school?"

"No dude, you're thinking of your cousin."

"Was he the kid we stole those dollar-store shoes from?"

"Bro, half the school wore dollar-store shoes. You're going to have to get more specific."

Honestly, aside from Eyelashes, there wasn't even all that much we could have said about Eli. I mean, we'd talked at him, sure, but it's not like most of us ever had what you could call an actual conversation with him. For most of middle school, Eli had been somewhere between amoeba and bottom feeder with those dolls in hand-sewn clothes his only lunchtime companions. As those occupying higher ecological niches, ranging from golden eagle (my brother) to at least scavenger (me, hanging around my brother and picking up his scraps of coolness), we'd believed it was the natural order of things that required us to kick the shit out of Eli on a weekly basis. We'd cornered him behind every portable, in the south stairwell, in the bathrooms farthest from the office, like those omnipresent, long-extinct terror birds Ms. D had taken us to see at the museum. That terror bird had had a mean glint in his reconstructed glass eyes as he mowed down on a much less impressive-looking stuffed jaguar, which stared at you in the same reflexively bestial silence as Eli every time we beat him down.

"Okay Girlie, you know why we're here, right?" Alex would say. We never called Eli by his name. It was Ellie, and once I told everyone "elle" was French for "she," it was "Girlie." "Girlie" was the biggest middle school insult we thought we could muster for a boy. And Eli would just stand there, nodding like one of those dipshit birds pretending to drink water on a desk up to the moment when we'd claw at him, shrieking and scratching and punching until he was reduced to a body gone slack and relaxed as a hypnotized chicken.

"Wasn't Ellie a foster kid?"

"Guys, I don't remember, but I think his dad was in the secret service and they had to go into some witness protection spy thing." This was from Dimez. Ryan groaned.

"You have no idea who we're talking about, do you? There is no way that happened. Ellie would have been cool."

"But he moved, right?" I asked.

"Are we seriously still talking about this kid?" my brother said, glaring at me. "Why you guys are so interested in him I don't know." I quickly shut my mouth.

(Reason two: None of us wanted to invoke his name like the *Candyman* curse, and then be accused of being exactly what Eli was. That was like willingly taking on the camouflage of a southern willow ptarmigan, who usually makes a nice dinner for a hawk, stupidly turning white before it even snows. And at least compared to Eli, I could actually pass for a bird of prey.)

Dimez, who'd had maybe four or five beers by now, picked up Eyelashes again. Then he started to howl. "Oh shit, it looks like this was Eli's girlfriend," he said, turning the doll over to reveal "Eli's" with a heart stitched on to the tag. It was the kind of heart we'd all seen girls doodling, complete with initials we always hoped were ours in the interior. Dimez bent the doll so that she was hanging over the log. Then, almost mechanically, he positioned the biggest doll, the one with the felt rooster comb headpiece, behind her. "Look guys. She's getting some cock!" And he opened his mouth to deliver the same director's commentary he used for everything ranging from porn to *Blue Planet*; "Aw, c'mon. Get her. Ya. Get her. C'mon... Oh yeah," looking at all of us, willing us to laugh, as though exhaling our laughter would help expand us outwards like balloons, regaining some of whatever we had lost to the dolls on *our* beach.

(Reason three: The guys must have remembered Eli couldn't swim. And maybe, for my brother and Dimez and Ryan, he had actually sunk soundlessly in their memories as they'd watched, coolly, like that shark underneath the water in *Jaws*.)

"Damn, Girlie must have been desperate."

"Yeah," my brother grinned, "being a weirdo like that I wonder why."

Then I heard the girl doll talk.

I mean, it had to have been her. "Quit it," I said. I could see the jerky movements of her mouth, like some claymation special, the "youyou youyou youyou" almost like hiccups.

"Quit what?" Ryan grinned. "What's your problem bro? You look paler than Michael Myers."

"Quit banging your hands on the rocks," I said to Ryan, "or whatever you're doing. Whatever's making that doll bounce around. I think you're breaking her record."

"Bro, you're hearing things. That doll was broken to begin with. Besides, I'm not banging anything."

"That's what she said."

"Shut up, Dimez."

"I'm pretty sure they moved," my brother said thoughtfully, picking up the doll and freeing her from what Dimez helpfully informed us was the camel-style position.

"The dolls?" For a second, I was so relieved he was going to admit he'd heard her too that I wanted to puke.

"I meant Ellie's family, dumbass," my brother scoffed. "Of course the dolls aren't going to move. If they ever did, their batteries are probably dead now." He put Eyelashes down thoughtfully next to the rooster doll and then stepped on her belly. Nothing came out.

"See?" I said. "Ryan broke her."

"I'm telling you she was already broken."

"Then maybe it was you," I said to my brother.

"Gavin, why do you care?" Alex tried stepping on her again

and then, disgusted, kicked her back into the pit. "She obviously isn't even supposed to talk."

By the time we left the beach, Alex was munching on our last bag of Doritos, and neon purples and pinks were fading out to cool grey blues, like those half-burned-out "open" signs in the strip mall. Ryan had to go to work, but Julie's parents were out of town so the rest of us took the tunnel under the bridge to her house because she was having a party. When we were kids, Alex and I used to go the long way home after school every day just so we could go through that tunnel. We'd screeched, "hello, hello, hey, hey," the echoes of our own voices coming back deepened, almost Dad-like, or at least how we thought Dad would sound. Sometimes it was even "I love you," although Alex used to make sure that was only if a cute girl was going the same way. I had to take Alex's word that we did sound like Dad. After all, out of the two of us, he was the only one who'd remember, and ever since Mom had dated Karl, the first of her drunk-as-fuck live-in boyfriends, Alex was the only one who prevented me from being the equivalent of a rabbit gallivanting across the lawn under the mildly peckish eyes of a raptor.

But not in the tunnel. In the tunnel at least I could sound like a hawk.

Tonight Alex was screaming, "hey hey hey," accompanied by what sounded like the whistle of a starling who'd learned how to imitate the wolf whistles he'd heard coming from construction sites. "C'mon little brother," he grinned. "We are going to party!" And I whooped along with him. Dimez joined in. On the other side of the tunnel, a couple of girls waiting at a bus stop held their breath in their shoulders until we passed as we ogled the one who bent over to get something from her bag. I didn't know, back then, how we must have sounded to those girls, like an unkindness of ravens mobbing a pity of doves. I couldn't even see myself in the reflections of the girls' glasses as they stared silently at the ground.

When we got to Julie's, a bunch of us took turns pouring the vodka we'd brought into what was left of our blue Gatorade and the Coke can mixers Julie left on the table next to a half-eaten bag of chips. Dimez was talking to some girl about going to smoke outside while my brother went off somewhere with Julie. I kind of wished Ava was there. None of the guys knew, but we'd even kissed. Once. After a fairly romantic environmental club garbage audit of the school cafeteria when she'd caught me throwing a chip bag on the ground on my way home.

"Think of the birds," she'd said seriously. "Birds have been falling out of the sky in the southwestern United States all summer. Bluebirds, warblers, starlings. And in Europe, there's the swifts. And the swallows. No one knows why. And seabirds," she'd said, pointing to the bag, "are especially vulnerable to the litter we leave behind. They've been known to choke on it."

"I swear," I'd blurted out, "I'll never eat Doritos ever again!"

"Well," she'd grinned a little, "I guess that's a start." And before I knew it was happening, Ava's lips had migrated toward mine, closing my mouth so that all I could hear was her fairly excited breathing and my own heart threatening to explode on me like the alien in *The Thing*. But I knew that at best my friends would see my love as ridiculous. Alex had tried to teach me camouflage, how to make sure that, if I wasn't quite the Andean cock-of-the-rock or the imposingly aloof terror bird (basically the Michael Myers of prehistoric mammals), I could still pass as a distant descendant, perhaps the cool-as-fuck shrike who impales its meals on a tree and gives as many shits as the metal-head kids who smoke cigarettes for lunch. But Ava was smart and interested in the ecological fate of birds; with Ava, I felt like I didn't have to try and transform from a fourteen-year-old boy whose voice was still cracking into a syrinx-using avian, able to sing two notes at once, saying one thing and meaning another. Standing at Julie's kitchen table, I tried to choke down the ball in my chest that was maybe the Gatorade, maybe the feeling that the grave we'd found was a lot less laughably bad *Pet Sematary* remake and a lot more, well, grave. As in serious.

"Bro, you okay? You want a smoke?" Dimez said, sounding a little concerned as I came out the back door.

"Naw man. I think I just need to puke," I lied.

"You probably don't want to go back there," Dimez said.

"Why?"

"Your bro is there with Julie." He waggled his eyebrows.

"Bro," I laughed, "Alex is so drunk right now he probably can't do anything, if you know what I mean." The truth was I was still creeped out by Eli's dolls and needed to empty my stomach in the bushes.

Julie's house was one of the nicer ones we'd been in; the yard of the place her parents rented was huge, backing onto a ravine that eventually connected to the parkette secluding our beach. I stumbled over to the hedge in the back, swaying a little, hoping I wasn't going to fall through the super flimsy fence separating me from the drop into the ravine that looked sharp enough for lemmings to accomplish their last fatalistic leap before some snowy owl snapped them up. Then I heard voices: my brother's, from somewhere behind one of the scraggly pine trees bordering the edge of the park. "Shhh," I could hear him say, "keep quiet. They'll hear you. Everyone will hear you." I couldn't hear exactly what Julie was saying, whether it was "Not you, not you. I don't want to. I don't want you," or "Youyou youyou. I want you. Just you," like my brother would later claim, but there was something, almost a wail, just under the surface of her voice. I stood there, as invisible as breathing, just like when my brother said I needed to choose whether I was going to get beat up or do the beating. And before my brother emerged from the trees, before we stumbled home to an empty, dark apartment with Mom working nights and Alex telling me we'd be fine if we just drank another beer because that's what Dad used to do and he said it cured all headaches, there was a choking squeak, the same as the sound when we'd stolen the canary toy from our neighbour's poodle and made a silencing hole, letting out all the air, easily mistaken for the wind.

* * *

When we got to the beach on Monday afternoon, the hole was larger. Once we walked the scraggly parkette path and poked through the bushes that hid our beach from view, we could see the grave was almost pit sized, less like the nesting hole of a kingfisher and more like the giant, gaping burrow of a badger. At the bottom of the pit was a crow. A big one. A dead one. It was a blasphemy of feathers sticking out at weird angles, the kind of crow they put in Halloween specials as a harbinger of definite potential doom. ("Gross," Ryan said, nodding approvingly.) All the dolls were gathered around the edge of the grave in an almost perfect semicircle facing inward. Even Eyelashes. I realized, with the same chicken skin crawling up my back as the time I was five and in bed and my brother told me Freddy could kill you while you slept, that she was not in the pit where my brother had dumped her. Eyelashes was standing slightly behind the rooster doll, and was the only one facing us, and not the crow. Somehow, overnight, the grave seemed to have deepened ominously into a chasm.

We talked theories; after all, there were plenty of reasons a dead crow would be lying in the middle of the beach. And there were plenty of reasons the dolls could have been moved and arranged in some kind of coven-esque satanic summoning semicircle. I could picture those reasons like movie scripts in my mind with their predictable characters, their expected endings, but the tenses kept getting jumbled, like half-remembered shows we'd all seen as little kids and couldn't quite remember afterwards if our dads had really dumped us on an island with reject toys or left us home alone to fend off burglars. These things could happen. But they shouldn't. They shouldn't happen. But they do.

Script one: It was some stupid kid thing. Little girls who liked dolls most likely. Nothing to be scared of. Maybe they were having a tea party or whatever little girls did. Maybe the dead crow was a coincidence. And they tried to bury it. Or maybe they just liked hurting small animals and were on track to starring as the next real-life Michael Myers, slightly worse than Jason Voorhees, who wouldn't kill a puppy.

Script two: It could have been a largish, slightly ravenous scavenging animal, most likely of the coyote or lupine variety, in any case with canine teeth. Or something tool-using that could pierce through feathers and skin without leaving any marks. If this was the case, it would have been like a whole documentary-type shoot, exploring the natural wonder of predatory instincts and territorial aggression, a fight to the death for the crow.

Script three: Someone filled the pit with whatever goo they could and tried to sink a dead crow, Mafia-style, in a kind of tribute to *I Know What You Did Last Summer* (which Ryan explained was somewhat of a cult classic), i.e., someone wanted us to find them. The dolls were gathered around in their vigilante wake to let us know the killer knew. It was a revenge plot, most likely orchestrated by someone who hated us.

Script four: Some *thing* was fucking with us. (Picture dark stairs into the classic haunted house basement, an uneasy camera over the shoulder. The dolls. Nothing. But fear.)

"But why kill a crow? That's like... like *you* levels of messed up," Dimez said to Ryan, who actually seemed pleased.

"How should I know? That Ellie kid was a weirdo."

"You think Girlie did this?" I tried not to sound surprised.

My brother shrugged. He'd been quiet all day. "Well, if it wasn't him, who was it? Who else knows the dolls are here?"

"We do," I said in a low voice, but my brother didn't seem to notice.

"And seriously, are we really still talking about that loser? Who cares?" my brother said. "And who cares if there's a dead bird? 'Cause *this* is the *only* body I'm interested in right now." He smirked, scrolling past the screenshot of the Kijiji ad for the guard dog he wanted to get for Mom. When he showed us the next pic on his phone, it featured more of a passed-out Julie than I had ever seen before. I mean you could see a barely covered everything, the stuff Dimez talked about whenever he mentioned the word anatomy. "Nice, huh?" Julie was nice. That was the problem. And here Alex was, zooming in and out to dissect Julie's posterior with the same stupid grin on his face that Ryan had when he got suspended for what the teacher called "disrespectfully" treating the frog he was dissecting in grade eight, spearing it with a ruler and then pretending it was a puppet.

But I didn't try to stop Alex.

I watched her too, a chicken-hearted watching, while my heart banged like a hummingbird in my chest. I watched with the same gut-sick excitement as all those times Dimez and I took Eli's arms and held them behind his back, waiting for Alex to land the first punch. It was totally natural, I tried to tell myself. Even if I felt a little queasiness staring at Julie, perpetually frozen in motion like those girls in slasher movies who scream and don't even try to run, it was probably just because I shouldn't have eaten that sketchy taquito at lunch.

I'd read somewhere that male zebra finches only develop their calls by imitating the calls of other males; zebra finches can tell in a second if you are part of their group by the calls you make. "Nice," I said, carefully, same way my brother had, echoing Dimez's porn-watching low wolf whistle.

"I thought you guys broke up," Ryan said offhandedly.

"Why?"

"I heard her mom wants to call police on you."

"Bullshit," my brother said. "That's my chick you're talking about."

"Why the police?" I asked.

"Like I said," my brother shrugged, "I don't know what you're talking about."

"Right bud," Ryan grinned, "just like you don't know Girlie's exactly the kind of weirdo who would go set up a picnic for his dollies. Heard you like having picnics with the ladies in ravines too, ya know."

"What are you trying to say?" my brother asked, assuming a defensive posture like he used to do when Karl came looking for us, like a bird spreading his wings to look larger. It used to make me feel a little less scared.

"C'mon bro, relax. You know I'm just playing," Ryan said uncomfortably. I remembered how Ryan had once had his mom pick me and Alex up in the middle of the night, when Alex texted after Karl had decided that the way my brother breathed in a hockey mask while we were watching *Friday the 13th* on our phones in bed was too loud, and he was going to make it quiet. We had slept on couch cushions on Ryan's living room floor, and Ryan had unearthed a sleeping bag from his mom's days as a camp counsellor to stay with us. "People talk lots of shit. You know I don't believe it."

I stared at Alex for a minute too. My brother might have dressed up as Voorhees once to scare the shit out of the Anderson twins on the fourth floor, but he used to wear that goalie mask and tell me to get behind him when Karl came home looking to give out black eyes so we could pretend the next day like nothing bad had happened. And even if he had said he didn't care that the crow was dead, it's not like he'd done it. Right? He wouldn't do something like that. Plus, the way the dolls looked, staring at the dead crow in the pit soundlessly, a thought I knew should be as dumb and unscientifically impossible as Michael Myers getting up from that fall off the second-storey balcony occurred to me.

Maybe *they* killed the bird.

I knew that sounded ridiculous, like kids' Halloween specials, not the sophisticated R-rated horror movies that actually showed blood and boobs which Ryan streamed for us now. Maybe it was ridiculous. But there was that nagging hopeful queasiness, a vague memory of Ryan telling us about how the world's worst Raggedy Ann doll had to be kept behind glass at an occult museum, or that there was this super evil sailor doll people were so scared of that they wrote apology letters to it. There was even a doll that made you sick if you looked at her online. Sometimes dolls did weird shit, just like how Alex said girls did shit you were never going to understand. Right? And if it was the dolls, none of this could be our faults.

"What if it wasn't someone who killed the crow?" I took a breath. "What if it was some *thing*?"

Then I heard the bushes rustling next to me and I jumped. Ryan almost killed himself laughing.

"Isn't that Julie's sister?" he said, gasping.

It *was* Ava, I realized, standing over a couple of the fairly large sunflowers in the only patch of mangy grass beside the bushes hiding the log and our tiny beach from view of the path. She was whispering, "Hi. Hello. Hello and how are you doing?" while in the background, a couple of ducks dove and resurfaced and dove and resurfaced, looking for whatever sketchy two-headed fish lived in the lake.

"Hey Ava," my brother screamed out in a mock singsong voice, "who you talking to?"

"The sunflowers," she said, coming over to the bushes and parting them to look at us. Ava's voice was thin and treble, an embarrassingly soft warbling species we would have tried to kill outright if it had belonged to another boy. I panicked. Quietly. That duck and I were on the same page, my stomach flipping wildly between wanting Ava to say hello to me, and wanting to make absolutely sure that, to the rest of my friends, the nauseously delirious feeling I got around her stayed completely invisible.

"The plants?" Ryan said incredulously. My brother, in mock shock, dropped his Doritos.

"Yes," she said calmly, "we've already lost over three billion birds since 1970."

"And talking to sunflowers is supposed to do what exactly?" my brother said, in a deliberately loud voice. I didn't know it then, but girls like Ava invoked a fear in us, not that we would have been able to identify it as fear; we didn't do scared. We mostly laughed during bodily amputation scenes in *Saw*, and the most jittery I'd ever seen us was when my brother full-on punched Dimez in the face for jumping out at him in the dark hallway coming back from the bathroom after a six-hour-straight slasher movie marathon.

"The Royal Horticultural Society did a study and found out that talking to plants really does help them grow faster. And the environmental club is doing a project on wild bird feeding; we want these seeds to be ready for all the cardinals and chickadees before they migrate. Gavin, you missed that meeting; I didn't know you knew. That's what you guys are doing here, right?" Ava stopped for a second, as though she was looking at my brother for the first time. "You're my sister's ex, aren't you?"

"No," my brother said. He sounded pissed. "I'm your sister's boyfriend. And none of us are a part of your little environmental club either." But my brother *looked* at me and I could feel myself beginning to sweat.

"No, you're not my sister's boyfriend. And your brother comes to environmental club all the time. Right Gavin?"

I knew, objectively, that a girl who talked to sunflowers was not supposed to be hot, even if normally, when I looked at Ava, I felt like I was inside the sun itself, getting close to that maximum temperature of fifteen million degrees. But when Ava looked at me now, I looked away. The rest of the guys howled and I gave a short, barking laugh while my stomach threatened to do its best impression of a fulmar chick and puke up that noxiously blue Gatorade and vodka I'd just finished. I tried not to picture it, an electric stream landing somewhere just around Ava's shoes.

"I have no idea what you're talking about," I mumbled as she stared at me and I looked away. I could hear Ava stomp off, her *thuds* somehow echoing louder than my brother's laughter.

"Weirdo," Alex said. "It was probably her."

"It's not. It's like..." I swallowed, "some *thing.*"

"Are you talking about... like... something *paranormal*?" Ryan said incredulously. Guys our age weren't supposed to believe in the invisible, the unseen antecedents behind a bunch of flying birds dropping dead from the sky, the cause and effects intangibly stretched out like the thick, dark smoke from the steel mill.

I shrugged. "What about the dolls?"

"Gavin Thompson," my brother said, shooting an unfathomably deep look of disappointment in my direction, while using my full name like it was the proper scientific genus and species for *Totalus nutso kiddus*, "that is the stupidest thing you've ever said. Seriously bro. Shut up."

* * *

The next few days unfolded like the script for an artsy horror film that Ryan would have turned off in the first ten minutes because honestly, nothing *really* happened. But it was terrifying all the same. By Monday *that* picture of Julie was all over school. At the beach we found two dead ravens in the pit and Eyelashes face down underneath both of them. The happy face doll was holding the little cocktail sword that had somehow come out of Baldy's belt, and was staring into the open mouth of the grave. And the rest of the dolls, of course, were arranged in their satanic semicircle which, it occurred to me, if this was a movie, would actually look hysterical, them in their tiny kindergarten-coloured outfits, their tiny little hands that couldn't even make a fist. They were a big joke. Only Dimez would let me see his grin shiver, stepping on the happy face doll so a faint *hee-haw, hee-haw* came squeaking out.

"Fuck man, that one laughs like you!" my brother said to him.

"Hey Dimez," Ryan grinned, trying to hold back a snicker, "guess you and Girlie are doing this together. I wonder if you can actually stab a bird to death with a plastic sword."

"Um, that's your sword. That belongs to Baldy over there," Dimez pointed out.

The dolls did look like us. Sure, none of us were natural-born wildlife killers, even if Alex had punched our neighbour's poodle in the face when it went to bite him and Ryan did that thing with the frog in middle school. But the doll with the happy face on its stomach did have the same hyena laugh Dimez was famous for, and Baldy matched Ryan's closely shaved head. The way the biggest, most rooster-like one sat, so assured, legs sprawling, was obviously my brother. And then there was the Echo doll, with no call of its own, quiet until repeating Dimez's *hee-haw*.

"How did Girlie even get down there? Like to arrange them on top of the doll?" Peering over the edge, Dimez had the same big-shock expression on his face as when we'd dared him to stick his finger in the electrical socket back in elementary school. "Damn, that pit goes down pretty deep."

"Didn't he take gymnastics or something?" I said, joining the guys in laughing, uncontrollably, dutifully.

"Yeah," my brother said slowly, wiping the tears from his eyes, "that one time, didn't we beat him up for wearing tights?"

On Tuesday there were three dead jays and possibly what used to be a pair of magpies. We howled. We gasped. We shrieked like a drongo bird imitating a hyena. Every time the sound came out of me it felt like a cheap echo, like if a parrot had an owner who watched *It* on DVD too many times, causing the bird to develop a calamitous cackle.

"How is he even doing this?"

"He probably slid down. His tights must look like they got shit stains all over them."

"But didn't he move just before high school?" I said. "How would he even get here in time for us to see it after school when he's across town?"

My brother looked at me like this was the stupidest thing I'd ever said. "Maybe he skipped?"

"Bro, Rooster over here looks straight up like he's crowing over this one!" Ryan pointed to the sunless side of the log, where the rooster doll sat smugly on top of Eyelashes' back. We all crowed too. Loudly. Nervously. After a while, I felt like the laughter didn't connect any of us. It was genuine imitation.

Dimez looked thoughtful. "If Girlie can slide down a hole like this and get back up, do you think he might have been the one to do... you know... what happened to Julie at the party?"

"What?" My brother's face was expressionless.

Dimez continued. "I mean, can you imagine some random trying to get out of Julie's backyard and sliding down a slope like her ravine has? Guy must be a goddamn circus acrobat."

"What are you talking about?" I said.

"Didn't you hear about what happened to Julie at the party?" Dimez said softly. "She got like, assaulted." Dimez paused and then shook his head. "I mean, I guess there's no way it was Girlie. He would have no idea what to do with a girl. Maybe it *was* just some guy trying to break in. Right?" Even though it was silent, I could hear my brother's anger, like when the music turns off in a slasher flick and all you hear is breathing behind a bush, or how, in late summer, all the birds stopped singing.

"Whoever's saying that happened to Julie is talking a bunch of bullshit." My brother stared blankly at Dimez. "I was with her the whole time."

"Maybe it's Girlie spreading rumours too," I said quickly.

"Alright." My brother gritted his teeth, hucking the dolls one by one out into the water like we were skipping stones. "Let's settle this, once and for all. We know that fucker Eli doesn't know how to swim."

I hadn't told the guys, but I had started dreaming about the dolls. In one dream, the dolls became life sized, and they worked on digging the grave themselves while a man-sized rooster got a crossbow and shot Miss Eyelashes through the heart. The arrow turned into Cupid's in the air. In another, the dolls were already buried, but from a bird's eye view the grave turned out to be the North Pacific Garbage Patch. And then I was inside Echo the doll, shooting arrows into seagulls and laughing about how they should be called shit hawks. When the arrowhead hit the seagull, it began to rain starlings and sparrows and warblers and bluebirds and jays. And a big dead crow. I cut open the crow and plastic pieces of dolls spilled out of his stomach, arms and legs and noses and strings. I realized I wasn't Echo anymore, but the zookeeper, feeding a captive Hawaiian crow I'd named Ava some doll pieces for breakfast. "Whose fault is it?" I'd asked, and she'd answered, "Youyou youyou youyou." And all I could think of was that wasn't a natural call for anything except a shit-disturbing jay when I realized I had just fed her Julie Caldo's butt. I woke up with the pillow in my mouth, unable to scream.

On Wednesday another dead crow lay on top of Eyelashes, spread eagle in the pit, surrounded by at least four jackdaws.

"Honestly, it's kind of sick," Ryan said, "especially if that little dolly was his girlfriend."

"Maybe she's into necrophilia."

"Shut up Dimez." Alex groaned.

"Why? It's funny." For a second, Dimez actually looked hurt.

"No, it's stupid," Ryan scoffed. "Maybe not as stupid as Gavin's theory that the dolls did this. But it's definitely stupid."

"Gav, man, don't let him talk to you like that," Dimez said quietly.

But the more I looked at the dolls, the more they looked like us. The one with the little plastic sword reminded me of the knife no one knew Ryan was carrying until we'd all seen him pull it out at some homeless guy who'd tried to grab Alex's wallet at the bus stop. And that half-sob laugh from the happy face doll reminded me of how Alex once told me their grade four teacher, Mr. Klaus, used to say Dimez tried to get people to laugh so they wouldn't notice he was crying inside. And as for the rooster, Ava said when roosters are trained for cock fighting, they carry blades strapped to their legs. And once, I saw Alex hold an X-Acto knife he'd stolen from the art supplies closet to a girl in elementary school; it was one of the days Mom hadn't packed us lunch and this girl had pizza. And I was the Echo doll, repeating ad nauseam, "Don't scream." "Just give it to him." "Don't be stupid."

"Whatever," I said hollowly. "It's still stupid."

My brother and I went home through the tunnel that night because he said he wanted to go by Julie's. We didn't talk, and I was suddenly very aware of how much I had no fucking clue what Dad's voice actually sounded like. It was the same squirming quiet after we'd delivered our final kicks to Eli and the kid tried to catch his breath, his stomach rising and falling in jerky movements, like when you tangle a puppet's strings. A part of me had always hovered, wanting to give him a Kleenex for his bloody nose (not that any of us carried Kleenex). I wondered how a wild oilbird or swiftlet would have read our signalled echolocations, the way my brother's feet stomped the pavement in the tunnel, like we used to do to anthills or little kids' sandcastles on our beach, the tiptoe of mine behind.

"Wait here," he said when we reached the bushes bordering the ravine in her backyard as he went up to the back door. Even as a kid, I had always thought of my brother as a lover, the way he whispered into our neighbour's poodle's ear to make her go belly up, the way he'd made coffee for hungover Mom, his whole angry-at-your-boyfriend-for-leaving-you-sad face softened, melting into some downy floof while he stirred in the milk. But now, with Julie, his smile hardened into a fake plastic doll mouth bump; "So you're going to talk to police?" "You really want to talk?" There was no way to hear Julie talking, just the sound of a small scream as he put his hand in the door, a bang as she shut it.

"What the hell did you do man?" I didn't know how, but I had this feeling, like watching one of the videos in Dimez's collection of truly sicko amateur porns, where the camera kept zooming in and out with that fluttering queasiness of a moth trapped inside a window pane. But Alex ignored me, heading straight for the tunnel, hoodie pulled over his head so it was impossible to see where or what he was looking at. Or if he was possibly (though probably not) crying.

"Nothing," he muttered when I caught up to him.

"That's a big nothing."

"Yeah. Exactly. It's a fucking big *nothing*." The way my brother said it, there was a complete lack of guilt, like when we used to play *Jaws* with our teenage cousin Becky at the beach, which basically meant Alex and I chased her around in quasi-aggro circles, doing our best impression of that aquatically carnivorous strain of nightmare, chomping the water near her ankles in a jilted rage. Becky always told Mom, "They're so cute." But under water, we were not cute. My brother was a mess of algae flowing around the back of his head, *Predator*-style. I was insectoid-eyed goggles, reminiscent of the Brundlefly with its prawn head. My brother and I would shark our way through Becky's legs, up to chest height, closing in on a primordial déjà vu; this had happened before, even if it was just the girls bouncing on that lifeguard show as one of the super ripped dudes threw a Frisbee and his eyes watched her with salt-diluted want. My brother would open his jaws and pull the lazy string holding up her bikini with his teeth, then grab her top.

He ate her, tearing skin, frightening girls in movie audiences everywhere so that she screamed.

Or at least she'd tried to scream. He'd pulled her under water. And then she was silent.

* * *

About that silence—sometimes that really was all I heard when Alex and I walked home through the tunnels. No echo, no pubertal and manly low-toned approximation of Dad, just the quiet of Eli breathing before the water engulfed his mouth. It was easy to blame him for it, that silence, his never saying anything. Whenever we had laid him flat on the school asphalt behind the portables, no teacher ever found out. Eli shut his mouth and made us think it was no big deal, that nothing bad had really happened. Bad things that happened had sound to them, explosions of guts and gore and blood, or at least a creepy soundtrack. Silence meant it wasn't so bad.

Silence almost meant that maybe it never even happened, like that secret memory of Eli I had. My brother had just started high school, and I was behind the portables at lunch because, despite Eli giving a presentation on crows for science, which involved him bringing an actual dollhouse to school (he called it a diorama), Michael D'Angelo had decided my brother's absence and me carrying an overdue library copy of *The Genius of Birds* meant that he would take it upon himself to pants me in the hallway outside the boy's bathroom. Once I'd hunkered down in our usual smoking space, away from teacher sight lines and D'Angelo's crew, I'd started crying. Silently, I'd thought. But then I'd heard a chokey kind of snot-filled cry coming from my own mouth, the kind that I would normally have done only behind the closed door of a bathroom at home so that every forensic piece of evidence associated with its existence could be easily disposed of in the toilet bowl.

When Eli had come around the corner, cradling one of his dolls, his eyes were also red from a whole bunch of not-weed. He'd stopped crying when he saw me, his eyes darting around hummingbird-fast. "Are you okay, Gavin?"

I'd held my breath and didn't answer, hoping that Eli hadn't seen my snot-filled T-shirt and would just go away so I could pretend none of this had happened. I had never realized how hard it must have been for him to be so quiet whenever we beat him up.

But Eli had sat down beside me instead, carefully wiping whatever boogers were running from his nose on his sleeve, making sure the doll was pristine. "I saw your book," Eli had sniffed, referring to *The Genius of Birds*. "That's not just for science is it?"

I'd shaken my head, not trusting myself to speak.

"So you're an expert. Good. I have a feather I wanted to give Miss Euphonia here," he'd said, holding up Eyelashes, who he'd been cradling like she was his first-born child.

"Euphonia?" I'd growled. "What kind of fucking name is that?"

"It means sounding pleasant. Do you think you can tell me what this is from?" Eli had said, opening his hand to reveal an iridescent black feather. I'd felt a little resentful that he was trying to quiet me down. I'd realized I had never heard Eli cry before. Despite the fact that I'd definitely felt his bodily fluids, snot or blood or even tears, on my fists when we beat him down, bringing a mucus-y joy to my own eyes, I had never heard the kind of gut-wailing banshee sobs that I'd just been producing.

"Yeah," I'd mumbled, "I guess." Eli had pressed the feather into the palm of my hand, which I hadn't even realized was open. I was almost scared to touch it. "Is that really a Hawaiian crow's feather?" They were almost extinct.

"It's from my dad. Isn't it cool?"

I actually thought it was, even if it decidedly did not belong in what my brother would consider the category of cool. But it's not like I could show him how excited I was. "That's bullshit. How did your dad even get that? That's gotta be fake. And why the hell are you going around playing with dolls anyways?"

After I'd said it, I felt like shit. I'd remembered dimly, how, in grade four, our teacher had made our class make a giant childishly glittery sympathy card for Eli and his family when his little sister drowned on a family beach vacation. After school, when my brother had grabbed the back of his coat and started laughing at how Eli had gotten glitter from the card all over his face, I'd taken a deep breath and laughed along with him, saying, "Sorry for your loss, Girlie. Looks like you're the little girl of the family now."

He'd shrugged, eyes silently boring into the ground. And there it was again, the silence I was used to from Eli, but this time all I could hear was my own shaky breath. Maybe Eli had cried all those times, and I'd never paid attention.

"That's fine. Whatever. You don't have to let me know shit about your dad. I mean, hell, I know my own dad as well as this cute little chicky pie here. Pleased to make your acquaintance, sweetheart," I'd said, giving a little mock bow to Miss Euphonia. For a second Eli and I were both silent, pretty much stunned that those words actually came out of my mouth, and then I was giggling, nervously, because what the fuck? Here I was, just like Eli, talking to a doll.

"Pleased to make yours," Eli had said, making the doll bow back. "You're a real doll." I'd stared at him. Then we'd started laughing hysterically.

I didn't know it was possible for a grin to be loud, but Eli's, stretched widely across his face, looked as ear-splitting as the white bellbird's 125 decibel call. "I have that feather because Mom said my dad is an ornithologist and that's why he doesn't live with us. She said he works for a conservation area. In Maui." Eli had said the name of a place I didn't even know how to begin finding on the battered globe Ms. D had in class, never mind envisioning what it actually looked like. "I've read everything she said he ever wrote about birds, but I want to get better at identifying the feathers so when he comes back we can talk about them." He'd paused, looking at me drooling a bit over the feather. "Do you really think it's a Hawaiian crow's feather?"

"Well, it's not a black-capped chickadee's!" I'd snapped. When he'd looked perplexed, I'd reminded him, "Those are the ones who sound like they're saying 'cheeseburger.'"

"Cheeseburger?"

"Cheeseburger."

"CHEEEEESSSEBUURRGERRRRRRR," he'd roared. By that time we were howling with laughter, the loudest noise I ever heard Eli make. "Do you want to keep it?" he'd said to me.

That question threw me. "Dude, this is a really rare feather. Are you sure?"

"I'll ask my dad for another one." All of a sudden Eli was looking at me with the wide eyes of a sick raptor. "What's the most interesting thing you know about crows?"

I'd taken the feather because I was scared to talk to him further about crows and black-capped chickadees and Maui, wherever the hell that was. I was scared that our weird little vacuum behind the portable wasn't as soundproof as maybe we thought it was. "Look man," I'd said uncomfortably, "let me tell you something about corvids alright? Corvids will abandon other members of their group if they think they're truly sick.

Crows do it all the time. They think predators will come find the whole group because of them." Eli had nodded, reminding me of that video of a duckling who tragically imprints on an electric train and gets run over by a kid's bike in the process. I'd wished he would say what we were both obviously thinking; no matter what, it's not like we could be friends.

But he didn't. And I'd put the feather in my jacket pocket as silently as when my brother had tried to squeeze Eyelashes, and nothing came out, as when I'd stood pretending to hear nothing outside those bushes.

* * *

On Thursday I didn't go to the beach after school. A police car sat outside the front office all day and my brother bragged all through lunch about how they got nothing out of him. Why? "Because nothing actually *bad* happened. I told you already," my brother said sternly, flicking a fry at me. "There's nothing to talk about."

I realized my brother's nothing was creeping me out like the type of horror movie where you don't see shit for the first hour. In math, I kept thinking about the silent spring Ava had mentioned, how there had stopped being bird songs in the nature recordings some guy had been doing for forty years. I got myself a detention in science for eating an entire bag of Doritos under the desk. After school, I listened to Ava talk about how birds were falling from the sky now because of fireworks that made them crash into buildings at night, or smoke and ash from wildfires interfering with migratory patterns. Or mass poisoning. Or climate change. There was no mention of doomed doppelganger dolls, or suicidal crows, or how Ryan and my brother and I once watched a seagull strangle itself on one of our six-pack holders, our only comment a halfway grunted "cool," which I almost choked on when I thought about that look of sad disappointment in Ava's eyes that time I threw a pop can in the garbage.

There was no mention of how maybe we'd released some evil spirit into the world that time we played with the Ouija board at Dimez's house on Halloween and never said goodbye because we got bored and ended up egging Mr. Klaus' house with the grossest egg; when we'd cracked it, it had a fetal chicken. But she was going on and on about how regardless, it was us who was killing these birds. I raised my hand. "So you gotta tell me. How exactly are these birds dropping out of the sky my fault?" And she completely ignored my question.

After the meeting was over, she marched up to me.

"Why are you here? You're not part of any environmental club. Remember?" she said, staring disgustedly at the empty chip bag in my desk.

I shrugged, carefully examining the dirty laces of my shoes. "Look, I'm sorry about how my brother talked to you," I said, "but there was nothing I could do."

"No. You just wouldn't."

"Look, it's not my fault you pissed him off..." I began, but she cut me off.

"Yeah, it is. I wouldn't have to be there if you guys took care of those sunflowers when you go smoke every day..." She took a deep breath. "And yeah. It is your fault. The birds are your fault. It's all our faults, don't you see? Our greenhouse gases account for up to fifty percent of global warming. The land is now thirty percent hotter which is melting the ice caps. You never quit eating Doritos. And," Ava's voice came out in a shaky waver, "you knew what happened to my sister. And you wouldn't say anything."

"What?"

I know my brother would have told her to shut up. But it was me with the nothing voice as she walked away, only quiet coming out of my mouth like wind.

On Friday there were four dead crows, a nutcracker, and what could have been a partridge, but on closer inspection was probably a pigeon. Or a dove. Eyelashes was cradling it dangerously close to the edge of the pit and looking in, while the rest of the dolls watched her from inside, limbs sprawled flexibly over their corvid kills like some kind of deranged ballet dancers. At what point, I thought, did the number of crows become an actual murder, with intentionality behind it? I stood there, looking into the pit, trying not to make eye contact with my brother, as though not seeing would mean not hearing either. Dimez joined me. "So if it's not Girlie who's doing this and who maybe broke into Julie's backyard," Dimez said slowly, "then who is it?"

"How do you know it's not him?" my brother said quickly.

"Guys," I said, still looking into the pit. "He can't swim? Remember? How would he have brought Miss Euphonia back?"

"Did you just give that doll a name? Are you defending Girlie?" my brother snapped. Then he looked at me as though he was a crow trying to recognize the face of someone they'd disliked months ago. "Remember how you begged Mom to take that stupid dance class that looked like gymnastics as a kid? How do we know you're not doing this?"

"Because you all saw me take gym and you know I can't climb."

"That's right, make us think we're crazy. Spoken like a true serial killer," my brother said, trying to make it sound like a joke. "Right Ryan?"

"That is the sound of guilt my friend."

"Yeah, but we all know you're the true sicko, Ryan," I shot

back. "Face it. You're the guy whose idea of a wet dream is *The Texas Chainsaw Massacre*. I mean *this*," I gestured, panicking slightly, to the very dead, partridge-faking dove, "has you writtcn all over it."

Ryan looked a little proud. "Please. If I was killing birds, I would definitely admit it."

"Guys, what if it was just some homeless guy living on the beach?" Dimez said, in the same desperate, peacemaking way Mom used to try to get us to talk to so many of her ex-boyfriends over dinner.

"I don't know man," Ryan said slowly. "I heard police said it was someone at the party, not some random who broke into Julie's backyard. And I'm not saying I know who," he said hurriedly, glancing at my brother. "I wasn't at the party because I had to work. Besides," Ryan said, pointing to the pit, "this whole bird-that-Gavin-thinks-is-a-partridge thing reminds me of the tree decorations in that stupid school play of *The Nutcracker* Gavin wanted to be in so badly in grade six."

"True," my brother said.

"Yeah," I snapped, "remember when you had to be the Rat King?"

Ryan crowed at that. "Bro, I mean Julie does say she smells a rat whenever you're around."

My brother ignored him, focusing on me. "Remember when we went to that farm in elementary school and you said you were in love with a sheep? Maybe you're the sicko."

"Please," I said, and it wasn't like I was thinking before I spoke; the words came out louder and faster than I had known they needed to, "at least I'm not the one who took pictures of some drunk chick after doing who knows what to her. In the bushes."

My brother's eyes narrowed as he picked up Miss Euphonia

like he was studying her, and I remembered Ms. D had said light travels faster than sound; action is faster than words. "Remember when you held Girlie's dolly like it was a real freaking baby? You acted just like him. Maybe this whole thing is your fault," he said, and before I could stop him, he twisted off her right arm, the one that was still covered by the dead blood of the dead dove, then threw the rest of her in the pit before tossing it to the ground.

And I just stood there. "That wasn't me! It wasn't." I could hear my voice rising. "That's like saying it's the fireworks guy's fault because he sold them to whoever set them off and caused those birds to drop dead from the sky in Arkansas. Or it's his neighbour's fault, because he didn't tell him to stop because his house was too close to a bird's nest. Or are you going to blame his kids because they wanted the fireworks in the first place?" I was babbling now; I realized my voice had an edge of truly sick panic to it, but I couldn't stop because what if it was us? What if it was all our faults? All the dead birds, all of what happened. In my brother's hands, was Julie a doll-shaped thing, as much a chick as Miss Euphonia lying slug-eyed on the beach? "I mean it's not my fault that our stupid grandfather worked in a steel mill and now there's blue-green algae all over the beach. And *that* wasn't even his fault. He needed a job. Right?" And did my brother make her body plastic, a used thing, his toxins leaching out while he claimed what was happening was nothing, the same way the steel plant used to blame the direction of the wind for the poison blob they found in the harbour?

"Gav, man, are you okay?" Dimez said, pretending to feel my forehead like I had a fever or something.

"Gavin," my brother said scornfully, "no one knows what the fuck you're talking about. And no one cares." But I heard his voice waver. I stared at him without speaking, then, without really knowing why I was doing it, I slowly went to pick up Miss Euphonia's arm.

That seemed to surprise my brother too. He gaped at me for a second, then picked up our last beer, and left.

"Bro, was he crying?" Dimez asked me curiously, sounding maybe a little worried.

"Shut up," I lied, turning around briefly before following my brother. "His eyes are just red because we smoked."

* * *

I caught up to Alex in the tunnel, puffing from the run but still clutching the broken doll arm tightly. "Why'd you do that?" I wanted to say, "You broke her." Just like the kingfisher eggs we'd skipped like stones across the beach. Just like Eli.

"Why'd I do what? Damage your precious dolly?"

"I meant Julie."

"Kid, you wouldn't understand. You're too young." I knew this should have made me feel like when he and Ryan caught me making that sandcastle with the Andersons last summer, separated infinitely by the moat of maturity as they'd hollered and laughed and stomped on our easily squashable turrets before going to smoke without me. But I knew this was a lie. Instead I felt like how I imagined the villagers who'd finally found the chainsaw-sounding lyrebird felt, or the final girl who stabs the killer in a slasher movie; the thing you were so scared to hear the sound of has lost all its power and all that's left is you, staring at something on the ground that now seems so much smaller.

"I know what happened," I said.

"Gav," my brother switched to a pleading whine, "bro, you can't tell anyone. You won't. Right? I mean, there's nothing you can do now. It's not going to undo it."

The way his voice sounded, it shocked me. My brother wasn't making sense. "Just admit you did it," I swallowed nervously.

Instead of a response, my brother chugged the rest of his roadie, gave me the finger, and crushed the can under his foot.

"For fuck's sake," I exploded, "at least pick up your fucking garbage!"

"You pick it up! If everything I'm doing is so bad, why didn't you try to stop me? Huh? Why'd you look at her pic too? You know, if you hadn't been watching like some sick perv, I would have just gone back to the party." He hesitated. "I didn't even really want to. I just thought I should."

"I wasn't watching," I said dumbfounded. "Dimez and I were just smoking." I couldn't believe my brother, who had always seemed so much bigger, had a voice so small it didn't even echo through the tunnel.

"Well it wasn't the fucking wind! I heard you," he said, slightly hurt, "when you rustled the bushes. You said I probably couldn't even do anything because I was too drunk. Well, I did," he said sadly, "and you were there. And you didn't say shit to stop me."

And you didn't say shit. And you didn't. It echoed, long after my brother turned away from me and walked to the end of the tunnel and after his voice, definitely not Dad's, began to fade. Sometimes I worry I'm still standing there, unable to move, listening to the reflection of his voice hitting the walls of the tunnel and ricocheting into me, over and over and over again, like the north wind grounding birds that should be in migration.

* * *

We'd all said it was the wind. The last day I ever saw Eli, the day after my brother had destroyed sandcastles on the beach, that's what we told people. The wind was why his doll ended up in the water. The wind was why he'd tried to swim out, why what had seemed like the lights of a billion fire trucks and ambulances ended up rescuing him from the incredibly toxic harbour water. That afternoon, Eli had followed us to the beach after school like, as Alex described it, "some sick puppy whose balls you cut off and it still licks your face." Actually, Eli had followed me.

"Hi," Eli had said, standing awkwardly as we sat on the log. "I wanted to show you something," he'd begun, holding out Eyelashes, the doll he'd called Miss Euphonia.

When Alex had moved aside to let me do the honours of the final kick to the stomach, he'd asked Eli, after Eli's face had already crash-landed on the ground, oozing in the cheap horror-movie glow of the fluorescent outdoor bathroom lights, if he knew why we were doing this to him. I don't even think we knew. But of course, Eli had answered. "Certainly. You're displaying typical corvid behaviour. You brother understands."

And when Alex had asked whether that was some kind of way of calling us idiots, I'd told him Eli was talking about crows. "Why do you even know that?" Alex had said, and I couldn't tell whether he was talking to Eli or me. This had enraged and frightened me at the same time, the idea that Eli and I shared anything but the air that we were breathing at the moment, as though, in my brother's blind rage, we were interchangeable.

"Shut up. Don't ever say I understand you, Girlie. No one understands you," I'd roared. "Shut up, shut up, shut up!" It was a flaccid, scrawny fake of a roar that broke the silence the same as Eli's nose when it hit the ground, echoed in that strange, slightly misshapen way parrots have of saying something the way they think a human would. I'd stood there, watching myself kick him over and over again, punctuating my final words by taking that stupid crow feather and snapping it in half, as though by cracking the vane, my memory could become smaller, a walnut, sealed, forgetting I had ever known what it was.

Then I'd seen Miss Euphonia. She had fallen out of Eli's grip when we'd pushed him to the ground. And all my rage had smothered my fear. "Did you use duck feathers for this?"

Eli had nodded, staring at me, all innocently wildlife-eyed from the ground while my brother watched me like a hawk.

"Well that's good I guess." I'd picked up Miss Euphonia, cradling her for a second. And I'd wondered if this was how an eagle felt, right before they push a fledgling out of the nest. "Because she's about to go for a swim."

I remember Eli said something, or at least his mouth moved in some approximation of "Don't. Please. Stop," but his voice wasn't full of the moaning vowels I'd expected; instead it was like one of these pre-recorded messages on the phone Mom used to get us to call when she had to talk to those credit card companies and you're just pushing buttons, not listening really. After I'd hucked his doll into the water, he screamed, the most soundless scream I've ever heard, like when you're taking a shit at school and you don't want anyone in the next stall to know. "Please! I can't swim!"

Eli wasn't lying when he said he really couldn't swim. We'd watched as Miss Euphonia bobbed along the surface of the water, as the blue-green algae circled in the tiny little whirlpools he was making with his hands. Eli took great big gulps of poo-water which filled his mouth, stripping any decibel level from his shouts for help.

I felt like screaming right along with him. But Miss Euphonia beat me to it. She let out a terrified wail at ear-shocking, almost screaming piha levels, and I started to run toward the shoreline but stopped when I realized I was the only one. I looked at the guys, but no one had moved. And I wanted to shout, "You fucking idiots, what if he drowns? What if he dies? Then it's our fault. It's all my fault," but I felt like in *A Nightmare on Elm Street*, when Freddy gets you in the loneliest of your dreams, and no one can hear you because there isn't any way to share the fear inside you.

Even now I don't know if I tried to call for help.

That night, something funny changed for me when it came to understanding the weight of keeping a silence. My brother said it was time to go and I'd nodded. It had felt safer than saying anything out loud. On the walk home, I'd watched birds flit soundlessly above the steady cloud of shit coming from the steel factory. By nodding, I somehow knew I'd entered that unspoken agreement with my brother and the rest of the guys, that we would never talk about this. To anyone. We would take the memory of that day and play it without sound in our minds, like an old Bela Lugosi silent film, maintaining our non-speaking agreement when Mom asked us where we'd been while we ate a cold slice of pizza for breakfast, or when our teachers glanced at us suspiciously once it was all over the news that Eli had to be rescued from the harbour, or even when Michael D'Angelo claimed he knew Eli "real well" so he could get on TV. We didn't say shit. That silence wrapped around me like the web of an orb-weaver spider catching a tiny thrush, and until tonight, I hadn't been able to connect it with the threads of my own memory.

But I was the one who threw Eli's doll in the water. Not Dimez or Ryan, or my brother. Not the sound of some stupid kids trading lunches behind the portable afterwards, when I thought I heard him whispering, "cheeseburger." Not the north wind, but the way my own voice sounded in the tunnel, little and small and scared.

* * *

And I was the one who would break the silence and go tell Julie
I would tell whoever she wanted what I had heard happen. I
told Ava the same thing. An idea had come to me Wednesday
night, a kind of curse-breaking atonement, but I needed Ava's
help to get down into the pit and lift out the dolls. "Please,"
I'd begged her, for once actually just attending environmental
club instead of trying to get a detention by waving around the
Bunsen burner, "the last thing we need is more plastic on the
shoreline, right?"

She'd sighed. "I do know an organization that recycles plastic toy parts."

I'd considered asking Dimez or Ryan to come help me and
unleash us from whatever silencing pact we'd made that day
at the beach that had turned us into the dolls, forever stuck
echoing the same juvenile cruelties. But Ryan said he had to
work and didn't have time for "kids' stuff," and when I texted
Dimez he didn't respond, whether it was because he was asleep
or didn't want to fight my brother, or didn't care, I don't know.
And maybe it was better they didn't come. Like in every horror
movie, I knew I was going to have to split up with the guys
eventually, go my separate way in order to defeat whatever it
was that possessed us that time on the beach with Eli, that night
with Julie, every time we'd dropped a Doritos bag and choked
a seagull.

We went to the beach at night, after Ava brought me to talk
to Julie, long after my brother had gone to smoke weed with
Dimez, and Ryan had gone to work. Ava, who went camping
every second weekend with the outdoor ed. club, brought the
rope and explained climbing knots, lowering me down about six
feet into the grave. Once I was in the pit, I took a deep breath in.
"Alright bro, here we go," I said, gritting my teeth and ripping

the arms off Baldy, using his little sword to cut the string that activated his voice before tossing it into the bag. I tore into the surprisingly soft stuffing stomach of the happy face doll so that his smiley button formed a sideways U or N, like at first he'd started to say no, but the word never really came out. Roosters are notorious for cawing for their territory, so for the rooster doll, I dismantled the scratched old-school record with his rooster's comb first, smashing it on a rock. "This isn't yours," I told him, gesturing to the pieces on the beach, to the beach itself, and then to Miss Euphonia, sort of half-expecting her to say something.

Actually, I don't know what I expected. Maybe something better than what I'd just said, some expert articulation from what turned out to be a cassette with its tape unwound. My voice rebounded through her cheap plastic arm like a makeshift loudspeaker. But she didn't say anything. And I realized maybe she couldn't. Maybe the blue-green goop had gummed up her tape, dampening her voice. "C'mon," I muttered, "c'mon, speak. Please." I realized I was begging. But no amount of sugar-coated cajoling was getting her to use her vocal cords. I was suddenly sad. It reminded me of how Ava had said that birds in Australian cities couldn't sing their alarm calls loud enough over the sounds of cars and buses and so many men talking, and so many of them had ended up dead.

"Gavin," Ava called down, "are you ready?"

"I don't know," I said. "Give me a minute."

I saved him for last, that doll-shaped me. I unscrewed Echo's legs, twisted off his hands. I took a black Sharpie and painted over his mouth in a large black O his own silent scream. After I popped off his head (like Mom would say, he wasn't using it anyways) I reached into his microchip insides and took them out. I did it, I thought. It was me that killed the dolls.

When I reached the surface with my backpack, I gave Miss

Euphonia to Ava. "I think this one we could fix up, you know. Give her to some kid maybe," I said awkwardly. "Only problem is right now is she doesn't talk."

"Let me try," Ava said, opening up the panel on Miss Euphonia's chest directly at heart level. Inside was a tape recorder, and the recording head had a bunch of that blue-green junk in it. Ava carefully wiped it out with her finger, the way they show wildlife rescuers cleaning seabirds, then wound the tape tighter before she replaced her chest. "Hello," she said. "Talk to me."

"Talk," Miss Euphonia answered back.

"See?" Ava said. "She's fine now."

"Really? She's talking?"

"She can," Ava grinned at me, "and she will. You know what you heard."

"You know what you heard," Miss Euphonia repeated, echoing through the tunnel, almost as though her voice came before mine. And it was me repeating her voice, even as I slipped a note to Ava to give her sister, even as I told my brother I had to speak against him, even when I nervously talked to the police and I told them yes, I was sure. I knew what I heard. It was me repeating her voice, the one saying, "I can." The one saying, "I will."

SO WHAT IF IT'S SUPPOSED TO RAIN

THERE IS SOMETHING WRONG with Yvie's mother and The Mother knows. The Mother always knows. The Mother knows it is Javier's mother, not Yvie's mother, who finds Yvie setting up camp Outside. It is Javier's mother, not Yvie's mother, Lil, who brings Yvie home with a respirator dangling from Lil's old backpack, wearing Lil's old camping boots, Lil's old UV-protective long-sleeve sun shirt like some kind of junk bug carrying the dead husk of a sucked-dry aphid on its back. It was Javier's mother who had to remind Lil that no one would expect her to go Outside eight months pregnant to find her daughter. Edwin's Mother, who used to be a pediatrician before she died and became a part of The Mother, had informed Javier's mother that air pollution could cause stillbirth. Or congenital heart failure. Or hernias. But still, Lil should have known Yvie, who used to be so terrified of mosquitoes in the night-time great Outdoors that she refused to go anywhere without wearing a beekeeping hat, was going Outside to camp in the bush tonight. Even if Yvie wasn't talking much to her mother these days anyways, what was Yvie's mother doing with her feet up on the couch, asleep, not knowing her teenage daughter was Outside, at risk of air poisoning or malaria or dengue fever or the rains to sweep her away like she had never existed? If Javier's mother hadn't seen Yvie leaving, there is no way of knowing what could have happened.

But that is no excuse; Lil should have known. A Mother should always know. *ERROR_GEN_FAILURE* flashes reprovingly across The Mother's face, accompanied by her signature, softly judgmental *ding*.

"Where were you?" Lil says to her daughter, who is dripping mud and disaster on the marble entranceway floor. Even though The Mother is on the couch in the living room across from the front hallway, Lil can still feel the accusing stare on her smoothly featureless face, the Error code flashing terrifyingly across what would have been her mouth. (Vaguely, Lil remembers how the nurse technician explained why The Mother remained devoid of human features; not to mimic some creepy arthropod-like alienness, but because her Silicon Valley creative team couldn't agree on whose deceased mother's nose she should have.) The Mother's hands end in perfectly manicured acrylic talons holding balance scales; the pan on the right is for Accomplished Duties, the pan on the left, which currently dips dangerously toward the ground, is for Errors.

"Out."

"Outside?" Lil can hear her voice rising to the pitch of the long-extinct cicada's song. Just like Ansley's Mother's and Barclay's Mother's and William's Mother's voices would.

Yvie shrugs. *ERROR_SHARING_PAUSED*.

Lil knows that Javier's mother (whose actual name Lil has forgotten; it starts with an L, she's almost sure of it. Leda? Lina? Javier's mother called her Lisa when they met. From what Lil's seen at the monthly Mother Calibration Meetings, most of the mothers only know each other by the names of their offspring) cannot see the Error messages on The Mother's screen from where she's standing in the hallway, but is already speculating about what each *ding* could mean. After all, The Mother in Lil's living room is the same as The Mother in Javier's mother's old-fashioned parlour (not living room). She is the same as The Mother in the house next door, the same as The Mother in every living room or kitchen in every house under the domed and purified airspace of The Nest. She is the same Mother who is composed of the whole-brain emulations of Monty's Mother and Roger's Mother and Tony's Mother and all the other dead Mothers of all those top CEOs, CFOs, politicians, judges, lawyers, doctors. The Mother is all of them combined. She is Edward's Mother and Harry's Mother and Charles' Mother and all the other Mothers with a capital M behind the men who'd kept the country running through the Great Heat Wave, the beginning of the Water Wars, the men who'd developed artificial air purifiers and temperature control and bought stock in respirators. She is the Mothers of the men who built The Nest as part of the Great Preservation, pumping in pure oxygen under its dome like casinos used to do in Vegas. The Mother is made of the voices of all these Mothers, and by uploading The Mother, all the mothers in The Nest can hear the wisdom of these Mothers inside their own heads. Because of The Mother, they can repeat this wisdom out of their own mouths. And all the mothers in The Nest agree, The Mother knows best.

Javier's mother gives a little gasp. "I hope you weren't intending to spend the night Outside," she says to Yvie, who rolls her eyes. "The tunnels aren't safe to travel in, not when there might be rains." She lowers her voice, talking now to Lil. "And judging by those beekeeping hats with veils I saw at their campsite, there might even have been Anties."

* * *

Anti-Emulation Activists, opposed to any kind of emulation—including the captivity of any remaining insects so that their "consciousness" could be emulated by drones for the purposes of pollination or, in the case of the dung beetle, animal husbandry—were the kind of people who lived on The Outside. They set up camps in swamps, still waters, the last wild meadows, anywhere there was a rumour of finding living mosquitoes or ladybugs or crickets or even, among those the most wild-eyed with hope as thick as the grey air they breathed, wild honeybees, ready to defend the last of the last from Trappers. Lil's stomach dive-bombs a little as she remembers how she'd made the mistake of telling her then ten-year-old daughter she wanted to talk to her about the birds and the bees. Yvie had sort of nodded at the right parts, looking glazed, and Lil had that same desperate feeling she'd had with her camera at a still unsunk Pismo Beach in what used to be California, anxiously scanning the sky for what should have been a migration of orange and black monarch wings, Yvie impatiently asking when they'd see any butterflies. "Do you have any questions?" Lil had fumbled, badly, at the end.

"No." Yvie had resented the bee metaphor; Lil was sure of it. At every stage—sweet powder snuggles and defiant bedtimes and childhood fairy princesses (which, according to Lil's daughter, were the only things other than butterflies, and maybe ladybugs, that deserved to have wings)—Yvie had battled Lil's love of what Yvie called her "uglies."

"Okay, well if you think of any—"

"I won't," her daughter had said bluntly. "Plus it's not like I have to care about bees. Aren't they mostly extinct?"

* * *

"Anties?" Lil tries to sound horrified at the thought of anyone deliberately trying to live on the Outside. When Yvie was eight,

Lil had been a wildlife photographer and activist, and they'd spent a summer living out of a van. Yvie, of course, had hated it. Lil had said, at the time, it was so Yvie could experience Nature before it was too late, but really, Lil knew that if she didn't do something that mattered now, when would she ever do it; would anyone remember her as anything other than a mother?

Javier's mother nods solemnly. "I have to tell you, I was surprised to find your daughter out there." Lil tries not to roll her eyes like Yvie. Javier's mother is never surprised; she was in a sorority in college, back when it was still possible to go away to college. Lil is almost sure of it. If you wanted to know which mothers drank copious amounts of white vino despite the grape shortage and two small children, which mothers were sleeping with men other than their rich husbands, or just even sleeping through the night (night doulas, Javier's mother loudly believed, were for the weak), you talked to Javier's mother. But more than that, Javier's mother was the best at expecting the worst. At the monthly Mother Calibration Meetings, Javier's mother led them all in discussing vaguely apocalyptic scenarios. A flash flood, the water table rises. A toddler can drown in less than five centimetres if left unattended. The Mothers, sitting behind each of their mothers in a circle, flashed in unison, *ERROR_DS_DRA_MISS-ING_PARENT*. Someone's daughter moves Outside; her skin is greying at twenty-five. *ERROR_BAD_ENVIRONMENT*. A mosquito bite on a child. West Nile. Malaria. *ERROR_VIRUS_INFECTED*. A lack of EpiPens carried by a mother and some brightly child-coloured flowers in a field with newly liberated farm bees, a true bouquet of horrors. *ERROR_NOT_READY*. In the background, the sepia-coloured posed family portraits (no new-fashioned, 3D, brightly coloured moving LifeLites for her) hang perfectly in agreement. A Mother needed to be prepared.

Lil is surprised though; Yvie had always been a girl's girl,

folding her sleeping bag up neatly in the back of the van, dec-
orating the mosquito netting over the mattress with bits of red
and yellow and pink metallic gift wrap ribbons so that it resembled the curtains of what Yvie called a princess bed, one of those
with drapes and a canopy made of silk, back when there were
still silk worms. Lil had dreamed their nights would be spent
chasing lone fireflies, trying to record the last cricket songs,
but Yvie had always refused to leave the van at night. "But there
might be mouse-ketos. And don't those mouse-keto things
carry diseases? Do you want me to risk my life for a little bug?"
Yvie would say, dramatically flopping back on the mattress in
the back of the van.

"It's mosquitoes. And you're wearing netting for that. You
know, all these bugs are going to be gone one day soon. Don't
you want the chance to see them?" Lil would ask hopefully.
With her daughter, Lil always felt herself becoming smaller, like
she'd used the wrong lens on an object that was too far away.

"And if the mouse-ketos bite me I could be gone one day
real soon. Don't you care about me?" Of course Lil wanted to
think Yvie knew she did. And of course Lil did. Even if there was
that time photographing the last of the spiderlings, a day that
was so hot that Lil took off her own respirator to get a better
view because the goggles were fogging up. Even though she
knew her eight-year-old daughter was watching. It was nothing, but it happened because Yvie was so quiet for once and
Lil had been so grateful for that quiet, for the chance to not
discuss how Yvie needed to finish her toast and stop refusing to
put on her respirator that, yes, Lil knew she didn't like wearing
because it was like breathing into a box, but she had to so they
could see the momma spider. Even if Yvie didn't want to go see
the momma spider, they were going to see the momma spider,
and Lil was sick of answering questions; if the momma spider

could die, did that mean Lil was going to die? Was Yvie going to die? And when she's dead what would happen; would she be like a popsicle and melt into the ground? An instant could be everything. Even if almost no time passed between when Lil took her respirator off and Yvie saw, between when Yvie must have taken off her own respirator to catch the Luna moth she thought was a butterfly, and when Lil saw Yvie trip, her respirator tumbling to the ground. Even if almost no time passed between Yvie inhaling the unfiltered dawn and Lil running to put her daughter's respirator back on.

"Why were you Outside?"

"It was a dare."

"Spending the night Outside, all by yourself, was a dare?" Lil tries to sound outraged, like Bradford's Mother and Carleton's Mother, but she can still feel the excitement of Outside herself. She can remember how she'd definitely, and okay, more than once, looked at the air quality rating and decided that it was still okay, especially if she bumped up the oxygen, especially if they had a back-up respirator, and maybe even if they didn't, maybe it was still worth the risk to her and Yvie back in their van days for the chance to preserve the already elusively rare dinosaur ant in LifeLite. It is as if Yvie has metamorphosized into a stranger that is excitingly familiar to her mother. One that wears hiking boots. One that can set up a tent. Lil can picture it now: mother-daughter picnic lunches of freshly greenhouse-grown fruit to attract any remaining pollinators, the two of them finally connecting over wearing matching respirators. She almost feels a swell of tender pride at Yvie's muddy footprints on the marble.

"I wasn't by myself. Theo was there too."

"Theo?" Lil pauses. Her heart drops like an adult Luna moth, who, lacking mouth parts, lives only a week in order to reproduce. "Who's Theo?"

"A guy I know who knows how to camp." Javier's mother looks appropriately horrified. Lil hopes she doesn't notice Lil's own mouth is open in shock.

A guy? Her daughter was doing this for a guy? Her daughter, whom she'd spent years trying to coax outside with the promises of finding real honey for her fake tea parties if Yvie would just come with her mother and look for the last wild honeybees? Her daughter, whom she'd once told moths turned into fairies during the day, and then had to create a whole homemade book of fairy names and backstories in order to photograph their last nighttime appearances? And now, some guy had suddenly made her love the nighttime great Outdoors when Lil couldn't even get her to look at a picture of a Luna moth?

Somehow, Lil feels more expendable than she ever has. Like the lost legs of a Matabele ant who barely notices their absence, can run almost as fast when they are gone.

"You went camping Outside with a strange guy?" And how dangerous was that? The Mother thinks it's very dangerous. The Mother knows because she is made of Wallace's Mother, who used to be a Girl Guide Troop Leader, and knows the dangers of campfires, especially in a drought; she is made of Justin's Mother who, as a sorority sister, knows it is easy to black out in the darkness with a strange boy. But who was Lil, Ms. Sleep-In-A-Van-For-Her-Art, to tell Yvie it was dangerous? The Mother wants Lil to know that Elton's Mother, who was a child psychologist, thinks Yvie is simply imitating her mother's bad habits, like that experiment with the clown doll and the hammer where the child beats up the doll only after they see the adult do it; Javier's mother is staring at Lil like she should definitely be doing more. "Did you use protection?"

"Mom!"

"I meant a respirator." The Mother has let Lil know that Manning's Mother, who was a pulmonologist, and Nyle's

Mother, who was a dermatologist, are both worried Yvie is looking a little grey already; Chad's Mother, who sold used sporting goods before marrying rich, is sure Yvie has no idea how to put on a respirator properly and she could have gotten air poisoning. She could have died. Could still die. Wasn't there secondary air poisoning, just like secondary drowning? This The Mother confirms that Parker's Mother knows: she used to scuba dive back when there were still coral reefs. "Did you use the respirator?"

"Since when do you care about me going Outside? Or are you just making a big deal of this because of her?" Javier's mother looks vaguely pleased, but Lil knows Yvie isn't talking about her. Yvie is talking about The Mother, whom she has started to call "the relic." As though she is old, instead of the newest state-of-the-art technology. As though she is outdated, instead of offering timeless wisdom. As though she has nothing left to offer, not in this world on fire.

Still, Javier's mother does not need to know this. "You need to go." Lil says, pointing upstairs, hoping she sounds as firm as Reginald's Mother, the former judge.

"Okay," Yvie says, sitting down on the stairs to pull her boots back on again.

"I meant to your room! You're grounded!" Lil shouts. Immediately she regrets it. As Yvie stomps up the stairs, she feels like an unnaturally lonely ant in a lab experiment, just waiting for the worst to happen. Even if Shipley's Mother and Mark's Mother say it's the right thing to do, this is stupid. Besides, The Nest has no real soil, only AstroTurf.

"I've got to go as well," Javier's mother says, sounding satisfied at least, "but if I were you, I would check those boots. Make sure she hasn't dragged anything in. You wouldn't want to end up with an infestation." She lets herself out.

At the last Calibration Meeting, Arvinder's mother, whose

name Lil definitely can't remember, had seemed nervous, even more than the other mothers discussing the doomsday rains scenario as their Mothers finished the Calibrations. Javier's mother told them what had happened three years ago; the rains had washed up through the tunnels to the Outside, backed up through basements. *ERROR_NOT_READY*. It should never happen again. The Mother had insisted on sump pumps, backflow valves, watertight shields sealing off the tunnel entrances. Emergency respirators at every tunnel entrance. Iodine pills in every bathroom in case the nuclear reactor powering The Nest's air purification system was damaged by a future deluge. Javier's mother had just asked Arvinder's whether she had attached hanging oxygen masks to her children's overhead bed compartments like they used to do on those old airplanes when the flashing Error began behind her head. *ERROR_DEBUG_ ATTACH_FAILED. ERROR_DEBUG_ATTACH_FAILED.* Something had squiggled on top of Arvinder's Mother Unit's shoulder, into a gap that should definitely not be there between the shoulder and arm. Her wires were exposed, writhing like spaghetti victimized by poltergeists. Fire ants! There was no mistaking their dully hellish-coloured bodies, antennae that ended in tiny shillelagh. Of course it would be fire ants. Fire ants and mosquitoes were the only insects still left in abundance. Fire ants loved mistakes. Natural disasters. Hurricanes. Human landscaping. Anything that makes the world more of an inferno. Hot enough that spiderlings will hatch in the balmy January temperatures of what used to be Buffalo. Hot enough that a girl would take off her fogged-up respirator goggles.

Lil hadn't understood when Javier's mother asked Arvinder's whether or not her son was enjoying the ant farm she'd seen delivered to their house last week.

Dutifully, Lil checks Yvie's boots, slightly disappointed that the only life form she seems to have dragged in is a scorched blade of grass. After, she goes upstairs, hovers at the half-open door to Yvie's room. "Who is Theo?"

"I told you," her daughter says, not looking up from where she's sprawled on her bed. "He's a guy I know."

"Just a guy?"

Yvie rolls her eyes again. "It's no big deal."

"Of course it is!" The Mother knows it is. Or at least it could have been. Every Mother knows there are a lifetime of terrifying coulds for every child, a whole world of under-the-bed arachnids to protect them from.

"Whatever," Yvie says, getting off the bed. "I need a tea. That okay? If I leave my room?" She doesn't wait for an answer before she heads for the kitchen. So Yvie is a tea drinker now. That was news to Lil. She'd practically had to beg Yvie not to throw out her stash of Earl Grey after Yvie had found out that tea bugs sometimes used to poop in the leaves.

"Yeah. That's fine," Lil calls after her, but it feels too late. Even if almost no time has passed, there was that small time between fine and not fine. It was the time it took to snap that final glorious picture of the spiderlings dispersing before the rain set in, their fine silk lines ballooning out in stunning eerie pearls against the breeze. It was the time it took for one more LifeLite, while Yvie's respirator was left on the ground. No time at all. Just enough for a raindrop to cut the thread.

* * *

This time, with this baby, Lil was going to be different. She has promised herself. She has promised Luc's father. She will wear aprons with strings and maybe learn to cook something other than instant ramen. She will try to give a shit about cliché macramé while the world is burning and there is no one to preserve the image of the ghost moth. She might even learn to sew, or at least fix holes in socks (with Yvie, she'd just told her they were ladybug spots coming in. Other than butterflies, ladybugs were the only arthropods Yvie could stand, mostly because of their name). "Only the best for our son," Luc's father had said with a wink. Luc's father was the best; or at least he was better than Yvie's father, a man Lil barely remembered from when she was twenty except when she looked at the way Yvie flared her nose when she was mad. Yvie's father had seduced Lil with talk of seeing a real viceroy butterfly chrysalis, but it had turned out to be fossilized bird poop. The relationship was more of the same and he'd left after a year, although Lil thought this was more his fault than hers. After all, Lil had always thought she would be the best at what she did. At least she'd told Luc's father she was the best when they met over her margaritas while she bartended some rich man's event. At least it was true when it came to her photography.

But this time, as a Mother, Lil was going to be the best of the best. She would hatch plans for baby photos instead of capturing the hatching of Joro spiders. She would learn to love board books, even if the cardboard they were printed on used to be the homes of thousands of leafcutter ants. She would be safe; the only arachnid she would put her baby in contact with would be the itsy bitsy spider. This time, she was going to be a Mother.

"Don't worry." The nurse technician had smiled her wrinkle-free smile during The Mother's installation. Lil had tried to focus on her, not the stack of unpacked boxes in the corner of the basement from when she and Yvie had moved to live with Luc's father in The Nest a month after Lil found out she was pregnant, the ones full of Yvie's wings and night lights and butterfly pyjamas recollected like the ever-vanishing bug smears on the van windshield, the ones full of newborn onesies and diapers Luc's father had started collecting for her as soon as they'd found out about Luc. Luc's father had been so excited; he'd insisted on naming the baby after the twenty-week ultrasound. He had to be a Luc, after his own father, after the light he was bringing into both of their lives. "Being a Mother should come naturally. And you'll have a built-in community." The nurse technician reminded Lil of an earthworm, grossly smooth. "You'll never have to do it alone, not with the Founders' Mothers actually becoming a part of your thought process. She's better than a parenting guide. Better than any advice your own mother could give you." After all, behind every great was a great Mother.

On the table, Lil had watched the scales dangle from a hunched-over pile of steel and wires. The nurse technician tapped them and they swung like a watch in an online hypnotism video. The cables which attached them to the beam looked like rope, Lil had realized, the kind Luc's father would have used on a child's tire swing in the yard. Except now there were no more bees left to pollinate the hemp plants.

"As Mothers, we all need guidance," the nurse technician had continued, "and that's what your Mother Unit is for. She's here to let you know how you're doing. Any time you do something that one of the Founder's Mothers wouldn't necessarily agree with, The Mother will let you know. An Error message will also appear on your Mother Unit's face and the Errors scale will tip. The sensors that link you and your Mother Unit will ensure you feel the weight as though you were carrying it yourself."

"What happens if I make too many Errors?"

"Well, it won't be comfortable. But you'll get used to it. Motherhood is full of so many changes, after all." Lil remembered being told motherhood would change her. With Yvie, she had waited for it, that startling transformation, the epiphany when she would melt into the toothless smile of her three-month-old gripping a rattle with less communicative capability than an army ant, her metamorphosis into a being who found a game of build-the-tower-knock-it-down more absorbing than tracking the migration route of the last monarchs. She'd waited for that moment when she would become like the common American field ant, gracefully capable of bearing the incessant weight of Yvie's bedtimes; "I need a glass of water," "I need another hug," "I need the light off," "I need the light on," "I need the door open," "I need the door closed," "Mommy if there's still an alphabet why aren't there bees anymore?" "Mommy why would the bees eat their own babies?" "Mommy, if I was sick like the baby bees, would you eat me?" The needs always seemed five thousand times heavier than Lil was sure her own neck was designed to bear. Lil had once photographed the strepsiptera, a legless, eyeless bag of eggs that let her offspring devour her from the inside out when they hatched. She'd found her far more alien than the all-but-extinct treehopper, who abandoned her larvae as soon as they hatched into the capable care of sap-sucking ants. "But don't worry too much about the bugs. You probably won't see too many of them. As a Mother, you'll know what's right."

"What bugs?" Lil had asked, slightly dazed.

"The Errors. We're talking about The Errors. Bugs is old-fashioned as a term, I know. But did you know, when one of the first computers malfunctioned, way back when, it was because of a moth in the relay?"

Lil had mumbled something about moths probably not being a problem anymore.

"Yes, but you do want to keep a close eye on the wires. I had a client a few years ago whose Mother was completely unravelled by these little ants. They just chewed her up and spit her out. When we found her, it was two in the afternoon and her baby was screaming and she was immobile on the couch with an empty bottle of wine."

In her morphine haze, Lil had dreamed of the pupae of the invasive garden ant, *Lasius neglectus*, which became sick with fungus and died as the uninfected sprayed formic acid into holes bitten through its cocoon for the good of the colony. Lil had dreamed of an army of fire ants, tracked in on her own boots, satanically chewing right through the cables of the Mother.

* * *

The Mother thinks Lil should demand to know who this Theo is; what is his GPA? What are his future career plans? Will he provide a perfectly air-filtered Nest home for her grandbabies? At the next Mother Calibration Meeting, when Javier's mother mentions the threat of Anties luring their offspring Outside to camp, just like they did with Yvie, one mother wants to know if Lil's even met Theo yet. In person. And is his skin ashy grey or grey-grey? Another wants to know if Theo has ever portaged. Backpacked? Does he own an off-road vehicle? If not, does his vehicle have a sticker in the back saying "My other car is a Jeep"? The mothers who are gathered at this meeting are all worried for Yvie, but especially for Lil. That is to say, they are worried for themselves, and Lil is one of them now. After all, every mother living in The Nest aspired to raise a Great Child, to have a chance at being a Mother with a capital M after she died, her consciousness living on in perpetuity as a part of the great conglomeration that was The Mother.

"I assume you're aware of Antie recruitment tactics," Javier's mother says quite seriously. Does Yvie display an unusual love of nature? A request for strange or exotic pets, such as beetles or tarantulas? Lil hasn't checked. Lil didn't know. As a mother, Lil doesn't even know what she does know anymore.

Lil hasn't felt this inadequate since Yvie was an infant. Staring into the other mothers' horrified faces, she remembers when Yvie was a newborn, that feeling of somehow missing something innately important. She didn't always wake up when Yvie cried at 4 a.m. because she hadn't heard her. She'd taken her daughter into the shower with her even though, more than once, she'd slipped and almost fallen on absolutely foreseeably wet tiles. She'd inexcusably bought a used crib. Does Yvie display a disregard or underappreciation for the lifestyle her parents have given her? A disregard for the values with which she was raised? Lil has no idea. Lil is a terrible mother; she could never be a Mother.

"Please," another mother in the blur of mothers, maybe Devon's, says, "you've just described every teenager I've ever known. My eighteen-year-old kid was out on Friday too. And because I trust him, I didn't even think to ask where he was going."

Javier's mother leads the mothers in looking aghast when the woman's Mother Unit dings *ERROR_NO_DATA*. Shockingly, Devon's mother seems not to care.

After the Calibrations, while everyone is helping themselves to mini sandwiches, Devon's mother touches Lil's arm lightly. "Is everything okay?"

Lil can't look at her. "I just need to get some air."

"Whatever you do, don't stress yourself too much. It's not good for the baby," Javier's mother calls out after her as Lil pretends not to fumble for a cigarette. With every inhalation on the back porch, The Mother *dings* in her ear. *ERROR_CONTINUE. ERROR_CONTINUE. ERROR_CONTINUE.*

* * *

Keep going. This is what a Mother does. Lil doesn't really know how to (at least not without all those verboten coffee and cigarettes), but the nurse technician told Lil that The Mother was designed for low energy situations. She was made to run on any energy she could find, on hydro even when the dams are broken by the floods, on solar power in an increasingly cloud-covered world. On back-up reserves in times of no power; thunder storms, electrical storms, monsoons. Once, on Yvie's first day at her new high school in The Nest, Lil brought The Mother along in the car. Lil had used the adapter to plug her into the cigarette lighter. She did not have the power to say: "I love you," "Be careful," "Please don't do what I did but please have the fun I did," "Please be the kid I raised," or "What have I done with my life?" But she managed a smile. A wave. Nothing too big or embarrassing in front of Yvie's new friends. Was it in that moment she'd lost her daughter? When Yvie didn't turn around or wave goodbye, The Mother Lil had crumpled over, just for a moment. But a Mother could not afford to be down, not for long. The Mother will always know what to do, and be able to do it, even when Lil can't. The Mother will always try reconnecting.

"Do you remember," The Mother tries from the doorway to Yvie's bedroom at night as Yvie looks up LifeLites of what used to be the Amazon, now TreeCorp, the tree-top encampments in the no-go zone surrounding the company fence, "when you were just a little girl and you loved your butterfly pyjamas until you saw pictures of them from up close and you said their faces looked too buggy? Do you remember the only bugs you would even think of touching were butterflies because you said they looked just like baby fairies?"

"Do you remember how I thought that Luna moth was a butterfly when I caught it for your birthday?"

"I mean Luna moths are so beautiful. It's a common mistake."

"Do you remember how you destroyed my canopy bed after you found out I killed it because I was scared it was going to eat right through it?"

"I felt terrible about that," The Mother lies. All Lil remembers is being angry, so very angry, when she'd found the empty mason jar with the wilting flowers, the squashed Luna moth on the bottom of Yvie's sneakers. She remembers ripping down a crying Yvie's canopy, smashing the jar against the van. At least she'd remembered to sweep up those tiny, discarded reflections of herself before Yvie cut her feet looking for the bathroom in the middle of the night. But The Mother makes her smile. "You were little. And you honestly thought it was going to ruin your Halloween Polar Fantasy Princess costume too."

Yvie rolls her eyes. "Enough with the stupid stories, Mom."

ERROR_PARENT_TO_CHILD_COMM

"You know you should probably eat something. You want me to make you a sandwich?" The Mother, in an act of true desperation, suggests Lil offer food.

"I'm not hungry."

"Do you remember when we were Outside and I'd make us spaghetti on the camping stove and I'd tell you stories about how there used to be mantises that looked like orchids, beetles that looked like gold lockets, stink bugs named after Picasso paintings? You liked my terrible cooking then."

Yvie grits her teeth. "Mom, I always hated the spaghetti. I thought it was earthworms covered in sauce."

ERROR_BAD_MEMORY.

At night, in the dark, The Mother is starting to look decidedly unbalanced. Every time Lil creeps downstairs to use the main floor bathroom (these days, it's every hour on the hour—

she doesn't want to wake Luc's father in the middle of night) Lil can see her Mother is ungracefully, impossibly lopsided, dragged down by the weight of the Error tray even though her body is supposed to be made of steel. She looks like a thrip trying to eat a mite with its asymmetrical mouth parts. She looks like a lone longhorn ant trying to carry a bowl of Cheerios. Has Lil really made that many mistakes? It is easy, so easy, to picture how The Mother could be knocked off her feet. It could be a rumour of Luna moths. A short sprint with her LifeLite to photograph them and Lil's water breaks. A month from now, Lil tries to find five minutes to take a picture of what could be one of those politically liberated bees trapped in Yvie's boots and forgets the baby monitor. Or a Lil, instead of sleeping when the baby does, exhausted from developing LifeLites, falls asleep with Luc on the couch. Only one of them wakes up.

Whatever it is, it would be the ugliest of the uglies. Lil is sure of that.

"Is everything okay?" Luc's father comes downstairs when Lil doesn't come back to bed.

"I'm fine." Lil tries to believe this; as Yvie's mother she'd been fine. Sure, there was that Halloween the air quality was good enough that Yvie should have been able to go trick-or-treating, but the fairy wings Lil had bought her reminded her teacher of a dragonfly and that was that; Yvie wouldn't wear them. And there was the time Lil had used Yvie's princess night-light to try and coax the singing cicadas out of hiding; Yvie had unfortunately discovered an earwig singing next to the bulb the morning after and it had been a good month of sleepless-ness for both of them when Yvie became convinced an earwig colony was living in her earlobe. So maybe she hadn't always understood Yvie. But what kind of mother didn't understand her own daughter? And who was Lil now, if not a mother? (Even if, after Lil had smashed the mason jar, Yvie had asked, "Are you still mad? Please don't be mad. Please, it was an accident. I didn't know." And Lil lied and said it was fine.) "I've just sacrificed my bladder to the baby god, that's all."

"That's what? The sixth time tonight? I could not do what you do," Luc's father says, kissing her on the top of the head and then gently placing a hand on her stomach. Lil can see the outline of The Mother from the living room, the reflection of the Error codes blinking in his glasses. "Your mother is the best, little man," he says, but all she can think is *who do you think you're talking to?* The Mother knows that Lil is not the best. She is not even fine. It was not fine that afterwards, Lil had been unable to crawl under the re-hung and slightly dilapidated canopy with cuddles and those incredibly expensive real cocoa chocolate chip cookies and do and say the mother words Yvie had needed to hear. Nothing was fine about how she was so angry she'd almost wished the shattered mason jar had hit her daughter. It was not fine that the next time they stopped for supplies, Lil told Yvie she couldn't have her chocolate chip cookies because the cocoa was pollinated by enslaved farm midges and she was just part of the problem.

And now, even when The Mother buys that same brand of cookies, Yvie won't even look at them. Lil eats them guiltily as Javier's mother discusses how Anties are destroying fields of cocoa, replanting them with self-pollinating coffee. Her extraordinarily long, fake eyelashes look like they perpetually quiver with fear. Right now, according to Javier's mother, Yvie could be buying beekeeping hats on the black market as part of a plan to free the last farming honeybees that wouldn't even know how to survive in the wild; Yvie could be having unprotected breaths. Now, if Lil wasn't careful, if she didn't start seeing the nefarious intent behind Theo's choice of camo pants, her daughter could even be crawling around in cow manure in the name of dung beetle liberation.

Lil, her own fake eyelashes threatening to come off because she doesn't know about the adhesive that all the other mothers with their solidly glued-on lashes seem to know, excuses herself to go the bathroom.

"Don't listen to her," says Devon's mother, who comes out to the veranda after Lil decides that, before she can face going back into the living room with a face whose fake eyelashes are not staying on no matter what she does, she needs a surreptitious cigarette. "We've all changed enough diapers to know a little poop never hurt anyone."

Lil has never been so relieved to discuss feces. "I'm just worried—" she begins.

Devon's mother cuts her off with a wave. Her fingernails, The Mother points out, thanks to Chase's Mother, the former esthetician, could really use a manicure. What must her children's nails be like? Does she let them bite their nails? Suck their thumbs? Maxwell's Mother was a dentist and is worried about their enamel, corrective braces, malocclusions, a word Lil doesn't know, even if she knows what a uselessly anachronistic epimeron is. "Of course you are. You've been hanging around Laura and the rest of them way too long."

"Who's Laura?" Lil asks before she thinks not to, and then feels stupid.

"Javier's mother. Don't worry, I know all she talks about is her son; I only know her name because I'm her massage therapist. I'm Vicki by the way."

"Lil. It's nice to know Devon's mother has a real name," she says awkwardly.

"Well, I'm not just Devon's mother," Vicki laughs, "and I've actually got four kids." Lil is trying very hard not to imagine four kids; Brandon's Mother and Bart's Mother and Bradley's Mother supply the petrifying details, enough to curl any woman into a fossil of her former self. A mother, running in four different directions when her children discover the manhole to the Outdoors, a mother—overtired from her youngest's late night teething, and her second oldest's refusal to read, and her oldest's summer indoor soccer league practices which had to be moved thirty minutes farther away due to the excessive heat— leaves the baby in the car when she thinks she has dropped him off at daycare. The windows are rolled up. "What's wrong?" And how many times had Lil left Yvie alone inside the van on a hot day? How many times could she forget with Luc before that one time, the final time, and it would be all her fault? Suddenly Lil is babbling her confession, oozing out a sticky, wet mess of fear and sad, like a startled stink bug. Vicki has done this four times and Lil can't do this again; she loved her daughter, no, that's wrong, she loves her daughter, will love her son, yes she knows that, but she can't seem to care about whether to do classic sepia-toned baby pictures or repaint the nursery with a mural of soon-to-be extinct robins and their classic little-boy-blue eggs now that the earthworm is vanishing at an alarming rate. With her daughter, she hadn't cared about teddies or princesses or even what happened to the pig in that stupidly sad bedtime book since there were so few Charlottes left in the world and now Lil can't even talk to her daughter! Lil can't even keep a tiny glass of water inside herself without peeing a little, for fuck's sake, and the worst part is The Mother knows all her can'ts; The Mother knows she can't possibly be good enough to one day be a Mother.

Vicki listens without batting a very short, unfake eyelash. "Hon, you need to get her out of your head. You need to take breaks. Trust me. I used to be a wreck."

"But... but how?"

"You know Arvinder's mother had a fire ant infestation." Lil nods slowly. She is not sure what Vicki is trying to say. "Thing is, fire ants are attracted to electrical devices. They chew right through wires if you can get them in. And even though The Nest is pretty self-sufficient, no one here works in manufacturing. It takes weeks, sometimes months, with all the supply chain Antie disruptions, to replace those wires." Lil hadn't noticed before, but she realizes that Arvinder's mother is missing from this meeting.

"But my son is about to be born. And my daughter—" And what kind of disaster would Lil be, again, without the guidance of The Mother? It feels a bit like looking into a black hole, or at least the depths of a fire ant colony, waiting to get brutally stung for disrupting the brood chamber of the queen.

Vicki cuts her off. "You're telling me none of those Mothers ever left their kids on the couch and looked away, just for a second, and bam! They fell off and hit their heads? You're telling me none of them pretended the story ended halfway through at bedtime because they were so tired, or screamed at their kid for rolling around in the sand during a drought and tracking it in the house when they'd already used their water rations for the day? You're telling me none of them thought *why did I do this* on a day when they're trapped in the house with a screaming baby and another on the way and it's above 50 degrees outside? But no Mother's gonna talk about that. Well, I've done every single one of those things. So go on. Tell me, with four kids, who are perfectly fine thank you, that I'm not a good enough mother. Tell me I'm not good enough," but still, she lowers her voice, "without The Mother."

Lil stares back at her. There is something in the way Vicki's face wrinkles when she smiles ("crow's feet," Javier's mother would probably call them. As though the footprints of the almost extinct, West Nile-suffering corvid were not a miracle. As though an ugliness could not be celebrated). For a second, it makes Lil believe maybe she is not the equivalent of a cockroach for not having bought her crying kid chocolate chip cookies. Maybe she is not the devil's flower mantis, not even a weevil, for wishing she was out photographing the end of the world instead of talking about red circles and green circles in a world where fires lick through what's left of the trees. Maybe it's not even the end of the world. Maybe it will be fine, like raising your kids in a little domed airspace in a world on fire. "But what if I'm not?" Lil whispers. "What if Yvie isn't fine?" Lil is not even really sure if she's asking if fine is okay.

Vicki holds a perfectly chipped nail over Lil's lips. "You're not the worst. Not by a long shot. She's just making you feel guilty."

"But what do I do?"

"You already know what to do. A Mother always knows," Vicki says as Javier's mother looks over. Wordlessly, Vicki grabs her purse and motions for Lil to follow her to the back porch where she takes out a small, glass-lidded box. Lil looks at the bustling, mini starter ant farm, small enough to fit inside a mother's purse.

"They breed like rabbits. Well, like rabbits used to," Vicki says as she hands Lil the farm. "Trust me hon. You're going to have to cut that cord sometime."

* * *

For a little while, Lil feels deliriously guilt free. So what if Luc's father isn't back until Saturday from his business trip and Lil promised she would finish painting the nursery so everything is ready in case she goes into labour early and she hasn't even started? So what if Yvie is going to a dung beetle protest Outside tonight? So what if it's supposed to rain? Lil tries to ignore Astin's Mother and Sherman's Mother, former designers and seamstresses for Modest Dresses, who both think Yvie's tank top is too low cut; Lil waddles to the couch, puts her swollen feet up, pretends not to notice the offending top. So what if, looking at her daughter, The Mother feels a strange ache? Where was the Yvie who was afraid for months of sitting outside because a June bug once dropped into her lap under a tree? Who cried at the thought of evening walks because she was convinced ghost moths would come back to haunt her and eat all her sweaters? Lil sits back, turns on a last-century documentary about Arctic bumblebees, which used to build their nests in the tunnels that belonged to lemmings. Lil thinks it's fine if Yvie goes Outside tonight, even though Spencer's Mother and Wesley's Mother and Rupert's Mother clearly think it isn't fine; since when does Lil know what is fine for a Mother? They have to ask, "Are you taking your respirator with you tonight? Do you have a back-up in case that one fails?"

"Mom. I'll be fine. Theo says most Anties don't even bother with respirators."

"You're not going to wear a respirator?!" There is a tinge of panic in this; Lil can hear Warren's Mother's and James' Mother's and Harvey's Mother's and Preston's Mother's voices rising. Lil isn't sure what's worse, that if The Mother could still cry she'd be in tears over the fact that Yvie is now a familiarly bug-loving stranger who doesn't need her mother to pitch her tent or refill her oxygen or cuddle her to sleep at night with cookies and now she'll never get to make up for the lack of unethically sourced chocolate chips in Yvie's childhood, or that Lil can barely recognize her own voice from Scott's Mother's and Truman's Mother's and Teddy's Mother's and Robert's Mother's and Carter's Mother's and Craig's Mother's and now, Luc's Mother's. It is anyone's but Yvie's mother's who cried that first night in the apartment with the cheap chiffon canopy bed, the concrete balcony with no grass. No potted plants even. Not a chance of creepy crawlies. Anyone's but Lil when she says, "And if most Anties jumped off a cliff like a bunch of lemmings, would you do it too?"

"Mom, I don't even know what a lemming is."

"Well you should." *ERROR_COULD_NOT_INTERPRET.*

"Look Mom, you're going to have to get used to this." So what if Yvie hugs her mother, then announces (yes, doesn't ask permission, just announces, as though she is six again and expecting her mother will unquestioningly go along with her plan for a non-tea tea party, where Lil and Yvie and all her stuffed animals drink teacups full of unpoop-filled Cokes) that she is going to whatever is left of the Amazon with Theo and they are going to stage a grieve-in for all the lost species of insects and amphibians? "I'll be gone in a couple of weeks. Theo and I are going right after graduation."

Staring at her daughter in this moment, Lil feels the same terrified pride mixed with rage that she felt when Yvie took off her respirator to catch the moth. When Yvie stubbornly insisted on wearing her butterfly pyjamas every night and Lil had to find a laundromat with working water in the middle of a desert so they wouldn't stink. When she caught Yvie researching honeybee farm conditions. When Yvie had become the person Lil had always hoped they both would be, and the part of her that is not proud is so sad that this is what a mother is; the woman who watches her life go on in her children without necessarily living it. That part of Lil really wishes she had a mason jar to smash. *ERROR_INVALID_UNWIND_TARGET.*

"Mom? You okay?"

"I'm fine. I just have to pee."

If Yvie notices, she doesn't say anything about Lil taking The Mother with her.

Lil doesn't go to the bathroom, however, she goes to the basement where she dumps The Mother in the corner. The Mother, Lil realizes, is hanging on by a thread. The weight of The Mother's Errors scale has loosened the joint connecting her arm to the socket; it hangs limply by her side, exposing her wiring. Lil feels a sudden urge to twist that arm, rip it right off, and she wonders if that urge is from the part of her that smashed the mason jar, or the part of her that had wished, holding her infant daughter every two hours, that Lil had broken her own arm, anything to not have to mother through those early days. Regardless, the Lil who is a jar smasher is proud of her daughter, even if the Lil that cleaned up those tiny glass shards is so, so sad that Lil is not that person anymore. *Yvie is going to be fine*, she tells The Mother, who stares at her blankly. *More than fine. She's doing great things.* It is almost like Lil is herself again through her daughter; after all, Yvie is successfully doing exactly what Lil taught her.

ERROR_SUCCESS.

No. Lil can feel herself vibrating like a cicada. *That's wrong.* But the Error message loops across The Mother's face, like the ball in roulette wheel.

Trembling, Lil grabs her purse and dumps out the mini fire ant farm that Vicki gave her that afternoon into the hanging arm of The Mother.

* * *

When Javier's mother calls, Yvie is getting ready to leave and the rain sheets are spider webs darkening the sky of The Nest, making it almost the colour of Outside. On screen, the bumblebee is doing the inevitable, getting eaten by the Arctic fox. "Is your power out?" Javier's mother says, clearly implying that Lil is in the dark about something.

"Yes," Lil lies before she realizes that onscreen, the fox is howling and her volume is turned up loud enough for Javier's mother to hear.

"So you're offline?" She can almost hear Javier's mother raising her eyebrows. Even Lil almost doesn't believe Lil would just do what she did.

"Uh-huh."

"Well then I'm glad I called. You know, Walton's Mother used to be a private investigator, and she said that the way you described Yvie at that last meeting... well, she definitely needs someone to keep an eye on her. And I know how hard it must be to do that for you, with the baby almost here." Lil feels the familiar gut-sick guilt slowly seeping back into her stomach. "And so I thought, let me ask around, because when I talked to Karanveer's mother—you know, who has the sign shop—she said Yvie was in the store printing something yesterday. So I talked to Jamal's mother who lives near the tunnel access—you know, the house on the end? Anyways, she saw your daughter and that Theo boy skulking around there this afternoon, storing those big cardboard signs in the bushes. Apparently there's a dung beetle protest Outside tonight. In this rain! If you don't stop your daughter, do you know what could happen?" Lung cancer by the time Yvie is twenty. Or death from West Nile. Has Lil considered the possibility of malaria, potential unwanted pregnancy, chronic debilitation from Lyme disease? Or sepsis from crawling around in a field of fecal matter?

"Laura, maybe you're taking this too seriously," Lil manages to whimper.

"It's Dolores. Not Laura. Did Vicki tell you it was Laura? Vicki always gets it wrong." An Arctic silence follows. "I don't think you're taking this seriously enough." Lil can picture how Javier's mother's eyes are narrowing, how she's folding her hands, which gives her the look of a praying mantis. "Before I was Javier's mother," she says slowly, "I was José's mother. José was my first son." Javier's mother swallows. "He died when he was two months old. SIDS. They said there was nothing I could have done. But for years and years after, I thought, what if I had breastfed exclusively instead of letting his father give him a bottle of formula when I was too tired? Did I put him on his back that one time? What if I left his stuffed bunny in his cradle after we played and I didn't remember to take it out?"

"I'm so sorry," Lil whispers. "But Dolores, there wasn't anything you could do."

"It doesn't matter. You'll never forgive yourself, losing a child," Javier's mother says tearfully. And what was Lil doing, letting Yvie out in that rain, in nothing but a tank top? No umbrella? What was Lil doing, lying on the couch while her daughter was planning to go out there? What Dolores says next makes Lil wish she could sink, quietly snail-like into herself. "Ask Vicki if she has. Her oldest daughter died in the last floods."

In the watery silence that follows, Lil can hear the robotic jangle of a million slot machines *dinging* slightly off key. *ERROR_CHILD_NOT_COMPLETE. ERROR_UNWIND. ERROR_MULTIPLE_FAULT_VIOLATION.*

And then the lights go out.

* * *

There is no time. The Mother knows this. The Mother doesn't know how much time she has left, with the fire ants slowly taking her over, and her back-up batteries that have rarely been recharged, and Yvie eighteen now and leaving for her protest-date out the garage door attached to the basement and about to make all the same mistakes her own mother did.

"Just tell me what you see in Theo," The Mother makes Lil say as Yvie is at least putting a jacket over that tank top. "What's so good about him that you'd risk drowning? Or dengue fever? Or air poisoning?"

"I thought you were cool with this." Yvie, pulling on Lil's old rain boots, seems slightly hurt.

"I am. I mean, I was. I mean, this just isn't you!" The Mother's voice is hysterical now, pleading, *Please no, not yet, you're still too young.*

"Maybe you don't know me as well as you think you do."

"It's just that you've changed so much." *And where oh where is the little girl I had to check to see if there were giant spiders under the bed for every night? Where is the little girl I had to pretend I would kill centipedes for in those gross campsite bathrooms?* "I just hope it isn't because of Theo. You shouldn't have to change for some boy." *You're still my young and I need to keep you safe.*

"Yeah well, I learned that from the best." And why is she looking at The Mother that way? Yvie's look says her mother is stupid, wearing that very airy maternity nightgown, unable to anticipate the danger of a tick climbing up her bare legs and parasitically burrowing itself into her body. "You know I'm only doing what you taught me to do. What you would do."

"I would never do what you're doing now. It's practically a monsoon out there already. It's way too dangerous." The Mother, with the little energy she has left, says this even though Lil thinks it's a lie. But it doesn't even matter if Lil *knows* this is a lie; it is too dangerous for her daughter. Like taking off a respirator, feeling the early morning sun.

"Sorry," Yvie says, in a voice that means she isn't at all, "I meant I'm just doing what you would have done. It's not my fault that you don't have the balls—" and even though The Mother automatically starts telling Yvie to watch her mouth, Yvie cuts her off "—*of dung*, to do anything worth doing anymore!"

"You're right." Here is where something snaps; the back-up batteries go dead, the fire ants finish gnawing through that final wire. The Mother is beside herself; her arm has collapsed to hit rock bottom, or at least the granite basement tile. *ERROR_ FAIL_SHUTDOWN.* "I don't. I had you instead." Here is where it is just Lil, with a dead Luna moth and a smashed-up mason jar and the daughter she swept aside most of those sharp pieces of Lil for, just leaving. And it's not like she can do anything about it.

The silence before Yvie tells her that she hates her, before Yvie slams the door, the one that follows is what Lil imagines a butterfly might hear right before the devil's flower mantis snatches it, midair, still in flight. It is just an instant. Not enough time. Never enough.

* * *

Now that the worst has happened, Lil realizes it is like burning toast. It's such a small thing until there are ants from the crumbs, and then mice from the ants, and then the diseases a toddler could get when they pick up a toy off the floor. And then and then and then. Even worse is when there are no more ants, at least not garden-variety ants. Worse is when there are just fire ants because there are no more gardens, just little safe pockets of roses and AstroTurf that almost looks like real grass except it is too perfect while the forests burn outside. The worst has happened. Yvie is gone, and Luc's father isn't here, and Lil is all alone because The Mother has shut down completely. The Mother is in over her head; The Mother is drowning in a basement flood, water pouring in from the semi-aboveground windows. The worst has happened and it will keep happening, over and over again, because nothing changes in a perfect world. The Mother cannot change, cannot afford her own human need while keeping her children safe.

Lil, defeated, watches from the second last step at the bottom of the basement stairs (the first is already submerged). The fire ants pour out of The Mother's arm, out of the wall, until Lil thinks all she is is a ball of wiggly horrors, thousands and thousands of searingly painful stings. There are hundreds and hundreds of them, all messing with how The Mother should be wired. Thousands and thousands, so many that it is impossible to see The Mother Lil has through all the bugs. This is not Cole's Mother, but Olivia, who, back when there were garden-variety ants to worry about, still never cleaned her floors properly and found her one-year-old son eating an ant and the piece of hard cheese it was carrying, just the right size for a choking hazard. This is not Mason's Mother, but Quinn, who left the laundry sink running during a drought and flooded the basement after bathing her four-month-old because she was so very tired. This is not Cooper's Mother, but Claire, who fantasized more than a little about her son cutting himself in the glass window he broke that she was left to clean up. This is not Luc's mother, or even Yvie's mother, just Lil. Lil, who once smashed a mason jar and wished it was her daughter's face. Lil, who didn't buy her daughter cookies, who didn't notice right away when her daughter couldn't breathe. This mother cannot go save her daughter. This mother can't even make it out of the basement.

Lil is this mother. She can't even go after Yvie because her water broke.

The old gym bag Lil was going to use for her hospital stay is already underwater, somehow wrapped around The Mother's bent shoulders like algae used to wrap around sunken ships. Lil tries using a broomstick, but it's not long enough. She tries a snooker cue, but it won't latch. The Mother, Lil can only imagine, would definitely beep about her son being born like this; *ERROR_BAD_START_POSITION*. Or *ERROR_BAD_ENVIRONMENT*. Everything is under water except for the ants: Yvie's old chiffon canopy, her precious childhood butterfly crayon drawings. *What do I do now? What do I do?* But it's not like The Mother is helping, all bent out of shape from being slammed into granite by the force of the water. Lil catches the butterfly wings she'd buried in the basement, the ones she'd bought the year after the dragonfly debacle, right when Yvie said she was too old to go trick-or-treating. She catches the 3D LifeLites of the spiderlings, the dead Luna moth; if she could, Lil is sure The Mother would hum so many mistakes, fire ants leaking out of her like Lil's amniotic fluid. *ERROR_DS_OBJ_NOT_FOUND. ERROR_REMOVE_FAILED*. The snooker cue itself is a mistake, the force of the water snaps it in half once Lil finally manages to catch something with straps. Lil grabs the pool skimmer, manages to turn The Mother face up, but it doesn't help. The bag slips off and sinks.

And Lil realizes that maybe, just maybe, there's nothing Lil can do.

This is when Lil notices the fire ants. Even if The Mother is sinking, the fire ants float. There are dozens and dozens and what looks like hundreds or thousands of fire ants, all climbing on top of each other, forming a life raft. All floating on top of the water, on top of The Mother. They are a rabble of insects. A plague of insects. But they are also a nest of insects. Olivia, not just Cole's Mother, reminds Lil that at least their children know what a nest of insects looks like, even if a nest of ants, or spider-lings, was a mistake. Even if the pollution and the smog and the end of the world was a mistake, Quinn, not just Mason's Mother, bought a kiddie pool and filled it with her water rations for the week; at least her children were going to learn how to float while the coastline sank. Claire taught her son to play baseball in the last blades of grass she could find. A single fire ant will drown. But together they form a break in the pattern, imperfect, like on those old, expensive rugs. They are a Lil who once smashed a mason jar but showed her daughter how to love a butterfly. A Lil who stupidly took off her goggles showed her daughter how to dare. If she hadn't done that, Yvie wouldn't have taken her respirator off. If she hadn't done that, Yvie wouldn't have taken off with a boy who still believed in possibilities. Yvie wouldn't be off, trying to save the world.

As a mother, Lil realizes, feeling the start of the dull pains in her lower back, she cannot go save her daughter. Her daughter doesn't need to be saved, not by someone else.

And Lil is done with being someone else.

Later, when Lil calls Vicki for a ride to the hospital, Vicki will ask, "Is everything okay?" Luc's father will ask her the same, watching his son's birth on a LifeLite while Lil gets to live it.

"Yes. I mean, I've been better. But I've also been worse."

Later, much later, Lil's yes will be a postcard from Brazil, a reassurance that, yes, Yvie is wearing her respirator, and even if it doesn't buy her that much time, maybe it will be enough for her to live her own life. Lil's yes will be a series of baby LifeLites done in tasteful black and monarch orange. Her yes will be a raft of fire ants, all those horrifically lovely red dots connecting her to her daughter, her to herself, her to the mother she is as she cradles her new baby boy.

AMONG CHAMELEONS AND OTHER SHADES

A GIRL, A BOY, AND THEIR SHADOWS are lying together in an unholy love quadrangle on the hood of their beater 2022 Honda Civic, watching the spaceport launch to Mars from a Walmart parking lot in Las Cruces. The boy is thinking the sky is a perfect baby blue today, almost like the interior of the car they'd bought for $300 when they landed in Austin, and everything he can see of the starship is excitingly new, and bright, and shiny. The girl is thinking she might throw up from last night's margaritas. Neither the boy nor the girl is concerned about the other's shadow; being scared of your own shadow is like being scared of ghosts, or the dark. Kids' stuff. All in the past. They both agree they are far too mature for any of that while eating their single-serving boxes of vintage Count Chocula for breakfast without any milk. The boy likes to think of himself as a man of science, and the only spirit haunting the girl is tequila; she is trying not to show she has a migraine, or look directly at the rocket glinting in the sunlight. "Just think," the boy squeezes the girl's hand, "once it's our turn in Boca Chica, it'll be like this every day. Mars doesn't even have rain."

"So it's going to be permanent sunshine for the rest of our lives?" the girl asks optimistically. The girl knows this boy likes her because he says she is cheerful and bright, just like so many other boys have, and the girl wants to be liked. She looks away from the reflective sun shade on their windshield as the hangover gathers behind her eyebrows.

"Well, I guess Mars has clouds. But not rain clouds. Nothing dark and stormy." The boy gently reaches over to her midthigh, placing his hand over the last word in the tattoo which runs backwards down to her midcalf; "Those Who Cannot Remember The Past." It was a quote he was sure he'd heard before, but when he'd asked, even she wasn't sure exactly where it was from. This trip from Toronto to Texas, destination SpaceX in Boca Chica for registration for the next available space launch to Mars, is supposed to be a honeymoon of sorts. The boy and girl are eloping. Sort of. They are not married, and the boy has agreed with the girl, at least out loud, that they never will be. But he'd checked online, and they still met the criteria for settlement on Mars. Previous romantic attachment. Demonstrated ability to cohabitate. At this point, with the number of already successful colonists, the government was willing to soften this requirement if money was involved; thanks to his parents' grocery store empire, the boy thinks the couple's romantic weekends in the girl's yurt will count. The last criterion, intentions of childbearing, he skips when he tells the girl. The boy, Adam, is a surprisingly young twenty-six even though he's been engaged once before, to his high school sweetheart, whom he thought shared his love of *Star Trek*. Near the end, even when they were always fighting, he still used to call her "Imzadi," and she'd pretend she didn't even know it meant "beloved." But he thinks this girl will be different, even if they've only known each other for a month. He thinks she wants the same as he does, what his parents have: a nice house, two kids, a tenuous agreement that even if things end up not great between them, it's far too late to start over and do things any differently. After all, the girl had told him it was *Star Trek: Voyager* that made her want to travel to space when she was a kid. And after all, the girl's favourite song,

"The Way We Were," is the same one he'd told his mother he would dance to at his own wedding when he was eight years old, and had finally gotten his pretty cousin to slow dance with him (even if she said it was just because she was practising for her grade eight dance with a boy named Danny). So when the girl had told him about her love for Streisand and Captain Janeway, he'd presented her with a detailed navigational plan (including both GPS and the celestial coordinates given by trigonometric parallax) for running away with her under the stars of a glow-in-the-dark mini-golf range on their second date.

"Hmm, nothing dark and stormy huh?" the girl tries to tease. "I thought Mars had a ghost lady."

"Sorry, I gotta dig my heels in on that one." Adam laughs as they get back in the car, turning the radio onto some oldies station. "That's bullshit. I already told you. She's nothing but people seeing patterns that aren't there in the rocks." He blasts the station, and all the cheesy pop songs about other people's loves sound the same. Boy meets girl, boy loves girl, boy loses girl or girl loses, the end. Because Adam has driven their entire trip so far, he's also decided on the radio. The girl had offered to drive when he'd looked like he was about to pass out as they'd rolled up Gravity Hill in El Paso on their tenth straight hour of driving, and he'd explained that it was the absence of a horizon that created the optical illusion of downhill really being uphill, even though the locals claimed spirits were responsible. He'd said it was okay, then told her some story about how his mother's driving used to drive his father crazy; "It's less stressful for me to drive," he'd said, yawning. "Besides, I didn't put you on the insurance." Now, she can see Adam mouthing the words to whatever song is currently on as he drives toward Big Bend. Instinctively she tries to hum along.

On the road ahead of them, the shadow of the flatbed truck with rails looks like it's saying a cheerful "hi" in the middle of the road. The girl tries to muster excitement under the increasingly high pressure of her pounding forehead. She has just learned that, on Mars, urine is often recycled into shower water. The girl, Maddy, is twenty-eight, and has never dug in her heels about anything; her ex-boyfriend, the dropout psychology major turned tattoo artist used to say she was a perfect example of the chameleon effect. With him, she'd tried to learn to draw. Her own mother had called her a drifter when she dropped out of circus school after breaking up with a fire-breathing busker. When Maddy was little, watching her father obsessively collect all of *Star Trek: The Original Series* on Blu-Ray even made her want to be an astronaut until she found out about how Laika, the space dog, had either starved or burned to death. "You think we'll be happy on Mars?"

"Of course."

"Sure you're tough enough to last?" she teases. Maddy knows she's only good at beginnings. She has a suitcase full of them, withdrawal letters from her environmental science degree, college brochures about the vet tech program she'd told the boy she might be interested in taking, tacky relics of old boyfriends. There is the *Intro to Psychology* textbook, dollar-store sunglasses from the boa constrictor–loving busker who wanted her to learn mime for his act (he used to watch his own reflection in those sunglasses, making sure she mimicked his moves exactly), the weight a physics grad student had dropped in her lap when he was trying to teach her about inertia. She'd stayed with him the longest, even though when they argued he called her stupid for not finishing her degree. She'd even once mistaken the opening credits to *Voyager* with the original series. Her father said he wasn't a fan of the female captain; he much preferred Kirk. Even when she'd handed him her telescope to show him where she'd spotted the Apollo 11 landing site, saying she was going to be the first woman ever to walk on the moon, he aimed it too low, and she'd noticed, in that instance, how his shadow engulfed her own in the moonlight on the driveway. Her father never found a way to see her reaching the stars. And when Maddy read about Ham, the chimp who went to space, only to suffer through electric shocks on his feet and die in a zoo at a young age afterwards, she stopped seeing herself ever casting a shadow on the moon.

Later on, with other men, Maddy was only vaguely aware of her own shadow; she'd met the tattoo artist during the overcast forecast of a tornado warning, the physics student in a thunderstorm. With the physics student, she had not noticed the tendency of her shadow to lie down horizontally on the ground, blending into the shitty parquet background of their apartment underneath his heels. But with this boy, maybe, it could be different. On their first date they went to the History of Space Travel exhibit at the museum. And he'd told Maddy that, if he could go through the time portal of the Guardian of Forever, like Kirk and Spock, he would have convinced Vladimir Yazdovsky, the astronaut who took Laika home in the last few days before her launch, to lose her back on the streets of Russia.

"You know her real name wasn't Laika?" she'd said. "I mean, everyone thinks it was, because it's so appropriate, calling a dog 'bark.' But her real name was Kudryavka."

"I know. They only called her Laika because she barked on the radio. Do you know," he'd said, as they'd exited the building at night, "when we look at stars, we're actually seeing the past light of the universe? Even though I understand how Laika made space travel a real possibility, I always thought it was weird to send a living dog to go land on something illuminated by the light of the past."

"But aren't we living in the past too then?" Maddy had frowned. "I mean, we get light from the sun. Which is a star."

He'd laughed then. Genuinely. "You know I never thought of that." The way he'd said it, the girl felt like a genius. "But I have to say," he'd said earnestly, leaning in for a kiss, "I prefer the present. And there's no sunlight out now."

On their second date, he'd talked about Mars, how maybe she could be the first vet in space. Make it so animals could live happily on another planet. And the girl had thought, despite the low light, that he had seen it in her, a hint of the Captain's red uniform against a backdrop of never-ending stars. After, they had gone back to her yurt, and he'd done so much more than trace the lines of her body, more than going through the motions. He'd looked at her eyes as though studying their details, although in retrospect she could not tell if he had seen her as she was, or if he'd been looking for stars in her eyes, the past in the present.

"I think I can last anywhere as long as I have you with me," Adam says now, gazing at her earnestly. He stares at the girl's bare legs as she props them up on the dashboard, feels an unexpected stab of happiness when she wiggles her toes at him. Even pointing at him with her toes, Maddy always made him feel like she saw him as smart, as a man and not just some annoying nerd boy who spent his weekends arguing the intricacies of fictional space universes. Vaguely, he remembers going to prom with his now ex-fiancée, and how, in embarrassment, she'd worn the matching *Star Trek* com badges he'd gotten for them as a necklace under the surprisingly high neckline of her dress. He hadn't noticed her hiding it until their first slow dance when she'd insisted on leading, not even leaning against his chest. But this girl was different. For Maddy, he would go anywhere in the world, in the known and unknown universe. On the dashboard, her thigh jiggles in a humanly reassuring way, making the word "remember" bounce hypnotically along to the beat. "Besides, the colony has been going for a long time now. And Mars is stupidly cool. Literally. When you're not inside the dome it's like negative sixty-three degrees Celsius."

He waits for her to laugh and of course, the girl does, even if her head is killing her. There is something in the boy's sweetness, the way he crinkles his nose when he gets excited or scared that he's said something stupid. She thinks the boy is genuinely sweet, giving up a chance to do his PhD in astronomy or astrophysics or something because she'd said she wanted them to start a life together. And at noon, the boy's shadow looks as powerlessly stumpy as the blighted succulent they pass on the side of the road. "You know," the girl says, "I was thinking, if Mars has no rain, does that mean it has no rainbows?"

"Of course Mars has rainbows." When he shows her the picture of a perfect ROYGBIV arc over Mars, he doesn't mention that NASA already confirmed it was just a lens flare. The girl doesn't say anything, even though she's already Googled it; she knows the boy is debilitatingly farsighted without his glasses. She thinks, maybe, she could learn to want to see things like this too. As they cross through the desert, she squints a little, so every distant patch of sand is a guzzle of blue lake, every lone cactus or palm tree a fairy-tale castle in the sky.

Adam's plan is to camp at Big Bend National Park for a couple of days on the way to Boca Chica. He tells the girl it's a dark skies park "with the best views of the stars until we get to Mars itself." He doesn't tell her that last year, a woman died from dehydration while hiking in climate-change induced temperatures of over 56 degrees Celsius. But when they arrive, the ranger does. "So we got some true explorers here huh? Not too many people come out to camp here anymore with this kind of heat." With muted horror, the couple nods along with the ranger's stories of real and imagined horrors: intoxicated hikers falling off ledges, Mojave rattlesnakes, scorpions, and black widow spiders that like to hide in sleeping bags. And then there are the creepy shadow people lurking in the darkness near the hot springs. "If you ask me," the ranger says, "probably just some kids on drugs. Don't let it keep you up at night."

"Don't worry," Adam grins, "we probably won't sleep much anyways. It's our honeymoon."

Maddy learns in the desert that shadows are longest in the morning and evening. In the morning, the outline of the cactus by their tent is the plant version of the wacky inflatable arm flailing tube man at the used car dealership where cars spew black clouds onto the road; in the evening, it is the undead octopus from an old pirate movie. As a kid, she used to search for that octopus under her bed every night, always exhaling with relief at the sight of an empty, though dusty, floor. In the morning, the boy and the girl both think they might make love like they used to, but it's almost 32 degrees out already, and by evening the boy is the only one still thinking of romance, the hot springs of the Rio Grande. The girl thinks the tent poles look like rigid-limbed projections of gigantic spiders in the sunset, and none of the hamburgers in the cooler are vegetarian. Out of the corner of her eye she sees a green anole, often mistakenly called a chameleon, being chased by a snake, their shadows blending and writhing together on the sand until the lizard drops her tail, darting away.

"I'm sorry," Adam says apologetically. "I thought that you just didn't eat pork. You know. Because pigs are just as smart as dogs, right?" he says, quoting one of the documentaries they'd watched together.

"Maybe we could go find a diner," she suggests.

"But I wanted us to be able to go to the hot springs tonight."

"Okay." The girl's shadow responds to this unconsciously. Although tethered to her heels, it still seeps out, slinking under the cooler, casting itself so that she blends into the boy sitting in one of their lawn chairs as he munches on a hot dog, even if Maddy doesn't notice. Just like when she'd been silently hungry for hours after her father used to say he'd take her to a movie if she stayed out of sight like a good girl while he was trying to watch the game. "I guess I'll be fine for tonight."

Ignoring her stomach, Maddy goes back inside the tent, lays out their sleeping bag on top of the air mattress.

Adam follows her inside, digging through his backpack for the ring. These past few nights have been the first time they have had a place together, the boy thinks. One they actually own, even if it is only a tent. This feels momentous somehow, like a step toward the homestead the boy imagined he'd buy for them on Mars, and he feels like he needs to mark the occasion somehow. Under the bizarre ocotillo, Adam gives Maddy the disco-ball ring he bought at the flea market in Austin. "It's a 3D model of the one on the 'I Heart DISCO' *Star Trek: Discovery* T-shirt you said you liked," he explains as he takes a selfie of them both. (Usually, the boy knows, legendary moments need to be captured on film to be believed, like wedding photos where the bride and groom are silhouettes in a gazebo against the sunset before the reception, or sightings of the inexplicably ghostly Marfa lights.) "To the end of a good beginning," he says, cracking them both a beer and quoting a line he remembers hearing at his cousin's wedding, "the best is yet to come."

"For sure," Maddy says. She wonders if she sounds less enthused, munching on an empty hamburger bun with mustard.

"You got some on your lip," Adam says, leaning in for a kiss. After sunset, the cacti's shadows have become the disembodied arms of a nightmare tentacle monster; even this morning's tailless lizard is elongating in the dark. And the boy's shadow is also taller, absorbing the clearly defined impression of her on the ground as they kiss. She pulls back a little, reflexively fearful, which she covers by wiping French's from her lip. Her fear causes even his shadow to tense, premeditating the action half a second before the boy stomps on the green anole who has darted underneath them.

Then the girl's mouth is open as wide as that picture of a snake eating a wallaby she'd showed him once from her trip in the Australian outback, the one that made him queasy.

"I thought the chameleon was a snake," Adam says defensively, seeing the look on her face. When he was younger, his father had yelled at him for not being able to kill the rattler which had gotten into their tent during a camping trip. It made his mother scream. His father had sliced it in half with a shovel. "Its tail looked like a snake. I didn't want it to bite you," he tries to explain.

But the girl still looks crushed. "But it wasn't a snake. And I had a chameleon as a kid. They don't drop their tails."

"So if chameleons don't drop their tails, this one was probably going to die anyways," he says, trying to sound as calmly logical as he can, sure this will make the girl feel better, "which means I put it out of its misery."

"It's not a real chameleon," she repeats. "It's only called an American chameleon because of the camouflage. It's a green anole. And they drop their tails all the time," she says, her voice rising. "It's autonomy. A survival mechanism."

"Why are you making such a big deal of this?" the boy says. He realizes he is angry, mostly because she doesn't see what he sees, how the thing moved like a snake, how he was only trying to protect her.

"Because it was going to be fine." It's heat exhaustion

maybe, but Maddy has the oddest sensation of a part of her lifting out of herself as though she was a balloon, hovering above them, watching Adam watch the empty space where her body should be. Or maybe she's hungry? She's not really sure why she's tearing up. "And now it's not."

"You're being overdramatic," the boy says in disgust. "Remember 'logic is the beginning of wisdom, not the end'?" He waits for her to recognize the quote from Spock. When she doesn't, he sighs. "Look, I'm going to the hot springs if you want to join me." The boy is still clenching his fists and the girl notices how the veins just below his knuckles bulge green in the glare of her phone.

Her shadow is still intertwined in his, even as he starts to walk in the opposite direction, refusing to make eye contact, getting smaller and smaller the farther he is from the light of her phone. "Fine," she shouts out after him. She waits for it, this gradual separation of hers from his, and a ball of ropey softness curls in her stomach, like one of those hermit crabs that mistake a plastic bottle for a shell and can't climb out again.

But then the girl's shadow does an unexpected thing. She splits herself somewhere along the prickly spines of the tentacled ocotillo, unearths herself from underneath the heels of the girl's thrift-store Birkenstocks. The girl and the shadow, without the umbilical cord of physics to hold them together, stare at each other for a moment, then the shadow begins to slink away, expanding into a toweringly two-dimensional woman-shaped void. The shadow has the same slow walk as the girl when she twisted her ankle trying to wear stupid five-inch leather heels to high school because Delilah Parsons said heels made your butt look better. The shadow has the same stooped shoulders as the girl when she first saw a pig slaughtered on YouTube and didn't know how to tell her boyfriend that she couldn't eat the sausages his family had grilled for their annual BBQ. The shadow has the same silent voice as when she'd tried to tell a boy she was too drunk to have sex that night. He still made her drink from a plastic water bottle even though she remembers them talking about the dangers they pose to hermit crabs. For a brief second, the girl can almost picture herself dissolving out here like the sand, those crushed eons of once-so-solid rocks mixed with the tiny remains of billion-year-old crustaceans and shellfish.

The shadow spreads its way farther and farther south until it reaches the edge of the Rio Grande where it slinks down onto the rocks with the boy. In a reversal of the natural order, the girl feels a tethering obligation to trail along behind. When this shadow of herself reaches the boy, the girl realizes it is not all deep umbra; she is a faint double, an almost-Maddy, a blurry outline of her mouth, her words, her eyes that the boy once, in a moment of cheesy romance, called the windows to her soul. And even though Maddy herself is completely separated from this silhouetted stranger, with no angle of moonlight to bind them, the boy does not address her solid girl-self. He does not seem to see Maddy, even when she steps out from hiding behind the rocks. Maybe, she thinks, it is too dark.

"I'm glad you came." The boy thinks nothing about this is strange at all, without realizing how his own shadow blocks the stars of the Milky Way, the Marfa lights, anything that could have been used as a source of illumination. Later the boy will say he had no clue that he was now a part of a foursome; he kissed a shadow of the girl he loved in the hot springs on their honeymoon, thinking it was the girl herself. "Remind me to get you pissed off more often," the boy teases, his eyes still closed.

"It's not your fault," the girl hears the shadow of herself whisper, far away from the lights of any starship or glinting reflections of a past or new civilization. Despite the heat rising from the water, she shudders. Her shadow does not. Later, the girl will say that it was here, between the hot spring rocks and their stories of darkly creepy shades, that wild child Madeline Paquin learned to be scared of her own shadow.

* * *

To trace a shadow to her source requires history. In Old English, circa 450 CE, a shadow meant the same as a shade; a shade is the same as a ghost. Stone Tape Theory suggests that some hauntings encode their sagas on objects or buildings, replaying their replicas of the same moment over and over again. The staff at The Driskill Hotel in Austin, Texas, for example, are no strangers to residual hauntings. By the late 1980s they'd reported many disturbances from the shades of women and girls, the inappropriately disembodied laughter of a little girl named Samantha who broke her neck falling down the stairs in pursuit of a ball, to the incessant weeping from the suite of a woman named Tara whose fiancé left her. In 1857 Archduke Maximilian married a woman named Charlotte from Belgium. After moving with him to Mexico, she became Carlota, a shadow of herself, paranoid and terrified after his execution, convinced a farmer was an assassin, refusing to eat because she believed she'd be poisoned by Napoleon III. She haunted a set of gold-leaf mirrors which were a belated wedding present in the Maximilian room of the Driskill. Alive, she never saw her own reflection in them.

At least that's what the ghost tour guide told the couple when they had stopped in Austin. They could have flown into El Paso, but the boy wanted to see the *Beyond Planet Earth* exhibit at The Bullock Texas State History Museum. All he would talk about was how it was bullshit that the Mars greenhouse effect was starting to get completely out of control; originally, it was deliberately triggered by obtaining methane gas from Titan to warm the surface, and then sustained by importing moose who could belch and shit out methane gas equivalent to 2,100 kg of carbon dioxide a year, more than twice the amount of a round-trip flight from Oslo to what used to be Chile before it was subsumed under water. "It's going to be fine. They're doing what they need to build a civilization." And the girl had a vague feeling that this was a mistake she'd heard before, but said nothing.

They ended up at the Driskill's hotel bar, where Adam detailed their trip plan on the back of a bar napkin. They were going to loop themselves around, from Austin to Las Cruces to the Chihuahuan Desert, and then down to South Padre and Port Isabel, and ever-so-eventually Mars; the girl could trace their ouroboros-style progress on Google maps. "Onwards to space: the final frontier!" Adam said, clinking his glass against hers.

Four old-fashioneds in, and Adam suggested going on the ghost tour. Maddy didn't really want to; she had never liked ghost stories, never felt their delicious terror, even as a child. The thought of being forever condemned to relive your last footsteps down the same hallway, turn the same key in the same lock of the same room, or even chase the same non-existent ball down the same staircase for eternity and beyond was more depressing, she was sure, than whatever the bourbon was going to do to her head tomorrow morning. But Adam had insisted; he thought ghost stories were funny. "Did you know," he said, "that it was the shadows on the rocks in one of those early satellite images of Mars that started the whole idea that Mars has a ghost lady? You'd be surprised at how many ghost stories can be explained by pareidolia, the human tendency to want to see patterns when there aren't any." He scoffed his way through the tour, the bouncing ball, the laughter, the wailing, that might all just be tinnitus experienced by the super tired night staff. And of course, the ghost of Carlota herself, well, that was probably just somebody experiencing the Caputo effect, the documented psychological phenomenon of the tendency to see a face other than your own if you stare at yourself in a mirror in a dark room for long enough.

Maddy wished she had never told him about the Caputo effect. It wasn't comforting at all, not after the ghost stories and the bourbon. In the Maximilian room, every time the girl looked in the mirrors, Adam poked his head into the frame, blocking out her image. "Do you see her?" he asked curiously, slurring a little.

"I see you," she said, a little exasperated. They stared into the mirrors positioned across from each other, creating a strange loop of reflections. When Maddy was twelve, she remembered going into the girls' washroom at lunch with Delilah Parsons. Delilah had her high school sister's lighter, and they faced the mirror like girls have been doing since the late 1800s to see their future husbands on Halloween night. "Say it." "You say it." Of course, nothing really happened when they repeated "Bloody Mary" three times. "You say it." They tried again. And again. And in that mirror, just like in the ones in the Maximilian room, Maddy's search for the figure of a woman she thought she'd see came up blank.

"Damn. You look good," the boy said, stepping aside to squeeze her arm as they both gazed into the mirrors. It's not like he could tell the difference between the real girl beside him and the fuzzy mirror alterations; they'd had a lot to drink, the lighting in the old hotel was dim. Half of her face was covered in shadow. If you'd asked him later, the boy couldn't have told you the details of her forehead, the slight acne, the out of place eyebrows, the arc of her nose. If you asked the girl later, she couldn't have told you why, staring at those images of herself which got less defined the farther back they went, she felt a shiver. Maybe it *was* a ghost, that poor rich empress, or the jilted fiancée, or the little girl, all condemned to an afterlife without autonomy, without the chance to do anything different. Just like how, despite Maddy's exasperation, when Adam squeezed her shoulder, she saw how their shadows leaned into each other on the ground reflexively in a movement she'd repeated so many times it was almost instinct. After all, Maddy's shadow may have been an outline of her, but it was nowhere near a perfect reflection. And in those reflections of her, going backwards until infinity, her face became less and less visible until she was just the suggestion of a woman, as nebulous as a shade, like that carving of Carlota's outline in gold leaf on top of every frame.

* * *

The Southwind Motel in Port Isabel is the kind of sun-bleached turquoise and beige shithole that no one, Maddy thinks, would ever mistake as being part of a rainbow. But it has air conditioning, a tourist trap ghost tour, and a greenish pool that may or may not be infested with brain-eating amoebas and which, the woman behind the counter with the jet-black nails warns them, definitely features black widow spiders where they store the pool noodles. "Just a warning," she winks at Adam, "they're fairly deadly to human males too." More importantly, however, their peeling motel balcony features a direct sight line of the Boca Chica launch site. Just think. They could look past the horizon from their bed, see the next glint of rocket and fuel aiming for the stars, and all for just sixty-seven dollars a night, reduced to forty-five if they are willing to stay on the third floor.

"On account of it not being, well, exactly private." The woman informs them the third floor features the ghost of a Victorian woman condemned to walk the same stretch of hallway for the rest of her earthly days.

The boy says it's perfect.

"Just like her," Adam says, squeezing Maddy's shoulder with one hand while trying to scrape off some stray ketchup on the thigh of his jeans. "Of course it takes one to know one. Right, babe?"

"I guess." Maddy unconsciously picks at the sunburn on her thigh; a thin layer of skin peels off next to the word "Past" of her tattoo. The plan was to stay close enough to the launch site so that when they came up on the waitlist, they could make any flight on twenty-four hours' notice. Her electronic signature on the online application for residency in the Mars colony they had filled out using McDonald's WiFi had looked so stunted next to Adam's, a clumsy outline of her normal letters, like when she had tried to picture tracing the shape of a double mountain while learning to print her name, almost the curves of those twin pillars of formerly explosive volcanic rock on Mule Ears Trail in Big Bend.

A week into their motel stay, Maddy attempts to get her shadow to rejoin her. Maddy would rather stream *The Nature of Things*, talk about the issues with captive moose on Mars, but Adam loves it when the shadow of herself silently folds the clothes he leaves on the floor, then makes them dinner. And even if her shadow is no longer shackled by the laws of science, Maddy doesn't want Adam to think there's something wrong; she feels powerless to investigate the changing eating habits of the ghost moose on Earth, to do anything except go along with making a diet that consists mostly of Kraft Dinner. After they eat, Adam's favourite thing is to sit out on the balcony in full sun and talk about their future life on Mars, which usually sounds like a cross somewhere between *Star Trek* and those reruns of *The Jetsons* she remembers watching on Saturday mornings. Maddy realizes, given how methane moose farms result in trauma to the ungulates, she cares less and less about simulated rotational gravity, or how *Star Trek* did it first. But Adam is so excited, talking about what they could be in the future. Her shadow leans forward, hanging on every word.

Maddy tries science; she tries reason. What if Mars was a mistake? What if it burned them up with its now uncontrollable greenhouse gases? What if, like Adam had been talking about with those studies on melanoma in astronauts, her skin got even thinner in space? What if she wasn't tough enough and ended up developing bone density issues, becoming thinner and thinner until she was as light as her own shadow? Maddy even tries sweet talk. She could go inside, get out of the sun, watch David Attenborough on her phone. Remember how she used to love that? Instead, Maddy and Adam fight over whether it is ecologically responsible to tap the ancient frozen oceans on Mars, and Adam says he wants to view the trapped marine life in the aquarium, then take a boat ride to see the dolphins. "They believe in not making sea life into souvenirs. It's your kind of place. Besides, I figured you might miss the animal variety on Mars." He steps all over her shadow on his way inside to get another beer. And when he comes back out, that stupid shadow of herself leans in closer to the boy, saying he always has such great ideas, smiling so anti-radiantly that Maddy has to give up her position, move closer to him, watch as the shadow casts herself more deeply across both of them as she thinks about the boy holding her hand while they pet the stingrays.

Maddy is starting to wonder if her shadow is eclipsing her. Like the time Adam buys her a shell-shaped tiara at the Rusty

Pelican gift shop because she'd once said she liked mermaids, and he says she looks like a bride. He says it's the way her scarf catches on the tiara in the wind as they are climbing up the outside stairs to their room, how it makes her shadow look veiled against the shadow of the stairs, which, when combined with the actual staircase, makes the symbol for infinity turned sideways. He says, almost wistfully, that his cousin had a beautiful Latin Mass for her wedding, and now she has three kids, while Maddy stomps on the edge of the scarf with her heel to pull it down, feeling a weight sinking in her own stomach.

The only time she doesn't feel this heaviness is with the green anole she privately calls Liz, who lives somewhere between the sink and the only slightly cracked bathroom mirror. Maddy watches her maintain her green countershading, her belly almost translucently light instead of fading into a stressed dark, unafraid of the girl while Maddy pees. When Liz scuttles across the floor, dark brown as soon as she sees Adam, he screams because he thinks she's a snake. And Maddy feels a coldness creep over her, like brain freeze from the unnaturally blue slushies she ate as a kid, or the extreme temperature drop from bright sunlight into the ominous shade of the supposedly haunted lighthouse in Port Isabel. As the late afternoon shadows spread over the girl, dragging her down until she is lying prone on her back on top of the dull jungle print bedspread, all she can remember is the familiar feeling of being unconsciously terrified, like when the busker used to let his boa constrictor stay out while she slept. Now, on top of this averagely terrible eighties comforter, she is surprised she can only dimly remember why she had loved this before, this tangle of the boy's legs around hers.

* * *

In the morning, Adam goes with Maddy and her shadow to the pool. They spend most of their mornings at the motel pool now, Maddy alternating between the umbrella areas and diving into the deepest part of the water to avoid any shaded entities from making their appearance. Maddy loves the pool, something about how her high school science teacher had once showed her that, at a certain depth of water, the shadow of a pencil will actually get so narrow it will disappear. But underwater, Adam's limbs feel heavier; he doesn't like how the reflection of the water makes him look skinnier and lankier, more like a teenager than he already does. Back when they'd left the airport for Texas, he'd told Maddy he had enough money saved to take care of both of them, echoing his own father who hadn't wanted his mother to go back to work after his younger sister was born. Now that the money's almost run out (his parents had not liked the idea of him running off to Mars with "some girl he barely knew"), all the days seem to go in slow motion. He knows that today, just like yesterday, the girl will insist on going back to the motel room right after noon. (Maddy has begun to time her exposure to the outdoors now in terms of the lengthening of umbras, mostly because Adam does not yet seem to have noticed her shadow's separation from herself; he addresses the shadow as though they are still one and the same. In the room, Maddy knows she can switch off the light source, draw the blackout blinds, make it so her shadow is completely gone.) Adam wonders if she feels it too, this inability to move forward. After all, the girl is worse off than him. He knows Maddy has no money, no job, no car to get back to Toronto. Dispassionately, he watches a ladybug struggle in the water until he tries to get the girl's attention with a cannonball.

"Yesterday was fun, but I thought this afternoon we could go to the beach," Adam says once they are back in the motel room.

"No," she says, reaching for her cheap sunglasses on the nightstand and putting them on, even though it's pitch black in the room. Adam can't even see the chameleon she insists on calling Liz like a pet. When he looks at the girl, he can't see her eyes, just the images of himself in the lenses, looking small, maybe even desperate.

"Okay. How about we go to Louie's Backyard for lunch? It's right on the water and, no offense, I'm kind of sick of Kraft Dinner. I'm thinking along the lines of semi-casual, but romantic. Less Kirk and Uhura's kiss in season 3 episode 10 and more like one of Riker and Troi's intimate meals on Ten Forward." He pauses, waits for a flicker of recognition, what he thought was their shared love of both the original series and *The Next Generation*. She stares at him blankly.

"You can go for lunch."

"So you'd rather just stay here with the blinds closed and the lights off?" Here the boy knows a new panic. The decisive outline of their new life he had so carefully navigated on the road map of Texas, the carefully plotted stops they'd talked about on South Padre Island and Port Isabel, then Boca Chica to Mars, all of it seems blurred in the darkness of the stupid motel room where he can't even recognize the shape of Texas on the road map lying somewhere on the night stand.

Whatever response Maddy gives is still muffled by the comforter.

"Fine. I don't even know who you are anymore. You're not the girl I fell in love with," Adam ends up yelling, louder than he'd even intended.

"You're scaring Liz," Maddy says softly.

"Yeah, well maybe Liz scares me!" The boy hates the way his voice quivers between Captain Kirk and Elroy Jetson in the pitch black room; he hates that if Liz was a deadly viper, he wasn't sure he could do it, save the girl like his dad had saved his mother from that rattlesnake in their tent. He slams the door when he leaves, blurting out, "Maddy, I'm leaving you." He could leave. He has the money. Sort of. If he calls his dad. He could always go do his PhD, and maybe by then they'd let single people go to Mars by themselves to work, and he could get away from all the snakes and lizards and stupid reptiles.

Instead, he gets a job taking tickets for the new mirror maze at Gravity Park. It troubles him, sometimes, when he stares into the entrance funhouse mirror, the one that makes him look like the rumour of an ex-wrestler turned carnie, or his own father while he was still boxing. But Adam could not say what in this antagonistically large illusion of himself unnerves him; the boy does not notice that the size of this image matches the scale of his silhouette just before it gets dark.

* * *

As soon as the boy leaves, the shadow of the girl tries to trail after him, bypassing the closed door. Maddy argues she shouldn't; the day is pretty overcast, and the more diffuse a source of lighting is, the more indistinct the outline of the girl on the ground will become, blending unconsciously into whoever is around. Maddy argues she can't; after all, a shadow casts upon the first opaque object in her path. Plus, somehow that would mean Adam was right; even though for Maddy, this is a feeling as ill-defined as the position of one of those God particles the physics student liked to go on and on about. Maddy even argues that maybe they would be better off if the boy leaves; it is always only with boys that she loses the ability to see herself as solid, capable in non-transparent ways of producing a reasonable outline of the girl she really is, the one she wants to be.

Maddy can argue all she wants, but this potentially demonic

shadow of herself is so hell-bent on going after the boy she slams the hallway closet door in frustration when she can't find the girl's sandals. Liz turns a shade of dark grey that matches the lettering of "Past" on Maddy's upper thigh, less faded than the other words, less exposed to the sun.

"I'm sorry," Maddy whispers as Liz turns into her darkly stressed self. She watches her scuttle quickly back to the bathroom, almost disappearing into one of the black bathroom tiles that make the shower look like a giant chessboard. The girl knows this could be for camouflage or to signal distress; the girl knows no one has done any kind of real study on why the green anole changes colour. The girl knows, but her shadow puts on her running shoes instead, heads down to the waterfront to be with Adam.

* * *

Adam discovers it is possible to love only part of someone. Not only the parts his pubertal self, stealing old copies of *Hustler* from his father before his cousins showed him Pornhub, would think about, but the lips and tongue and silent teeth on his skin. When he insists on turning on the lights at night, Maddy is backlit by the single-bulb bedside lamp underneath the covers; he can see her as only the outline of a woman in the dark. *Okay*, the boy thinks. *It's going to be okay. We're going back to how things were.*

But the Maddy of afternoons is a different creature entirely. Bright sunlight is anathema to her now, all those clearly noticeable late afternoon umbras and penumbras stretched out over the sand. This Maddy curls up under the covers into a damp, thundercloud-style lump in the middle of the comforter. She insists on having the black-out blinds drawn, the lights off any time the sun is out. Most of the time now, party girl Maddy

Paquin, who once told him she'd stayed up for a month straight in Cancun and he'd joked that maybe she'd thought she was preparing to live on Neptune instead of Mars, sleeps listlessly in the middle of the afternoons. Adam wonders if any of this will get better when she finds out that dust storms block out most of the sunlight on Mars.

When Adam gets back to the motel after work, he usually goes to the pool instead of upstairs. Maddy has left her sandals there (again) and the way their shadows hit the wet deck, it looks like the inversion of a person, fully formed. All the anger he has been too scared to feel comes flooding back. And why wouldn't the girl walk in the sun with him? She always had before. Why should he ever need to care that the stupid lizard squatting in their bathroom was scared because of him? If only he had seen his own shadow lengthening into a reasonable copy of the Mojave rattlesnake on the bottom of the pool; he stomps over to the equipment shed, snapping a multicoloured soggy noodle in half to wield as an impromptu Klingon bat'leth sword, ready to take out any black widow spider. When he doesn't see any, he squashes a couple of ladybugs instead. And everywhere there are faded foam bits of rainbow littering the deck surrounding him like the saddest birthday confetti. Or nuclear fallout.

"Are you okay?" he hears a voice murmur from inside the darkness of the shed, so softly it doesn't even come close to over-powering his breathing. "I'm sorry honey," and "Don't worry. We're okay. We're going to be just fine."

It never occurs to the boy that this shadow of a woman is not the girl he thinks he loves, that this is the same old story. Boy meets girl. Boy loves girl. Her end, whether the girl wears a Victorian bustle, or just a sundress she thought she'd buy to go sightseeing on her honeymoon but mostly wore huddled underneath the faded motel blankets in the heat of the after-noon. The end, until it happens again.

* * *

On her good days, Maddy tries to battle the supernatural entity she is convinced is directing her shadow's movements. She buys cedar, lavender, and violet oil online with Adam's credit card from Marie Leveau's in the dark safety of their motel bed. She rewatches *The Exorcist: The Version You've Never Seen* on the motel's pay-per-view service, and Googles "Reiki Masters," trying to find one within a 10 km radius. Instead of Mars, she thinks about suggesting that they go to India, or anywhere between the Tropics of Cancer and Capricorn, just so she can be there for Zero Shadow Day. She even buys the sixty-eight white candles some bride is reselling on Craigslist, makes a mental note to have them blessed by a local priest. "Are you trying to burn this place down?" Adam asks when he sees the candles, and Maddy throws them all out.

The problem is Maddy thinks Adam is in love with her shadow. From her burrow on the motel bed, she's watched Adam respond to what he perceives as her shadow's comforting levels of poltergeist-like activity; when the forks and knives clink against each other like windchimes he says, "Remember how you used to play my stomach like bongos in bed?" She remembers how he'd said, "Jesus. If our future offspring plays the drums, I'll know where they got it from." When there is a soft wailing from the kitchenette as Maddy tries cooking a dinner that doesn't come from a package, he says, "Remember the time we were going to cook lobster together and you cried hysterically trying to put them in the pot, so I told you I would take them to a friend's who had a saltwater aquarium and would release them when he drove home to PEI?"

Even in broad daylight, the boy doesn't notice the shadow and the girl are two different entities. He crinkles his nose and smiles when the shadow turns the lights on every time the girl turns them off, waiting for him to come back to bed at night. "Were you waiting for me?" he murmurs. He grins when her shadow appears behind him without warning and envelops him despite the direction of the sun, despite how they've argued all afternoon. Maddy wonders if this reminds Adam of how, when they'd decided to run away together, she had come up silently behind him, even glowing a little from the mini-golf black light, covered his eyes and said, "Guess who?" As though, back then, there could not have been any question that it would be her, the woman he'd said he fell in love with.

Worse, the boy's shadow has begun to combine with her own, the two of them getting bigger and bigger, dragging Maddy down. Like that one time on the balcony that Adam mentioned children, sooner rather than later, even though they'd agreed on waiting at least a few years. His shadow enlarged via unholy matrimony with hers as she'd nodded, "Yes, of course." Combined, their shadows were so big that they fell off the edge of the balcony and Maddy had headed straight to the front desk, asked the woman with the Goth nails to recommend a local Catholic church. Maddy figured, by testing her shadow against the interior of a sacred space, she could sort out whether or not she was a victim of spiritual possession requiring a demonic exorcism. But despite incense, copious Latin from the priest, and Maddy dipping her fingers in the holy water, nothing yielded burning or hissing screeches, no smoke appeared like dry ice from an eighties wedding.

* * *

"Why'd you leave this morning?" Adam is somewhat annoyed as he picks her up outside the church. He'd insisted on coming after waking up late to discover Maddy missing from their motel bed, a woman-shaped crater. What if the girl had left him? What if she'd wanted space, and not the kind he'd promised when they got to Mars? What if she'd had enough of hearing about the space he envisioned for them under the colony dome, a three-bedroom, two-car garage, at least two bathrooms, even if they were run on grey water? This had awakened a kind of motel bedside table-flipping panic which caused her stupid lizard to go all dark and brood creepily on the shower curtain. "I didn't even know you believed," he says.

"In what?" Maddy says defensively. "The holy ghost? The whole new life everlasting thing, amen?" She does not quite know how to explain the fluffy dread awaiting her underneath the fluorescent motel bedside lamps, the way the boy is not even aware of the engorgement of his own shadow. It swallows her up when they are in bed together and he playfully mentions Kirk is his hero for sleeping with all those alien women.

"I meant I didn't know you were raised Catholic too." In this, Maddy can see the echoes of him wistfully describing his cousin's church wedding; his shadow presses into her as she stares into the rear-view mirror. Her own shadow responds, curling into his. Adam smiles at them in the mirror and she knows he thinks the girl and her shadow are the same; he thinks she's checking her makeup even though Maddy hasn't worn any kind of makeup since she found out about animal testing in grade six. But the boy's shadow and her own, united to cast across her face, make it look like she's wearing eyeshadow and Maddy briefly contemplates jumping into the middle of the road at the next stoplight.

Her own shadow is surprisingly opaque, stubbornly blocking the car door. "Yeah, well, there's lots we don't know about each other," Maddy mumbles.

* * *

Once and only once does Adam feel as though he knows who the reclusive Maddy of those long motel afternoons actually is. Adam works until four, and when he returns to the motel, Maddy has their application to Mars spread out over the retro green carpet like one of those oddly shaped throw rugs his mother had in her living room. Or a chalk outline.

"So you want kids," she says flatly.

"You don't?" Adam feels the slow-burn panic creeping up his throat again, the same feeling as being out in the sun too long.

"You know every child has an ecological footprint of over nine thousand metric tonnes."

"Sure, on Earth," he rationalizes. "Obviously it's going to be different on Mars."

"Is it?"

Of course he doesn't know. And he knows she knows he doesn't. Suddenly, all Adam can think about are those pictures of Earth taken from Mars, how it's a speck, how very small, even microscopic, he would look from the same angle. Maddy continues and he can tell that rather than looking at him, she is looking at the lizard crawling in countershade to the folds of their blinds. "And what if I still want to be a vet?"

"I never would have suggested us going to Mars if there weren't moose. You can still be a vet to the moose."

"Yeah, but it's not like anyone on Mars really cares if the moose are okay." Adam sees her eyes follow the shadow as it crawls down the faded green curtains. He knows it isn't a snake, but even if it was, she wouldn't need him; she'd already told him that in the desert. Watching her watch whatever it is instead of him, he feels tiny, adrift, like there is too much space, and he'll never fill it. Even with his shadow, he has only the faintest impression of being larger than he could ever be in the direct sunlight. He rips the curtains open, pulling down the string in a blind fury. He isn't sure if the lizard comes down with it. The girl's feet tangle in the curtain as she tries to free herself.

"I think," Maddy whispers, looking horrified, "I stepped on Liz." The boy is not sure if the look is directed at him or not as she bends down to look at the lizard's body, which now seems smaller, perhaps because of the way the remaining curtain falls around her, blocking out the light.

"It's okay. You didn't see her. Neither of us did. She just kind of blended into the background. I mean, even if she's an American chameleon that's still a kind of chameleon, right?" The boy thinks the girl looks just like his childhood photo, buried in the blue blanket he'd needed to help him fall asleep until he was nine. She needs him now. That's what his shadow thinks. The boy's shadow wants to envelop her and so, unconsciously, the boy crouches down too, gently taking the edge of the curtain from her hand, drawing it around them both. He kisses her until they are both wrapped in the smell of old-lady mothballs. "It's okay," he says gently, "it's not your fault. It's not like there's anything you can do now. You're not a miracle worker," he tries to joke. It doesn't work. "Or even a vet."

"I know," she says. Same old story. This one the girl has heard before. Boy loves what happens to her face backlit by the sun, the brightness of her bleached-out fading purple hair contrasted with her features blended into the dark. Boy doesn't notice how undefined her nose, her lips, her eyes are, the same shade as that dead lizard, as he takes the selfie of them in his mind against the spectacular ocean view. Boy loses girl. Girl loses. The end.

* * *

Two weeks later, The End is actually upon them. Actually, they are on it; the girl finds herself on the gondola pendulum-type inversion ride after the boy convinces her to go to Gravity Park. Adam has free tickets from work, and he wants to go mini-golfing. "It was one of our first dates, remember?"

The girl's shadow does. She ripples with joy. She jumps up and down, squealing with excitement even as the girl shifts toward blue, exhibiting the Doppler effect for both light and sound simultaneously. She even agrees to go with the boy to the park before sunset, when their shadows grow and grow, while Adam reminisces. "Do you remember the seventh hole when I got the water gun to go off and it soaked you completely and I still said you were the most beautiful woman in the world? Do you remember how we slow danced at the fourteenth hole to 'Don't Stop Believin'' under the glow of the dark stars and I said all I wanted to do was be in the now with you?" On the ride, the girl feels like her shadow is playing a wraithy whack-a-mole with her stomach, turning her whole world upside down as she flips into the boy's penumbra. She is probably going to throw up. And from what she knows of Linda Blair, vomiting is a sure sign of possession, immunity to High Mass or not. After they stumble off into the line for mini-golf, Adam grabs her hand directly underneath the glow of the neon red sign for the Haunted House of Mirrors. Maddy exhibits all the typical weak-kneedness of an upset stomach but Adam, a little unsure, gazes at her rose-hued shadow, and interprets it as love.

"Look," he begins, "I know I gave you the ring like a month ago, but I... uh... I want you to be mine always."

"What?"

"Madeline Paquin," he says, getting down on one knee with

the help of the mini-golf putter, "will you boldly go where no one has gone before with me?"

"Are we talking about Mars again?"

"No! I mean yes. I mean, will you marry me before we go to Mars? I just got word today. We're scheduled," he pauses for dramatic effect, "to leave next Thursday."

Here, the shadow experiences her greatest victory over the girl. The natural order is reversed; Maddy becomes a perfect mime of this shadow of herself. Instead of her jaw reflexively opening into a rounded hallway of horrified shock, it becomes the joyous "Oh!" of a snake swallowing its prey whole. Instead of her feet rooted slightly apart in paralyzed surprise, the shadow's hips shift inwards to the boy, the start of an embrace. Maddy's gesture of surprise, her hand held to her mouth in terror-ish dismay, becomes her shadow, lightly and somewhat oxymoronically caressing Adam's hair with her penumbral fingers, whispering, "I'm so excited." This shadow of the girl wraps her fingers tightly around the ring, and all Maddy can remember now is how it felt waking up with a boa constrictor around her neck, the disco-ball ring tightening against her heat-swollen fingers. Her shadow says, "You might as well ask the traditional way then," prying the ring off the girl's finger and moving to hand it to the boy, forcing the girl into his shadow.

The boy reaches out his hand to take it. The girl drops the ring.

For the first time in months, the girl and her shadow are synchronous in their movements. As the ring falls to the ground like the tail of any reptile engaged in the process of autonomy, her shadow leaps forward, overshooting the dark pit of the boy's, becoming lost in the shade of the bridge underneath the go-kart ramp. There, the girl instinctively seeks refuge away from the glaringly nostalgic Friday night lights of what she thinks must have been some defunct high school football field.

"Crap! I got it now. Okay, do-over. Come on, there's better lighting over here," the boy says, waving her back. He probably wants a selfie of them. And the girl wonders, when they look back at that picture from the future, will he see her? Really see her? Will she even see herself? His shadow stretches toward her, its edges jaggedly blurring into the shadow of the icicles on the slushie stand, an array of mini knives.

"I can't go back," she says.

The boy bristles and pulls up his hoodie as he walks closer to the bridge. And how could he not see his weak shadow do its best cobra impression, which, lacking the definition of stadium-type lights, makes him look like a limply stretched-out sock? "I mean, I know this wasn't as good as our first mini-golf date, but you don't have to ruin the mood."

"Adam, that's not what I meant."

"And what exactly do you mean?" he says. "You don't want a picture of us getting officially engaged? You don't want to go back to mini-golfing? You don't want to go back to Canada? Because I'm with you on that one, in case you haven't noticed. We're leaving for Mars next week! And technically, we've never been to Mars. So we're not going *back* anywhere."

"Adam, look, it's just... maybe Mars isn't so great."

"How?"

Underneath the bridge, where her shadow only shows up as the faintest outline on the ground, the girl can remember hating *The Jetsons* when she was a kid, feeling so angry for Jane, whose driving they said was so bad bank robbers would rather go to jail than spend more time in a car with her. "It's just... maybe I don't want to shower in recycled pee water for the rest of my life!" She makes a face, wanting him to see disgust in all the exquisite detail of her nose wrinkling, the corners of her mouth turning down. At least, that's the face she hopes she's making. She's not really used to making disgust faces. And she can't understand how the boy doesn't see it, even if his own shadow engulfs the area around her while he steps back.

"I thought," the boy scowls, "that you were an environmentalist."

"I am." But is she sure, deciding to leave for a planet where moose are exploited for poop? Because a boy said that maybe she'd be the first woman in space to be a vet? And how many things had she done or not done because of a boy? Maybe it had been easier to see herself like boys saw her, a shadowy figure, hovering in the background, undefined unless in reflection of their well-defined selves. Maybe it had been easier than seeing herself drift away. Than not recognizing herself at all. But now, Maddy realizes, it wouldn't be easier to drift through the orbit of space, away from everything she could have been. Even if the starship was super reflective, glinting in the sun. And how could he recognize she would be as out of place as a ghost lady on Mars, how could he see that was definitely not where she belonged when she couldn't even see herself clearly anywhere else?

"I don't know what you want anymore," the boy says.

"Adam," she says softly, "what if I don't want to go with you to Mars?"

"What?" He can feel their once-so-solid plans dissolving, like the heat haze he'd mistaken for a lake during one of their walks in Big Bend. His own shadow sinks deep into the AstroTurf, searching for terra firma. Dimly the boy can feel it, something weighing him down. "But... you said you did. That's what you said before. Can't we go back to that?" the boy says. A seismic tremor in his voice makes him grab her hand to try to pull the girl out from under the shelter of the bridge, place the ring back on her finger. All the cracks in the concrete become fault lines, or snakes as they wind their way through the desert; the boy feels sicker than when they went upside down on The End. He steps directly into the fluorescent glow of the Haunted Mirrors, reminding himself to maintain the semblance of eye contact, staring just beyond her head, a trick he'd learned when nervous about public speaking. Just don't look down and he won't throw up. His shadow casts as wide as he can.

And how many times does the process of autonomy not go as planned for a chameleon or a green anole? How many times does the shadow of a writhing tail fail to distract a snake? The girl's shadow pools into a uselessly melted puddle as the boy says, "You know I love you right?"; the boy's shadow swallows up her own. The girl knows what happens to a reptile when autonomy fails. The girl knows she needs to get out of the direct line of the light source. She knows as the boy grabs her hand, as she pulls back, the boy does not see how his own shadow and hers combine to cast her into the realm of the indistinct, impossible to make out against the backlighting of the Ferris wheel, its lights illuminating an infinitely nauseating circular motion. All the boy sees is them together. He reaches for her hand again, and of course his shadow follows, closing in on her.

The girl stares at the ring for a second before she bolts toward the mirror maze, as fast as any arboreal lizard. She couldn't see a clear image of herself in any of the disco-ball faces, no matter how hard she tried.

* * *

Of course if you stare at yourself long enough in a dark room, you'll see a face other than your own. "Maddy. Maddy. Maddy," the girl whispers at her infinite mirror reflections, moving closer. As though some kind of Bloody Mary incantation had a chance of producing the girl who would have finished her environmental science degree, except her boyfriend got her a job making good money at his tattoo parlour where they used pigments made from heavy metals, animal fat and bone. As though she'd see a trace of the girl who understood the second law of motion, or the girl who would have learned to breathe fire back, except she was too scared of getting burned. Or the girl who would have applied to be a vet tech, who would have said she was sick and tired of mirrors back when Adam suggested a road trip through Texas to Mars, starting with the haunted Maximilian room at the Driskill Hotel.

The mirror maze, unfortunately, is less darkly haunted though, and more filled with lasers. Maddy's shadow casts long, wedging herself between the girl and the mirror. *Where'd you go, Maddy?* When a chameleon sees herself in the mirror, no one really knows what will happen. A male will go an aggressive shade of yellow, a fight reaction triggered by nanocrystals. They say the females get yellow spots to signal sexual receptivity, but no one studies what happens to the female's reflection. No one has ever watched to see whether a female chameleon recognizes herself in the mirror.

"Maddy? Maddy, where are you?" She can hear the boy's echo bouncing through the dark.

The boy feels unnaturally creeped out by all the dark corners of the mirror maze, illuminated with ghastly green lasers that remind him too much of the identity-stealing Borg impersonating Romero's zombies in *Night of the Living Dead*. "Maddy?" And what is he doing, mimicking caveman Commander Riker in episode 171 with his loud yells? What is he doing, going after the girl as though this is *The Flintstones*, not *The Jetsons*, and he's going to throw her over his shoulder and drag her back? It is then the boy sees his shadow, slow-crawling in his spread over and into the shadow of the girl. His shadow finds the girl's, and assimilates her completely, like the tree a chameleon has to change its pattern for. Like his father telling his mother to go change her dress. "Are you still there?"

Her shadow loves this, goes all soft penumbra in the knees when she hears the boy's voice. And how could the girl not go where the boy was? Where he wanted to be, even if it was Mars? It's not like she'd had any sense of direction before she met him; it didn't matter if she'd been drunk when she'd gotten lost trying to find her way back to the yurt at night. The dark had overwhelmed her then, just like now, pulling her to places she didn't want to go.

"Fuck, Maddy, stop playing around. I can't see you. Just come back."

Except the girl knows that when a female chameleon goes dark, she will fight to the death for her territory. For a male not to touch her. For her own spot to bask in the sun, regardless of whether its light comes from the past or not.

The girl knows if she can't recognize herself now, there's no way he can.

The boy knows it is illogical to be scared of the dark, of shadows, but when he looks in the mirror he barely recognizes his own face, the bulging veins of his hand that tried to grab the girl's, framed by so many dark corners. In this light, he is an anxious, lanky boy who still looks too much like his father; in this light, all he can see is his shadow reaching the girl, attempting a poltergeist-like rampage. He rattles the mirror frames. He bangs on the maze walls. The boy remembers how his father once broke his mother's vase by throwing Adam's Enterprise-shaped pizza cutter at the wall. A shadow can cast on the surface of a mirror, but this isn't him, no matter what's reflected. In this light, he looks hideous, looming over the weirdly reflected images of the girl like some phantasmic phony, or a snake that strangles you with closeness. "Where are you?" And he realizes, for so long now, he's been looking down on her, focusing instead on her umbral projection.

And then, somewhere in her infinite reflections, way way in the back, Maddy sees it. Her. The defined figure of a woman, what she had expected all those months ago in Austin, the one who must have been there if she'd only looked closely enough. "I'm here," she calls out, cautiously waving her hand, realizing her shadow has no choice but to wave back. She shifts a little to the right, so that it is impossible to see the laser light rays in the mirror; her shadow disappears and all she can see is her midthigh, "Remember" illuminated through the hole in her jeans. And here, without her shadow, she can see herself clearly. She can see herself standing solidly on the Earth, on her own two feet. She can only see herself staying on this planet, trying to help undo some damage done. She can only see herself with this boy, who, after all, did say he could see her being a vet, if she can stay with the animals on this planet. And there is no trace of the girl who'd stopped at Newtonian physics and inertia instead of researching the multiple possible endings of string theory. There is no trace of the girl who'd silently sat through all three seasons of the original *Star Trek* with her father, watching as Captain Kirk slept his way through every alien imaginable, or the girl who'd agreed to go to Mars.

The girl remembers how a chameleon becomes more visible, turning bright red, when the lizard makes up her mind to fight.

"I'm here," she says.

"Where's here? Stop moving. I can't find you."

"Around the corner. In the mirror maze. In Gravity Park,

South Padre, Texas." The boy doesn't answer her; can't he read her accurately reflected lips? "USA, North America," she says, exasperated. "Earth. And I'm not moving. I mean, I haven't moved since you've been trying to find me. But also, I'm not going to Mars."

A shadow can cast on the surface of a mirror, but in mirrors light only travels in one forward direction. When Maddy steps into the light, blocking the laser at the source, when Adam decides to change direction, backing up to give her space, her shadow, and his, both disappear. Seeing that he has seen her, she leads them toward the end.

"I'm out," Maddy says, reaching the exit of the maze. "I'm here." Outside, her shadow falls in line underneath her feet, dissolving into the evening.

* * *

Maddy and Adam are lying on the hood of their shitty car just outside of Marfa, waiting for the mystery lights while munching on falafel next to the food trucks. On the reflective patio, old beer bottles are transformed into pebbles at their feet. Adam stares at the image of Maddy, the clear reflection of the sunburn on her nose, the details of several arm freckles. The boy sees the girl. The girl sees the girl. It could be love. Maddy has said she wants to wait and see, never mind that, like the radio says, love is blind. And pretty much inexplicable. Just like the lights. They could be reflections of car high-beams, or maybe a launch from the spaceport, all those rockets going to Mars thinking that getting far enough away could fix the problem. They could be a flare from a gas compressor along the Trans-Pecos pipeline. Same old story.

One thing's for sure though. The Marfa lights are not

starlight, the lights of the distant past. For sure Maddy is now on top of her shadow and she knows that Adam is too. And their shadows, blocked out by the realness of their bodies on the hood of the car, even cause the recently non-air-conditioned interior to actually cool down a bit. Win-win.

"You know," Adam whispers, "the Curiosity rover discovered a weird light on Mars. But it was just a cosmic ray. Or a really shiny rock reflecting the sunlight. Could be the case here."

"Maybe," Maddy says, "but I still think the Marfa lights are some new form of life." She thinks about her not so sci-fi future, her plan of going back to Canada, getting her own apartment. Registering for college.

"You talking UFOs?"

"Not necessarily. Just something we've never seen before."

She thinks of how when she told Adam her new plan on their way out of Boca Chica, he'd said, "I'd still like to see you," knowing how she saw him. She'd grinned, told him that even if they were officially unengaged, the answer was yes. Mostly because she believed that at this point, him seeing her could actually be possible. She grins now too, knowing the darkness of their shadows is behind them in the selfie she takes of them against the setting sun.

And it could have been a lens flare, but the farther Maddy drives away from the motel, from Boca Chica, the more her pictures seem to catch their reflections in amazing rainbow detail; outside the house of mirrors, in the desert oasis next to the water in Big Bend, tonight in the pebbles on the ground. They are faint, but there. More real than a rainbow on Mars. Or the shadows of a boy and girl at night, with no lights from the towers, or houses, or apartments of an old civilization to create them.

ACKNOWLEDGEMENTS

My biggest thanks to the entire team at Book*hug Press for your work on this book. To Hazel and Jay, thank you for agreeing to bring this book into the world. To Charlene, thank you for your keen insights. I owe a huge debt to my editor, Malcolm Sutton, for the deep discussion and questions that made these stories the best they could be. Thank you, as well, for designing this perfectly surreal dream of a cover.

So much gratitude to my fantastic agents, Marilyn Biderman and Amanda Orozco at Transatlantic Agency.

I am also deeply grateful to the jurors of the 2020 Journey Prize, Doretta Lau, Amy Jones, and Téa Mutonji, for including "When Foxes Die Electric" in the pages of the Journey Prize anthology. Thank you to *The New Quarterly* and *Room Magazine* for seeing something in my stories that was worth noticing with your fiction awards, and thank you also to *PRISM International*, *Canthius*, *North American Review*, *Joyland*, and *Overland*, where some of these stories were first published. My gratitude goes out to André Forget and Carmine Starnino at Véhicule Press for choosing to include "The Underside of a Wing" in the phenomenal *After Realism: 24 Stories for the 21st Century*, and to the new generation of Canadian writers and readers who love speculative fiction.

Thank you to Russell Smith for mentoring me as I learned

to clarify all my fantastical ideas, and wrestle with the shape of these stories. I am grateful to Kathryn Mockler as well, for your early mentorship that taught me different forms of flash and short fiction, and for always being so supportive and making me feel like I belonged in the literary community, even in those early days.

My deepest thanks to the early readers of these stories, the Eastwood Writers Collective, Dawn Chapman, Grace MacCall, Alison Frost, Susanna Molinolo, Lee Parpart, and Kate Finegan; the animals in this book would be roaming far too wildly without your writerly support and critique. Thank you also for having the best celebration bubbly ever. Kate Finegan, these stories would be nowhere without your obsession with animal facts and your knowledge of American ghosts. Thank you for not only literally scaling walls with me, but for doing the same metaphorically whenever we sat down to discuss those early drafts.

My gratitude goes out as well to the all the writers and readers who have made me feel a part of this community, especially to Sara Mang, for being not only a wonderful writer but someone who knows how and when to give a writerly lift (as well as the best Toronto Korean restaurants), and to Kirby, for your friendship, your knowing insight, your community, your lasagna, and all those balcony talks where you saw into my soul.

Thank you to Rob Skuja, for oh-so-patiently taking my author photo. And deep gratitude to the Canada Council for the Arts, the Ontario Arts Council, and the Toronto Arts Council for supporting the development of this book financially.

Thank you isn't enough, but I will say it anyways. Thank you to my partner Mat for your patience, for your time, for hooking me on *Star Trek: Voyager*, for the campfire ghost stories, and for all the love that let me write this book.

PAOLA FERRANTE is a writer living with depression. Her debut poetry collection, *What to Wear When Surviving a Lion Attack* (2019), was shortlisted for the Gerald Lampert Memorial Prize. She has won *Grain Magazine*'s Short Grain Contest for Poetry, *The New Quarterly*'s Peter Hinchcliffe Short Fiction Award, *Room Magazine*'s Fiction Contest, and was longlisted for the 2020 Journey Prize for the story "When Foxes Die Electric." Her work appears in *After Realism: 24 Stories for the 21st Century* (2022), *Best Canadian Poetry 2021* (2021), *North American Review, PRISM International*, and elsewhere. She was born, and still resides in, Toronto.

Colophon

Manufactured as the first edition of
Her Body Among Animals
in the fall of 2023 by Book*hug Press

Edited for the press by Malcolm Sutton
Copy edited by Jo Ramsay
Proofread by Charlene Chow
Type + design by Malcolm Sutton

Cover photo of waves by Dmitry Makeev.
Used under CC-BY-SA-4.0.

Printed in Canada

bookhugpress.ca